B+T
6/29/12

W9-BQZ-983

NO LONGER THE PROPERTY OF
BALDWIN PUBLIC LIBRARY

HELLBOX

"NAMELESS DETECTIVE" MYSTERIES BY BILL PRONZINI

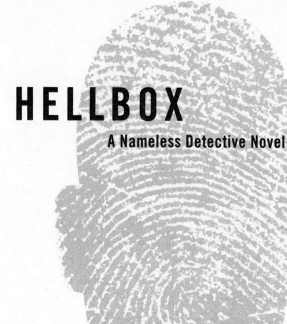

HELLBOX

A Nameless Detective Novel

Bill Pronzini

A Tom Doherty Associates Book
New York

BALDWIN PUBLIC LiBRARY

This is a work of fiction. All of the characters, organizations, and events portrayed in this novel are either products of the author's imagination or are used fictitiously.

HELLBOX: A NAMELESS DETECTIVE NOVEL

Copyright © 2012 by the Pronzini-Muller Family Trust

All rights reserved.

A Forge Book
Published by Tom Doherty Associates, LLC
175 Fifth Avenue
New York, NY 10010

www.tor-forge.com

Forge® is a registered trademark of Tom Doherty Associates, LLC.

Library of Congress Cataloging-in-Publication Data

Pronzini, Bill.
    Hellbox / Bill Pronzini.—1st ed.
        p. cm.
    "A Tom Doherty Associates book."
    ISBN 978-0-7653-2565-5 (hardcover)
    ISBN 978-1-4299-4723-7 (e-book)
    1. Nameless Detective (Fictitious character)—Fiction.   2. Private
investigators—Fiction.   I. Title.
    PS3566.R67H45 2012
    813'.54—dc23

                                                        2012011650

First Edition: July 2012

Printed in the United States of America

0   9   8   7   6   5   4   3   2   1

BALDWIN PUBLIC LIBRARY

For Marcia

HELLBOX

PROLOGUE

PETE BALFOUR

They shouldn't of kept making fun of him like that. Not like *that*.

It was all Ned Verriker's fault. Bastard shouldn't of hung that label around his neck like a goddamn dead bird. That was what took it right over the line.

Bad enough, all the crap Balfour'd had to take most of his life about the way he looked. Man couldn't help the face he was born with, could he? But he'd got so he could stand the ragging pretty well, even joke about it himself when he'd had a few. Like the night at the Miners Club when he was half in the bag and he come out and said he hadn't had a woman in so long he'd started carrying a picture of his right hand around in his wallet. Everybody got a good laugh out of that. Hell, he'd joined right in that night, and again the time somebody asked him if he was still dating old Five Fingers.

But after a while, when he was alone at night in his house, he didn't think that was funny, neither. Plain damn truth. Only woman he'd ever laid that he hadn't had to pay for was Charlotte, his ex-wife, and she'd been lousy in bed. Weighed more than he did, too, and had a face like a foot. Plus a mouth that never stayed shut. Nag, nag, nag the whole eighteen months they were married. Banner day when she walked out on him after the last of their fights, wearing a black eye and a smashed nose. He hadn't missed her one minute since.

The way he figured it now, he'd never have another woman except a second-class whore. Just too butt-ugly. No getting away from it—there were mirrors in the house, he saw his reflection in store windows, he knew what he looked like. Short, puffy body on stubby legs, not much chin, mouth like a gaffed bass, knobby head with a patch of hair like moss growing on a tree stump. Somebody'd said that to him once, someplace or other. "You know something, Pete? You got a head looks like moss growing on a fuckin' tree stump."

Mostly it hadn't bothered him, how he looked. And for a long time, he'd figured his life was tolerable enough. No real friends except for Bruno, and that was just because he fed and watered the dog and knew how to handle him. Treat a pit bull right and he'd lick your hand; treat him wrong and he'd tear your throat out. But that was all right, he didn't need anybody to hang around with except a few half-assed drinking and poker and bowling buddies now and then. He liked his house, a fixer-upper he'd turned into a real livable place with his own two hands. He liked working construction and being his own boss. He liked hunting and camping in the backwoods, and collecting guns, and shooting pool, and watching baseball on TV, and bowling a few lines at Freedom Lanes and playing stud at Henson's Card Room, and watching martial arts' flicks on the tube, and reading a Louis L'Amour western if he was in the mood for a good book. And when he got horny, well, he could drive down to Sacramento and spend thirty or forty bucks on a teenage hooker, or if he didn't feel like making the effort, he had his collection of porn videos, and he could go on the Internet and surf through the porn sites.

But sometimes, even before that night at the Buckhorn six weeks ago, it all backed up on him like a clogged septic system. More and more, he felt like hitting something, breaking something out of sheer frustration. Wished he was still married to Charlotte so he could beat the crap out of her again. Times like those, he knew how much his life here sucked. Really *sucked*.

It got so he couldn't stand the thought that things would go on pretty much as they always had for him, one day the same as another right up until he croaked. Weekdays working his construction jobs, working his little scams, and when he knocked off it'd be the Miners Club or the Buckhorn or Freedom Lanes or Henson's, and then home to watch a DVD or fool around online and then straight to bed. Weekends watching a ball game, sipping some brews, playing poker, playing pool, playing with his computer, playing with himself. Sure, he was used to it and he was better off than a lot of poor, jobless bastards living on welfare or sleeping on the streets, but that didn't make it any less boring.

Only then it stopped being boring and got ugly instead.

He remembered that night like it was yesterday. Friday night, and he'd been drinking Bud and shooting pool with three of the Buckhorn regulars. Just happened to wander in there that night and Frank Ramsey couldn't find nobody else to partner up, so he'd got asked and he figured, why not, it'd give him a chance to show up Verriker. Two of them never got along. Verriker thought he was funny as hell, a regular stand-up comedian, always cracking stupid jokes at somebody else's expense, even when he was at work at Builders Supply. Holier than thou, too. Drunk Friday and Saturday nights, first one in church on Sunday morning. Didn't like the way Balfour Construction did business and told him so more than once. Like *he* never cut a few corners in his life. Man has a right to live the best way he can and he don't need anybody else trying to tell him how to do it.

That afternoon, he'd finished the repairs on old Mrs. Evans' sunporch, and she'd paid him in cash like he asked her, and he was feeling good. So he thought the hell with Verriker and stayed put in the Buckhorn to celebrate. He'd've got out of there damn quick if he'd had any idea what Verriker was gonna do to him.

Other two in the group were Ramsey and Tony Lucchesi, with Ernie Stivic, who didn't know a pool cue from a golf club, kibitzing. Balfour had always got along with Ramsey, and Lucchesi was all right for a dago, even if he was a lousy barber. Didn't like Stivic much better than he did Verriker. Fry cook at the Burgers and More greasy spoon, asked him once if he knew the difference between a hamburger and a Polack burger, just kidding around, and Stivic got right in his face and threatened to bust his arm if he said "Polack" again. Two of the same, him and Verriker. Smart guys that didn't care about nobody but themselves.

It was about nine o'clock when they switched from partners Rotation to one-on-one Eight-Ball. Verriker's idea. When he was half in the bag, he thought he was Fast Eddie Felson. Fact was, none of them shot a better stick than Pete Balfour, so it was him Verriker challenged first. He smoked the bugger for five bucks and pissed him off. Verriker claimed he moved the cue ball on one of his shots, but none of the others saw it. He moved it, all right, but he never did see no reason why a man shouldn't have an edge if he could take it. That went double against a prick like Verriker.

Well, they played and drank and talked the way you do in bars. Pro football, a game he never liked much—too violent. A few jokes from Verriker, none of them funny no matter what the rest thought. Politics. Verriker and Lucchesi were bleeding hearts, and wouldn't you just figure on that? Him, he hated the politicians on all sides, except maybe for the Tea Baggers—some of them made sense. The rest . . . always raising taxes and passing bullshit laws that made it harder for a man to live. Always trying to take away your civil rights, like the right to own and carry guns.

Work was another topic they got into, and Balfour was just enough in his cups to tell how he'd phonied up an invoice to make an extra thousand on time and materials off old lady rich-bitch Evans. Didn't see no reason why he shouldn't talk about it; it was a good trick and a good story, and besides, he knew it'd piss Verriker off. It did, all right. Verriker said, "Suppose I tell Mrs. Evans what you did." Balfour said, "Suppose I tell your boss you like young boys." Verriker got hot, called him a dirty son of a bitch and said how about they go outside so he could kick some Balfour ass. He worked up a laugh, said he was only kidding around about the young boys, said he'd lied about screwing Mrs. Evans, even though it was the plain truth. He wasn't a coward, but Verriker had twenty pounds and ten years on him, and he knew he'd get his clock cleaned if he fought him. Pete Balfour's mama didn't raise no damn fools.

Verriker said, "You're an asshole, Pete, you know that?" but not like he wanted to fight anymore. He chewed his back teeth, but let it go unchallenged. That time, he did. Didn't want to light Verriker's fire again.

He turned his stick over to Lucchesi, and while the dago and Verriker were shooting, Ramsey got off on a story about how a tourist almost run him off the road that afternoon, some suit in a BMW going about twenty-five miles per hour over the speed limit. Ramsey drove a mail delivery truck, drove it like an old lady, so it was no surprise he'd near got forced off the road. Twenty-five over the limit was nothing on the good roads they had in Green Valley. Gone as much as fifty over himself when he was sure there wasn't any sheriff's patrols around. But the others were on Ramsey's side.

Lucchesi said, "Yeah, you got to watch yourself every minute these days. People driving too fast, talking on cell phones and not paying attention, jumping lights, cutting you off to save one car length and five seconds of time."

"You got that right," Stivic said. "Seems there's more assholes on the road every day."

"Not just the roads," Ramsey said. "Everywhere you go. It's like some sort of disease, you know? An epidemic of assholes."

Everybody laughed but Balfour. He didn't see what was so funny.

Stivic said, "Christ, you don't suppose they're organized? I mean, a union and everything?"

That got some more laughs. So did what Lucchesi said next: "We ought to put up a sign outside town. Big bare buns in a circle with a line through it. No Assholes Allowed."

Subject might've been finished then if it hadn't been for Verriker. Wiseass had to stick his oar in, had to make the kind of joke out of it that cut right to the bone. Just had to do it.

Said, "I got a better idea. What we should do, we should round up all the assholes in the state, maybe even the whole country, and stick 'em together some place in the middle of nowhere. Valley like this one, say, only bigger. Have armed guards on duty full time, make sure they all stay put. Call the place Asshole Valley, so there wouldn't be any mistake about who lived there."

"I like it," Stivic said. "By God, I do."

"Well, I don't." Balfour knew he should've kept his lip buttoned, but he was half in the bag himself and couldn't help it. "I think it's a stupid idea, that's what I think."

"Sure you do, Pete," Verriker said, grinning. "I figured you would."

"What's that supposed to mean?"

"Like I said before. You're an asshole."

The words come out loud and they brought down the

house. Fifteen or twenty other drinkers in there, every one flapping an ear, and they all busted out laughing, too. At what Verriker'd said, but it was Pete Balfour they were looking and howling at.

He wanted to smash the bastard's face in. If he'd had a bottle in his hand, he might've done it. But he just stood there with the blood coming hot up his neck and said, "I'm not an asshole," in a voice as loud as Verriker's.

"Bet if we took a vote on that, you'd lose."

"I'm *not* an asshole!"

"So you say. I say you're the biggest one I know, maybe even the biggest one in the county."

"You shut up, Verriker. You shut up—"

But Verriker didn't shut up. He was on his feet, moving around, grinning all over his face, playing it up to the crowd. Said, "Matter of fact, if we rounded up all the assholes in the state and put 'em in that valley I was talking about, I bet somebody'd nominate you for mayor. And I bet you'd win, hands down. Pete Balfour, the first mayor of Asshole Valley."

Brought the house down again. It made Balfour want to puke, the way they all hooted and high-fived and hooted some more. Looking at him and laughing *at* him the whole time. Made him so hot, he was afraid he'd pop a blood vessel if he didn't get out of there quick.

Must've looked to Verriker and the rest like he was running away, tail between his legs like a kicked dog. He could hear them laughing even after he was out the door. All the way home, he heard the laughter and Verriker calling him an asshole, hanging that mayor tag on him.

He didn't sleep much that night. Still felt lousy in the

morning. But he had work to do, a repair job on the restrooms and concession booths at the fairgrounds—a good
deal because he'd factored a gimmick into his bid to the
county where he'd buy some cheap-grade lumber that'd
pass for high-grade, make himself another couple of
grand. So he went out on the job, and the half-wit kid
he'd hired to help out on this one, and Tarboe, the faggot
fairgrounds director, were both standing there grinning.
The faggot said, "Good morning, Your Honor," and the
kid laughed fit to be tied. That was how fast word got
around in a small town like Six Pines. He snapped at them
to knock that crap off, it wasn't funny, and they saw he
meant business and left him alone. So did Eladio Perez,
his regular helper. The old Mex did his work and kept his
mouth shut, about the only one Balfour knew who did.
But all day long, he caught the kid hiding a smirk and
knew just what he was thinking. He could almost hear it
going round and round inside the half-wit's head like it
was going round and round inside his own.

Pete Balfour, mayor of Asshole Valley.

He knew he was in for a bad time for a while, but he
didn't figure on how bad. It was like a wildfire, the way
the bad joke spread around town, the valley, probably the
whole damn county. Everybody out there getting their
funny bones tickled at his expense. The fat slob at the
store where he did his grocery shopping. Harry Logan at
Harry's House of Guns, a guy who'd always been decent
to him. Luke Penny at the Shell station. Others who'd
been in the Buckhorn that night. First thing Tony Lucchesi said to him was, "Well, if it isn't Hizzoner." And
Frank Ramsey, all smirk and smart-ass with "You got your

political platform worked out yet, Pete?" And one more that was even harder to take. Charlotte, his cow of an ex-wife, so fat now her ass looked like the back end of a bus, standing in front of City Hall where she worked and making *ha-ha* noises with all her chins jiggling.

He did all he could to avoid Verriker, but that didn't stop the bugger from telling and retelling the story to anybody who'd listen. Keeping it alive. Keeping the knife stuck in him right up to the hilt, so the hoo-ha didn't go away after a few days the way he expected it would. No, it got worse. Seemed like everywhere he went, everybody he come in contact with—grins, giggles, stares, pointing fingers. Kids, even. Some snotnose couldn't of been more than ten, giving him a look that said plain as day, "Hey, there's the dude got elected mayor of the assholes."

Goddamn people! Didn't they know how much a name like that could *hurt*? Calling somebody an asshole to his face was bad enough, but saying he was the biggest ass-hole around, leader of the pack, making a big joke out of him and never letting him have any peace, that was the worst you could do to anybody. It sliced deep into a man, carved out chunks of his insides. Made him half crazy.

It got so bad he couldn't stand to go out of the house. Just holed up except when he was working, and some days, he could hardly make himself drive over to the job site. The half-wit kid kept looking at him smarmy all the time, hiding a grin and laughing with his eyes. He'd of fired the dumb-ass quick if he hadn't needed him to get the work done. Tarboe was just as bad. Started ragging on him about not getting the grandstand and concession repairs finished in time for the big Independence Day celebration, yap, yap, yap. Dressing him down with half his mouth, laughing at him out the other half.

Balfour had plenty of time to think, holed up in his house, nothing to do but drink too much whiskey and stare at the TV. He didn't even have any interest in looking at the porn sites on his computer anymore. More he thought, the madder he got. He shouldn't have to take this kind of crap. What'd he do to deserve it? Nothing. Bad enough he had one cross to bear, his butt-ugly looks, but this new one weighed twice as heavy, and hurt a lot more because it wasn't true, he wasn't what they were all saying he was. No way. He was just a guy trying to get along the best he could, same as everybody else. None of this was his fault.

He *couldn't* keep on taking the abuse. He had to do something about it, pay Verriker back for making him a laughingstock.

Yeah—payback.

Question was, what kind?

1

Kerry was sitting at the table on the long front porch, drinking coffee and taking in the view, when I came out in my robe and slippers. It was only a little after nine Sunday morning, another cloudless, end-of-June day; the temperature was already in the seventies, though it would probably get up near ninety by midafternoon. Usually I don't deal well with heat, but somehow hot days in the mountains don't seem quite as bothersome.

" 'Morning," she said as I sat down. "I wondered how long you were going to stay in bed. Sleep well?"

"Yup. Must be the mountain air." I snuffled up a deep breath of it, yawned, and sniffed in some more. The resinous pine smell was sharp and clean; you could smell the gathering heat, too, a pleasantly dusty summer odor. I grinned at her and added, "Among other things."

"Uh-huh."

"How long have you been up?"

"Oh, an hour or so. Nice out here."

"Nice," I agreed. I helped myself to coffee from the pot she'd brewed and brought out on a tray.

"You really do like this place?"

"Yup. So far, so good."

"Me, too. I wish Emily had been able to come with us. We don't want to take the plunge without her seeing the place first."

"*If* we take the plunge. I still think the owners are asking too much."

"Sam Budlong said they'd take less."

"But not a lot less. At least, that was the impression I got."

"If the Murrays want to sell badly enough, they'll be reasonable. It's been on the market a long time."

"So we don't need to rush."

"No, but if the rest of this little vacation goes well, and if Emily likes the property as much as we do and we can negotiate an affordable price, there's no reason to keep looking, is there? Frankly, I've grown a little tired of the hunt."

So had I, patience not being one of my long suits. Off and on over the past three months, we'd spent weekends in different areas within a few hours' driving distance from San Francisco—Lake County, the north coast along Highway 1, Big Basin and Santa Cruz, Penn Valley—and looked at maybe a score of properties, none of which had come close to our ideal second home. Emily had been with us before, but she was away all of this week: Her school glee club had been invited to take part in a state-sponsored summer music festival in Southern California. Singing was her first love and career goal.

It had been one of Kerry's ad agency clients who'd suggested we consider Green Valley, in the Sierra foothills northeast of Placerville: quiet, scenic, remote enough for solitude, but still reasonably close to Highway 50, and a relatively easy three-hour drive from the city. So we'd come up, looked around, and liked what we saw enough to contact a real estate agent in the valley town of Six Pines. I'd been skeptical when Sam Budlong said, "I think I have just the place you're looking for," but once he showed it to us, my skepticism went away pretty fast.

The house—cabin, really—wasn't such-a-much. Built thirty-some years back of redwood with fieldstone trim and fireplace—holding up, but in need of repairs here and there. Six smallish rooms, including a bathroom with chattery plumbing. No garage, the only outbuilding a combination storage and woodshed on the south side, but that was a minor drawback. The location was the real selling point. The place sat on a grassy knoll, pine woods on three sides, a couple of gnarled old apple trees at the rear; and in front, a mostly unobstructed view of the valley, sections of the Rubicon River that ran through it, and forested hills and snow-topped mountain peaks along the western horizon. You had a sense of rural isolation, yet it was only three miles to Six Pines. There were other homes scattered along Ridge Hill Road, a narrow secondary artery that wound along the hillside below, but none of them were visible from here. Live in a city all your life as I had, with neighbors piled up all around, some of them separated from you by nothing more than walls and areaways, and hundreds of yards of open space on all sides were pure luxury.

Another plus was that there was plenty to do in the region. Trout fishing in the Rubicon and dozens of mountain streams that threaded the valley and the hills and mountains surrounding it. Hiking. Hunting, if you were into blood sports, which we weren't. A variety of local activities that included a gala (the real estate agent's word) Fourth of July celebration. And Placerville, Auburn, the Amador County wine country were all day-trip close.

The only thing that gave me pause, aside from the selling price the owners were asking, was that Green Valley was less than fifty miles from the isolated section of the Gold Country where I'd been held captive, chained to a cabin wall by an ex-convict bent on revenge, for three hellish months several years back. For some time after the ordeal ended, I was unable to venture into the Sierra foothills; just thinking about it would bring on flashbacks and cold sweats. Gradually, the residual fear and loathing had worn off, but I still couldn't and wouldn't travel anywhere near the area north of Murphys. Fifty miles, though . . . a long way from Deer Run, too far for me to let it be a factor in the decision-making process.

Neither Kerry nor I was willing to commit to buying the property without spending some time there to get the feel of the area, make certain it was right for us. It had been up for sale long enough so that the Murrays, who lived in Sacramento, were willing to rent it to us for a few days, with the rental fee to be deducted from the purchase price if we made an acceptable offer. So instead of going back home after a two-night stay, as we'd originally planned, we'd decided to take advantage of the rental deal. The timing for an extended getaway couldn't have been better: neither of us had any pressing business this week. Brief vacation for us while Emily was away enjoying hers.

I finished my coffee, refilled my cup and Kerry's. She said, "What do you want to do today? Explore a little or just relax?"

"Both. Relax first, though. Maybe go back to bed for a while."

"Didn't you get enough sleep?"

"I wasn't thinking about sleeping."

She laughed. "You look like a demented old lecher when you do that."

"Do what?"

"Waggle your eyebrows that way."

"'Lecher,' maybe, but not so old. And I refute 'demented.'"

"Wasn't last night enough for you?"

"Hah," I said.

"People our age aren't supposed to have such active sex lives."

"Hah."

"What's got you so revved up this morning anyhow?"

"The mountain air, and the way your hair shines in the sunlight."

"My God," she said with mock awe, "where did *that* come from?"

"Part of my new seduction package." I did some more eyebrow waggling. "So what do you say, sweet thing? Want to go play our song again on that saggy old mattress in there?"

"Sweet thing. Oh, brother."

"Best offer you'll get all day. Better take advantage."

"Are you sure you'll be up to it again so soon?"

"Double hah," I said. "I'm Italian, remember?"

"How could I forget?"

I stood, stretched, waggled my eyebrows again, and held out my hand.

"If this is the effect Green Valley is having on you," Kerry said, "maybe we ought to rethink buying this place." But she got right up and twined her fingers in mine and let me lead her off to the bedroom.

While Kerry took her turn showering and dressing, I headed out to the deck again. On the way, my cell phone cut loose with its burbling summons, barely audible inside my jacket where I'd hung it on the peg inside the door. I'd almost forgotten I had the thing with me; had definitely forgotten it was still turned on. Cell phones don't always work in mountainous country, but this was not one of those satellite dead zones. I almost wished it was until I got the cell out and checked the caller's name on the screen. Tamara. Oh, Lord, I thought, not some sort of emergency. But it wasn't.

"I didn't think you'd pick up," she said. "Just wanted to leave a callback message for you. Didn't interrupt anything, did I?"

"You might have if you'd called half an hour ago," I said. "What's up?"

"Question on the Western Maritime fraud case you handled. I'm trying to get caught up on our billing."

"Haven't you heard? Sunday's supposed to be a day of rest."

"Yeah, sure. Like Saturday night's supposed to be boogie time."

"Meaning yours wasn't?"

"Not hardly. Two glasses of wine, a bad rental flick, and in bed by eleven. All by my lonesome."

Not good, I thought. She was drifting back into the semi-reclusive, workaholic shell that she'd closed herself into after her longtime cellist boyfriend, Horace, moved back east and then dumped her for a second violinist in the Philadelphia Philharmonic. A brief hookup with a man who called himself Lucas Zeller had brought her out of it for a while, until he turned out to be a con man and worse; the none-too-pleasant events that followed had taught her some hard lessons. She still hadn't quite recovered from the damage to her self-confidence and self-esteem. Still wasn't ready to put her trust in anybody she didn't already know and know well, particularly a member of the male sex. Caution and skepticism were healthy attitudes up to a point, but not if she let them make her a social outcast. She had a great deal to offer any man with the sense and sensitivity to treat her right. What she needed to do was put herself in a position to find him, and be willing to let him into her life when she did.

She hadn't asked for my advice, though, and I hadn't volunteered it. Nor would I. We had a kind of de facto father-daughter relationship, in addition to our professional bond, but I had to be careful not to come on too strong with her. Her relationship with her own father was prickly, and now and then she carried it over to me. Best for both of us if I kept my mouth shut, let her work out her personal problems on her own.

Fortunately, she changed the subject by asking, "So how's your weekend been?"

"Good. Very good. Looks like we've found our second home."

"All right! Where?"

I gave her the relevant details. "We're staying a few more days to make sure. Nothing urgent to drag me back sooner, I take it?"

"Nope. Everything under control."

"What's the problem with the insurance case?"

It had to do with a foul-up on the expense account charges—my fault. When we got it straightened out, I asked, "Any new clients?" because I hadn't spoken to her since Thursday.

"Couple," she said. "One routine; Alex is handling it. The other . . . well, Jake's plate's pretty full, and the new client's black. So I rang up Deron Stewart and gave it to him."

"I thought you didn't like Stewart."

"Don't much, but he did a good professional job on that Delman mess, and he didn't try to hit on me. So I figured I'd throw him another bone."

Stewart was a qualified operative, an ex-cop who'd worked eight years for the San Francisco office of a large national agency. Tamara and I had come close to hiring him over Jake Runyon when we expanded operations a few years ago. She was the one who'd vetoed him; too slick, too much ego, too much a womanizer for her liking. Stewart hadn't had any luck finding a permanent spot with another agency in the interim, owing to the lousy economy and with some outfits, maybe, a veiled racial bias. He free-lanced now, much as Alex Chavez had before we'd put him on full time a couple of months ago.

"What kind of case?" I asked.

"Nasty one. Excelsior woman being stalked by an ex-husband."

"Pro bono?"

"Not quite. Reduced fee. She's got a good job, but she's also a single mom—two kids. Her ex is one of those early-release, violent crimes' offenders the goddamn state keeps turning loose. 'No menace to public safety,' my ass. Police haven't been much help because the guy hasn't done anything yet, except hang around and make veiled threats. Woman swears it's only a matter of time. She's scared half out of her head."

"You think Stewart can handle the situation without escalating it?"

"Says he can. He'd better, if he wants any more bones tossed his way. Not a lot of freelance detective work out there these days."

"That's for sure."

We talked a little more, then let each other get on with our respective Sundays. I put the phone back into my jacket pocket, went out and leaned on the porch railing and thought about the cases Runyon and Chavez, and now Deron Stewart, were dealing with. As much as I liked this property, as much as I was glad to be away from the city and the daily grind, I still had a left-out, pastured feeling now and then. Officially semi-retired now, with a maximum two days a week at the office and mostly routine stuff when I was there. Okay, good. It was what I wanted, what Kerry and Emily wanted; I'd made my decision and I didn't regret it. But when you've been in the same business for two-thirds of your life, and found it rewarding and satisfying, despite a number of unpleasant situations and brushes with violence, it's hard to let go.

Maybe I wouldn't feel that tug, that vague sense of past-my-prime-and-no-longer-needed in six months, a year, two years. I hoped so. But if it lingered, I was not going to backslide again. There's nothing more pathetic than an old plowhorse hobbling around trying to function at the same level of competence as he had in his younger days, and accomplishing little except getting in everybody's way.

2

Six Pines was at the south end of the valley, a high school flanked by a baseball diamond and football field at the upper edge, the business district flanking the main road farther along, homes and cottages built up along one hillside, a church and what looked like a community center on the more gradual rising slope opposite. The population was 2,200 year-round residents, but it was evident that second-homers, tourists, and sportsmen swelled that number considerably during trout fishing season and in the peak summer months. A banner strung across the middle of Main Street advertised the annual Independence Day celebration Budlong had told us about—parade, carnival, picnic barbeque. Most of the business establishments looked open today, and there were a lot of people out and about when we rolled in a little past noon.

The town had a pleasant, century-past look and feel. This was old mining country and vestiges of the Gold Country heritage had been carefully preserved here—false-fronted and native stone buildings, a local museum that had once been a blacksmith's shop, galleried board-walks instead of paved sidewalks on Main Street and a couple of the side streets. The more modern structures sprinkled among the venerable ones seemed out of place, anachronistic. They did to me, anyway. But then, I prefer the old to the new in most things. Kerry says I'm hope-lessly old-fashioned, a wallower in nostalgia—compliments, as far as I'm concerned.

We parked in a public lot behind the museum and went in for a look around. It wasn't much—standard Gold Country items like mining equipment, faded photo-graphs and daguerreotypes, a Wells Fargo safe, and a collection of dusty old bottles. Then we walked down along that side of the four-block main drag, looking at storefronts and examining the preserved buildings up close. Part of getting a better feel for the town and the valley. We'd done a little of that the day before, prior to the visit to Budlong Realty, but you need time and par-ticipation to get to know a place.

There was an antique shop Kerry wanted to look into. While she did that, I went back to a sporting goods store we'd passed and asked the guy behind the counter about trout fishing in the area. He sold me a map and pointed out a couple of locations he said were prime, which I fig-ured meant tourist prime and should probably be avoided. The locals would keep the best spots to themselves and trial and error was the only way outsiders like me were likely to find them. He also sold me a fishing license, and tried to sell me "the best trout rod on the market," but I already owned a better fly rod made thirty years earlier.

It was in the trunk of the car along with my Daiwa reel and box of hand-tied trout flies.

Kerry was waiting when I came out. "Fine antiques" was a misnomer, she said; "useless junk" was much more appropriate. We went on down to the end of the business district, crossed over and wandered up the other side. In the middle of the third block was a three-story structure with a sign on the front that read: THE MINERS HOTEL— FOUNDED 1882. Next to the front entrance, another sign advertised lunch, dinner, and an all-you-can-eat Sunday brunch in the Miners Hotel Restaurant.

Kerry said, "I'm starving. Let's try it," and we went in. But we didn't get to try the Sunday brunch. The restaurant off the lobby was small and jam-packed, with a half-hour waiting list. Normally, Kerry's patience level is several points above mine, but she didn't feel like hanging around any more than I did; all we'd had besides the morning coffee was a glass of orange juice each. We could sample the hotel fare another day.

Next block up was another eatery, the Green Valley Café. Crowded, too, but a couple of customers were just leaving and we managed to snag the booth they'd vacated. The place's air-conditioning was cranked up higher than the hotel's, a welcome relief: the temperature outside was already in the high eighties. Judging from the look and dress of the patrons in the other booths and lined together at a long counter, the café was a favorite with the locals. Which usually meant the food was both very good and inexpensive, and that was the case here.

We were in the middle of mushroom omelettes with

fruit—I wanted home-fried potatoes with mine, but Kerry was always after me to limit my starch and carb intake—when the heavyset guy came in. I noticed him because I was facing toward the entrance and he made some noise shutting the door behind him. He was in his forties, homely to the point of ugliness, wearing old clothes and a scowl on a mouth the size of a small trough. He stood for a few seconds scanning the room, spotted an empty stool at the near end of the counter, and made for it in hard, almost aggressive strides. Man not having a good day, I thought. Or a good life, for that matter.

As soon as he climbed onto the stool, one of a group of three men in the booth behind him and next to ours said in a carrying voice, "Well, look who just came in. The mayor himself."

The heavyset guy stiffened, turned his head slightly to mutter something, then turned it back as one of the waitresses, a plump blonde, approached him.

"Haven't seen much of you lately, Your Honor," the same man in the booth said to his back. "You been away on official business?"

"Coffee," Heavyset growled at the waitress.

"Anything to eat?"

"Chocolate donut, if you got any left."

"We don't. Sorry."

"Just as well," the talkative one said. "Chocolate donuts're bad for your waistline, Mr. Mayor. What'll your constituents think?"

Heavyset spun on his stool, high color blotching his cheeks, and half shouted, "Knock that mayor shit off, goddamn it!"

The noise level in there went down quick. One of the women customers made an offended noise; a father sitting with his wife and two small daughters called out an angry "Hey!" The redhaired waitress said sharply, "You watch your language in here, Pete. This is a family restaurant."

"Tell that to Verriker and his buddies there."

"Lighten up, why don't you?" another of the men said.

"I'll lighten up when you all leave me the hell alone. All of you. *All* of you."

"Hey, take it easy—"

Heavyset said, "I ain't taking crap from nobody anymore," and jerked off his stool, glared at the three men, threw a couple of random glares around the room, and stalked out.

As soon as he was gone, the atmosphere in there climbed back up to normal. The man named Verriker said, "Balfour gets weirder and weirder all the time."

"Well, you keep yanking his chain, Ned," one of his friends said.

"Hell, it's just a joke. He used to be able to take being kidded."

"Not anymore. He always was a hothead, but now it's like he thinks everybody's out to get him."

"Brought it on himself, didn't he? The way he does business, treats people?"

The other friend said, "Never know what a guy like that's liable to do. I say it'd be smart to cut him some slack."

"Maybe you're right."

Conversation among the three lagged after that. A

couple of minutes later, they paid their bill and went out in a bunch.

Kerry said, "Now what do you suppose that was all about?"

"No idea."

"People here don't seem to like their mayor very much."

"If he is the mayor. Didn't look like a politician to me."

He wasn't one. When the waitress came over with our check, Kerry, who is neither shy nor retiring, asked her if Pete Balfour was the mayor of Six Pines. The question brought a wry and somewhat sour chuckle.

"Not hardly. That man couldn't get elected dogcatcher if we needed one."

"He's not running for mayor, then?"

"Not of Six Pines," the waitress said. "He wouldn't get fifty votes."

So we still didn't know what it was all about. Not that it mattered or was worth pursuing. Local business and none of ours.

After lunch, Kerry and I drove down to the south end of town. Just before you got to the Six Pines Fairgrounds, there were a couple of stands selling fireworks. Both had prominently displayed signs written in large letters: WARNING! FOR USE IN DESIGNATED AREAS ONLY! HEAVY FINES FOR UNAUTHORIZED USE!

Kerry said, "The fire danger must be high this time of year."

"Probably is, as hot and dry as it is."

"I wonder why they allow fireworks at all."

"If they weren't allowed, people would just go buy them somewhere else and bring them in. This way, the authorities can exercise some control."

"We're not going to let that effect our decision to buy here, are we? The fire danger, I mean."

"I don't see why we should," I said. "The earthquake threat doesn't keep us from living in San Francisco."

The fairgrounds were built on several acres of flatland just before the county road began its climb up out of the valley. What we could see from the road was a single set of pale green bleachers alongside an oval track and field, a handful of low shedlike buildings and animal pens, part of an open grassy area ringed by picnic tables where a flea market was going on, and a wide hardpan parking area. A marquee sign on a couple of tall poles announced the Fourth of July festivities, and advertised stock car racing the last Saturday of every month through September and a flea market every Sunday.

There were quite a few people wandering among the vendor tables in the flea market. Kerry suggested we go in and see what they had for sale.

"More useless junk, probably," I said.

"They might have some local produce. Flea markets usually do."

I turned into the lot and we wandered around among the two dozen or so vendors sweltering under awnings and umbrellas and not doing much business. A lot of junk, all right, but Kerry was right about local produce; she bought a carton of ripe strawberries and some vegetables. I didn't expect to buy anything . . . until I spotted an old guy who had a bunch of old paperback books spread out on a table and in boxes underneath. I hadn't brought along anything to read, figuring on just an overnight stay, but now that we were going to be here for a few days, I would need some escapist entertainment. Most of the paperbacks were westerns in ratty condition, but I rummaged up a couple of mysteries by Fredric Brown and Day Keene, pulp writers I'd read and admired.

We didn't stay long—too hot out in the open field. After we left, I drove us a few miles up the county road to where a small lake was tucked in among the pines, around the lake, then back into Six Pines. We made a brief stop to pick up some additional groceries, did a little roaming in the hillsides above the town, and finally headed up-valley to the rented cabin. Enough exploring for one day.

The cabin faced west, into the blistery eye of the sun, so we stayed inside, sipping cold drinks and reading until early evening. Kerry made a light supper, and by then it was cool enough to eat on the deck. Afterward, we sat and watched the sun fall below the westward mountains, the sky taking on a smoky red color. A light breeze kicked up and it was much cooler as dusk began to settle.

"Nice day," Kerry said. "Just about perfect except for that little incident in the café."

"Jerks everywhere. The other locals seem friendly enough."

"I thought so, too. The more I see of Green Valley, the more I like it. If Emily wasn't coming home Sunday, I wouldn't mind staying over the Fourth. The parade and picnic sound like fun."

"Well, we could stay for that and drive back early Saturday."

"Yes, we could, but the traffic is sure to be horrendous. Anyhow, we don't have to decide yet. Let's just take it one day at a time."

"I'm all for that," I said. "What I'd like to do tomorrow is check out the river and the trout streams."

"Go right ahead. No fishing for me."

"You might enjoy it if you'd just give it a try."

"Stand in an icy stream and murder some poor trout? I don't think so."

"I don't keep or eat them anymore," I said. "Catch and release."

"The hooks still tear up their mouths. I just don't see the fun in it."

The fun was in tramping through the woods, communing with nature, as much as in testing your skill with a fly rod. But I'd made that point to her before and it wasn't worth repeating. You either had the fishing gene or you didn't.

After a time she said, "Shall we go ahead and make an offer before we leave? Or should we wait until Emily sees the place?"

"She'll like it all right, but there's no need to rush. If we seem too eager, the owners may try to hold out for their asking price."

"But you do want to make an offer?"

"Pretty sure."

"Then we'll come back up next week with Emily and do it then. Agreed?"

"Agreed."

She nodded and smiled. "We really are going to love it here," she said, as if the offer had already been made and accepted and the property was ours. "Beautiful views, peace and quiet, and only three hours from home. What more could we ask for?"

3

PETE BALFOUR

Verriker again. Verriker and those sons of bitches Ramsey and Lucchesi. Humiliating him in the café in front of all the locals and tourists. He could imagine what it'd been like in there after he stomped out. Verriker saying in that loudmouth voice of his, "There he goes, folks, there goes the Mayor of Asshole Valley," and everybody hooting it up then, even the goddamn tourists, hooting and making fun of him behind his back.

Verriker, Verriker, Verriker.

He kept seeing that smug face, hearing that cackling laugh burn in his ears like acid. Saw that face and heard that laugh no matter where he went, in his truck, in his own house, in his sleep. Christ, how he hated that bastard! He'd never hated anybody as much as he hated Ned Verriker.

The only way he could breathe again, start living a normal life again, was to get rid of the hate by getting rid of the poison from that mayor label. But how? There wasn't any way. Not as long as Ned Verriker was alive, there wasn't.

As long as Verriker was alive.

But what if he wasn't anymore? If Verriker was dead, the label would die with him. And so would the laughter. And Pete Balfour wouldn't be a joke anymore.

Payback.

Payback in spades.

The notion came into Balfour's head just like that after he got home, and he couldn't of got rid of it then if he'd wanted to. And he didn't want to. He'd never killed anybody before, nothing human, just deer and ducks and old man Henderson's cat that kept coming around and making Bruno bark half the night so a man couldn't sleep. He never wanted to kill anybody so bad before. But he had a real hunger for Verriker's blood. Imagined him on the ground, the blood running out of him, eyes all wide and starey like a gutshot buck.

Verriker dead.

He grabbed up an invoice pad and a felt-tip from the table next to his chair, wrote **Verriker dead** half a dozen times in big black letters. The words looked good written down like that. Looked fine.

So fine that he said them out loud. "Verriker dead, Verriker dead." Sweetest taste he'd had in his mouth in a long time.

That afternoon, sitting in his easy chair with his feet up and a cold Bud in his hand, he thought about ways to do it. A gun, sure, that was the simplest, and he had plenty to choose from. He liked guns, liked the feel of them, the recoil, the smell after he'd triggered off a round.

He had revolvers, a couple of deer rifles, a regular pump shotgun and a sawed-off, the Bushmaster assault rifle and Sterling MK-7 semiautomatic pistol that he'd bought from that black market Russian, Rosnikov, who Harry Logan had steered him to down in Stockton.

But hell, he couldn't do it with a gun, not any kind. If he just went out and shot the son of a bitch, no matter how careful he was, he'd be the number one suspect. Everybody knew how he felt about Verriker and having that mayor tag slung around his neck. Bugger turned up shot, the county cops'd come straight to his door. Same if he used a knife or a hatchet or a hunk of firewood.

Accident.

That was the ticket. Make it look like an accident. Accidents can happen to anybody, any time. They couldn't blame Pete Balfour if he was nowhere around when Verriker had a fatal one.

Took him the rest of the afternoon and a full six-pack to work out a plan. It was a good one, slick and not too risky, and it'd fix Verriker better than a gun or some other weapon. The only problem with it was he wouldn't be there to see it happen, but that was all right. He could live with that as long as Verriker died with it.

Verriker's wife, Alice, would get it, too, but Balfour didn't care about her. She was almost as vicious and mouthy as her husband, with a tongue as sharp as a razor. Humiliated him once herself, he remembered, that time in high school when he'd hit on her before she started going with Verriker. Laughed at him in front of a bunch of other girls, called him Frogface and told him his breath smelled bad, why didn't he go home and drink a gallon of Listerine? Bitch. She had it coming to her same as Verriker did.

How soon? Hell, sooner the better.

Balfour popped another Bud and leaned back with his eyes closed, picturing how it would be. How he'd work it, step by step, and what he'd do afterward and the high he'd feel when he got the news. Biggest high of his life. It'd last a long, long time, too, he'd make sure of that. Go about his business, pretend to be real sad when somebody mentioned what'd happened. Keep a straight face and laugh like hell behind it, the way Verriker and the rest had been laughing at him.

Just thinking about it started him chuckling. And once he got started, he couldn't seem to stop. The chuckles turned into snickers and the snickers into guffaws.

He laughed so hard thinking about Verriker dead, he almost peed his pants.

4

KERRY

They stayed in bed late again Monday morning. No sex today, just cuddling and dozing. Weekend getaways were all well and good, but one or two nights wasn't really enough time to relax and unwind. Even if they only spent a few more days in Green Valley, it would still have the feel of a real vacation—the first one she and Bill had had in a long time.

Well, that was her fault as much as his. He'd been a workaholic most of his adult life and so had she. Long hours at Bates and Carpenter as a copywriter, even longer ones after last year's promotion to vice president. The advertising business, like the detective business, put demands on a person that had more to do with passion and dedication than a striving for financial security. Ad woman wasn't what she did for a living; it was who she was, what she'd been born to be. Same with Bill in the detective profession—the reason he'd been having so much trouble following through on his vow of semiretirement.

But there came a time when you had to back off at least a little, take some time for yourself before you burned out physically, mentally, or both. Start seeing what else life had to offer while you were still young enough and healthy enough to enjoy the experiences. The breast cancer had taught her that. She'd been fortunate to survive the months of surgery and chemotherapy and psychic drain, even more fortunate that there had been no recurrence (knock wood) and the cancer seemed to be in permanent remission. Still, she hadn't learned the slow-down lesson as well as she should have. Continued to work too hard, still didn't treat herself to enough TLC. Bill's decision to limit his agency time to two days a week had been something of a wake-up call for her. She hadn't thought he would stick to it this time, any more than he had on his previous pledge, but so far he had. And if he could, so could she.

A second home in Green Valley would be a good start. Quiet, stress-free environment, a place to relax, recharge your batteries whenever you felt the need. It would be good for Emily, too, in smaller doses. Thirteen-almost-fourteen-year-old girls were tightly wedded to their home turf and their circle of friends, but exposure to country life now and then ought to provide some perspective. Emily was extremely bright and well-grounded, but nonetheless impressionable and edging into a difficult period of adolescence. Kerry remembered her own early teens, the peer influences and the raging hormones, the silly choices and mistakes she'd made. Oh, yes, difficult and worrisome both.

Having a second home didn't mean that you couldn't

or shouldn't go anywhere else. She'd always had a mild yen to travel, visit England, western Europe, parts of Canada, but she and Bill had been such urban-dwelling, work-driven homebodies that they'd never made any plans that went beyond the casual discussion stage. Talk herself into spending a couple of weeks on foreign soil and she'd be able to talk him into it, too. At least one trip before Emily left the nest in another four or five years.

First things first, though. Make an offer on this cabin, and establish themselves here. The rest would take care of itself in due course. There was plenty of time (knock wood again).

Bill was still asleep when she got up. Good for him; he didn't get enough sleep at home. Even when he wasn't working, he was up early and rattling around looking for something to occupy his time. Definite Type A when she first met him; that and the long hours and job stress and his less-than-sensible eating habits had made him a heart attack or stroke candidate. He'd slowed down some in recent years, after Emily had come into their lives and then her long struggle with the breast cancer, but she still worried about him. Another reason, the main one, for owning a place like this.

Thinking about Bill's health led her to start worrying again about Cybil's. Her mother was in her late eighties, still mentally sharp, at least most of the time, but frail and too stubborn and independent to move into an assisted living facililty. Redwood Village, the retirement community in Larkspur, was her home now she said, and she fully intended to live there until she died. She had close neighbors, including one in the other half of her duplex, and they all watched out for each other. That was fine in theory. So was the fact that Redwood Village had a small clinic with a physician and nurse on twenty-four-hour call. But she'd had two falls in the past five months, and on the second, she'd banged her head on a table leg, blacked out, and lain on the floor for God knew how long—Cybil wouldn't say—before coming around. Cybil made light of the episode because that was her way, but the fact remained that she could have hurt herself a lot more seriously than she had. Could have died there on her living room floor.

Kerry had called her Thursday night to tell her about the trip to Green Valley, and she'd been all right then. A little vague in her responses, though, as if what she was hearing didn't fully compute. Call her again this morning? Two things Cybil didn't like (well, two among several): being a burden to anyone and being checked up on. Any more than one call a week, unless she was the one who initiated it, fell into the checking-up category. But under the circumstances . . .

When she finished making coffee, Kerry took a cup and her cell phone out onto the front deck. Another glorious morning, already very warm. Too warm to sit in the sun, she moved her chair over into a patch of shade. Her excuse for calling, she thought, would be to report that their second home search was finally over. It wasn't strictly true yet, but a little while lie was better than incurring her mother's wrath by saying, "I just called to see how you're doing."

She made the call, waited through six, seven, eight rings. No answer. That didn't have to mean anything ominous— Cybil might be out shopping or for a walk with a friend, or puttering in her small garden—but it was a little nervous-making just the same. Kerry let the line buzz emptily four more times before she disconnected, telling herself not to worry, if anything had happened, she would have had emergency notification. But she couldn't help thinking about those two falls, Cybil lying unconscious on the floor . . .

Bill was up; she could hear him singing inside. Singing . . . my God, it sounded more like a rooster being strangled. He was a wonderful man in most ways and he genuinely loved music, especially jazz, but he couldn't carry a tune in a bucket.

She finished her coffee and tried Cybil's number again. Still no answer. She had numbers for two of her mother's neighbors; maybe she should call one of them—No, that was a panic reaction. Cybil was all right, just out somewhere. She'd be furious if Kerry started contacting neighbors without definite cause. Just keep trying until she answered.

Bill was in high spirits when he appeared and Kerry didn't want to dampen them by voicing her concerns about Cybil. He was wearing old clothes, his hiking boots, and that godawful droopy green hat with the moldy feather he'd dredged up out of the trunk of the car—his standard fishing outfit.

"I'm ready to head out," he said, "do battle with some trout. Sure you won't come along?"

"I'm sure."

"It'll be cooler down in the valley."

"I don't mind the heat as much as you do," she said. "I made you a couple of sandwiches. They're in the fridge."

"*Grazie.* What would I do without you?"

"Make your own sandwiches and load them up with too much butter and mayonnaise."

He laughed. "So what're you going to do with yourself here alone?"

"Read, relax. Maybe take a walk in the woods."

"Watch out for bears."

"Uh-huh. Bears. If I see one, I'll imitate one of your growls and scare the wits out of it."

As soon as he was gone, she tried Cybil's number again. Still no answer. Oh, Cybil, come on! she thought. Then chided herself for being such a worrywart. But when you had an elderly, fiercely headstrong, frail, and fall-prone mother that you loved dearly, it was increasingly difficult not to worry.

She read for a while, stretched out on one of the deck chairs, but she couldn't seem to concentrate. Another unanswered call. An unbidden image of Cybil sprawled out on the duplex floor flashed across her mind; immediately, she blanked it out. Too much imagination, dammit, inherited from Cybil—one of the 1940's most accomplished pulp fiction writers and the author of two well-received mystery novels written in her late seventies. The Writing Wades, mother and daughter. Although in Cybil's not-so-humble opinion, a series of stories and two books about a tough-talking private eye named Samuel Leatherman was superior work to the creation of advertising slogans and campaigns. "We both write fiction," she'd said once, "but when you get right down to it, my kind's more honest." Well, maybe she had a point. A debatable one, anyway.

Lunch was a dish of strawberries. At one o'clock, another call went unanswered. Then, at one-thirty—

"Hello?" Cybil's voice, sounding perfectly fine.

"There you are," Kerry said, relieved. "I called a couple of times earlier—"

"Did you? Why?"

"Oh, just to let you know that we're still in Green Valley—"

"Where?"

"Green Valley. In the Sierras near Placerville."

"What're you doing up there?"

Oh, Lord. "Looking for a second home. I told you that the last time we talked, remember?"

"Of course I remember. I think it's a good idea."

"What is?"

"That you have a second home."

"Well, I think we finally found one that suits us. That's why we're still here—staying a few days to make sure we like the place enough to make an offer. It's a hillside cabin with a valley view—"

"Good, I'm glad. You can tell me all about it when I see you. When are you coming home?"

"Well, we're not sure yet. We were planning on Thursday, but we may stay over the Fourth and drive back Saturday. If there's anything you need—"

"Why should I need anything?"

"I just thought there might be." Don't ask where she's been, Kerry thought. But a question slipped out in spite of herself. "Were you out shopping?"

"Shopping?"

"This morning . . . today."

"Yes. Jane Greeley and I went to lunch afterward. Why?"

"I just wondered."

"Where I was and what I was doing. Checking up?"

"No, no . . ."

"Yes, yes. Well, I'm fine. No falls lately. But I did cut my thumb slicing a tomato last night. Bandaged it all by myself, too."

"Don't be testy, Cybil. I was just—"

"I'm not testy. When did you say you were coming home? After the Fourth?"

"We're not sure yet. Either Thursday or Saturday."

"Is Emily up there with you?"

"No. She's in Los Angeles with her school glee club. I told you that before we left, didn't I?"

"No, I don't think so. When will she be home?"

"Sunday."

"That long?"

"Well, they're giving a holiday performance—"

"When are you going to bring her over for a visit? I haven't seen the child, or you or that husband of yours, in weeks."

One week, to be exact. Cybil really was getting vague, her memory slipping badly. No use trying to deny it.

Kerry said carefully, keeping the concern out of her voice, "One day next week, whichever one's good for you."

"Any day is fine. I'm always here, you know that. Except when I go out to shop and have lunch with Jane Greeley. Call first, before you come."

"Of course I will."

"Good-bye, dear. Enjoy the rest of your little vacation."

"'Bye, take care," Kerry said, but her mother had already broken the connection.

She sighed as she tucked her cell into her purse. The thought that Cybil might not be with them much longer crossed her mind; instantly, she rejected it. Just because her mother was showing signs of senility didn't mean she was teetering on the edge of the grave. Her father's death had been difficult enough to deal with, even though they hadn't been close, but it had happened so many years ago, her memories of him were faint and fuzzy, like images in very old photographs. It was different with Cybil. Friend and mentor, a woman she admired and respected—yes, and needed—as well as loved. Losing her would be as painful as losing Bill or Emily.

But it wasn't going to happen soon. It simply wasn't. Why start hanging crepe needlessly?

Time to go for her walk. Worry always made her restless, and the only cure for that was exercise. Besides, the cabin had grown stuffy with trapped heat. It'd be much cooler in among the pines that crowded around the edges of the property.

Bill probably wouldn't be back before she was, but just in case, she wrote him a short note and left it on the kitchen table. Then she rubbed some sunblock on her face and bare arms, put on her wide-brimmed sun hat, closed all the windows, and locked up after she went out—a precaution because she didn't see any need to take her purse along. Bill had a key; Sam Budlong had given them two.

Where to go? The woods behind the house seemed the most inviting. She went up past the gnarled old apple trees and through the gate in the sagging perimeter fence. A barely discernible path, man-made or animal-made, meandered through the timber beyond: she'd spotted it on Saturday's inspection. She picked her way along it for a hundred yards or so, to where it split into two sharply divergent forks. Arbitrary choice: the right one. She turned that way, and the forest closed in around her.

Much cooler in among the old-growth pines, the air scented with a mixture of resin and needle and leaf mold. The cool semidarkness, the cathedral-like quiet, reminded her of Yosemite—a camping trip she'd been taken on there as a child, not by Cybil and her father—he hadn't been an outdoorsman in any sense of the word—but by the family of a school friend. Fabulous mountain vistas and ice-blue lakes that she could still recall with a sense of wonder, but it had been the forests, dark and deep and hushed, that had impressed her the most. She never tired of walking in forests vast like those or small like these, reexperiencing that childhood pleasure.

Dark, deep woods. The phrase made her think of the poem by Robert Frost about woods—walking on a snowy winter's evening. A poem that was also a metaphor about life, the long travel from beginning to end and the promises you made along the way. Promises like hers to Bill and Emily and Cybil and herself, the meaningful ones that she had kept and would continue to keep if she could, if only there were enough time.

Gloomy reflections, harking back to her concern for Cybil. She erased them the way Cybil had taught her to erase unpleasant thoughts as a child—with one mental swipe, as if they were chalked words on a blackboard.

The path continued to meander, growing fainter and

harder to follow in the darkish light. Kerry wondered if she ought to mark trees or snap off twigs or fern fronds in case she lost her way. Not necessary, she decided. Her sense of direction was good and she wouldn't wander far. Besides, it wasn't as if she were walking through miles of unbroken forest. There were other homes in the area. If she did lose her way, she was bound to stumble upon one of them.

Beyond a mostly dry streambed, the tree growth thinned into a long rocky meadow. Once she'd crossed it, the terrain gradually sloped upward through another stand of timber. The trail disappeared partway up the incline and she found herself plowing through tightly packed trees and thickening ground cover. She stopped finally, and would have turned back if she hadn't seen what looked like a road through a break in the pines at the top of the incline.

It was a road, she found when she'd climbed up the rest of the way—what looked to be the rutted remains of an old logging road. At first look, it seemed long disused, but then she spied evidence of recent passage in the ragged carpeting of pine needles and decaying vegetation that covered it. A shortcut to someone's home, possibly. Or maybe a local lover's lane.

Might as well follow it a ways. A dead pine branch covered with decaying cones lay next to the spot where she'd emerged; she noted it, then set off to her left, walking on the verge to avoid ruts and potholes.

She'd gone a hundred yards or so when she saw the pickup.

It was drawn in on a grassy area on the right-hand side of the road, so that only a small section of its rear end was visible from a distance. Kerry moved ahead until she was abreast of the vehicle. Dirty white pickup, several years old, its bed empty. There didn't seem to be anybody inside, either.

She hesitated, then moved out into the middle of the road. There was nothing to see anywhere around the truck, nothing to hear except the chatter of a jay. Don't be nosy, she told herself. But she'd always had a lively curiosity, another inheritance from her mother, and it got the best of her.

Slowly, she advanced until she was standing next to the driver's door. She bent to peer through the dirt-streaked side window. The cab was empty except for fast-food remains, bags and rags and miscellaneous clutter. Whoever owned the pickup was a sloppy housekeeper.

On impulse, she reached down and tried the door. Locked. Just as well; she shouldn't be poking around private property. The pickup didn't look abandoned. Probably parked here by a hiker like herself.

She still had her hand on the door handle when she heard rustling sounds behind her. She jerked upright, turning, just as a man's voice said harshly, "What the hell you doing there, lady?"

He'd come up out of the trees on this side of the road, no more than twenty feet away. A big man, dressed in khaki work clothes, carrying a toolbox in one hand. When he started toward her, glowering, she recognized him: the unattractive, middle-aged man who'd been called mayor in the Green Valley Café yesterday. Balfour, wasn't it? Pete Balfour?

"I said what you doing, snooping in my truck?"

"I wasn't snooping," she said. "I saw it parked here, and I thought it might be abandoned—"

"Who are you? I never seen you before."

He was still moving toward her. The ferocity of his expression made her back away from him, along the side of the pickup.

"I don't live here. My husband and I are renting the Murray cabin—"

"What you doing in these woods?"

"Walking, that's all. Hiking."

He stopped abruptly, staring hard at her, his mouth twisted into a grimace that gave him a troll-like aspect. Kerry stopped, too. She felt the urge to turn and hurry away from him, but not because she was afraid. Nervous and embarrassed, yes, but not afraid—not yet.

"Why the hell'd you have to show up here, now?"

"I don't understand what you mean, Mr. Balfour. I—"

"What? What'd you say?"

"I said—"

He yelled, "Screwing everything up, goddamn you!" and dropped the toolbox and lunged at her.

The sudden attack caught her completely off guard; she had no time to run or try to defend herself. He caught hold of her, threw her sideways into the pickup's rear gate, jamming her elbow, wrenching her back, ripping loose a cry of pain and surging terror. He crowded in against her, spewing sour breath into her face. She tried to claw him, tried to scream, but by then, his body was wedged against hers and his thick hands were tight around her throat.

Squeezing, squeezing, until his face, the trees, the daylight all faded to black—

5

It was a quarter after four when I got back to the cabin. The locked front door surprised me a little because it meant Kerry wasn't there. I let myself in, and on the kitchen table I found a note: *Out for my walk. Back soon.* So she must have gone later than she'd indicated she would. Probably spent most of the day lazing around, maybe had herself a nice long nap.

In any case, she'd been away for a while because the cabin was muggy with all the windows closed. I opened four of them to let in the light afternoon breeze, provide some cross ventilation. Then I got a bottle of Sierra Nevada out of the rattling old refrigerator and took it onto the deck.

Cooling some now, with the breeze and the down-sliding sun. Hot day in the valley. Much of the terrain I'd explored had been open and unshaded, and I'd worked up a pretty good sweat. Tired myself out, too. I could feel the stiffness in my legs and back from all the tramping over uneven ground. I must've walked four or five miles, a lot more distance than I was used to.

But I'd found a couple of likely fishing spots, neither of them on the map I'd bought in the sporting goods store in Six Pines—one along a clear, shallow, fast-moving stream, the other a tree-shaded, moss-banked pool. Plenty of trout moving in and out of that pool; you couldn't quite see them, except as faint shadows gliding among darker shadows beneath the surface, but they were there all right. I'd figured a Blue Quill or Thorax Dun would work well in the stream, and a Gray Hackle just right for the pool. Wrong on all three counts. Or maybe the fish just weren't biting today. I hadn't even had a decent nibble.

Tomorrow morning early, I thought, if I could haul my creaky old carcass out of bed in the cold light of dawn, I'd go out again. Today was the first time I'd been trout fishing in years, ever since that harrowing time at Deep Mountain Lake high up in the Sierras near Quincy. Thought I'd lost my zest for the sport, but today's outing was proof that I hadn't; I had just needed some time away from it, was all. If we did end up buying this place, I'd probably indulge in quite a bit of catch and release in the future. As much as I'd once enjoyed fresh trout pan-fried in butter, I'd reached the point in my life where I could no longer willingly take a life of any kind.

I'd have one more try at talking Kerry into coming with me tomorrow. She wouldn't have to put a line out herself, just be there to keep me company and share the experience. Convince her to try it once, and she'd be as hooked as one of the rainbows or browns I planned to catch.

I finished my beer, went inside for another. Moved my chair to the far side of the deck, put my feet up on the rail, and sat there sipping and taking in the view. The beer and the day's exercise made me drowsy; I nodded off for a while, until an ear-buzzing mosquito jerked me out of it. The low angle of the sun told me it must be close to six o'clock. A glance at my watch confirmed it.

And still no Kerry. She must have left just before I got back, I thought. Then I thought no, she had to've been out for at least a half hour by then or it wouldn't have been so stuffy inside.

Some walk. But how far could she have gone? Quite a ways if she'd taken the secondary road below; it meandered along the hillside for a considerable distance in both directions before dropping down to the main valley road. But she'd said something this morning about a walk in the woods. Which woods? There was timber all around the property, all along Ridge Hill Road.

Possible she'd gotten herself lost, but that wasn't likely. There were other houses tucked in among most of the nearby forestland, except for the section that ran along the ridge above and down the other side, and she wouldn't have gone up that far. Kerry was not a risk-taker for one thing, and for another, she had a built-in compass that operated even in unfamiliar surroundings.

Some kind of accident? Tripped, fell, hurt herself badly enough so that she couldn't make it back? That possibility was what worried me the most. Accidents could happen to anybody at any time, no matter how careful you were.

I let another fifteen minutes go by, my nerves jumping, the fear of some sort of accident jabbing at my mind. And when she still didn't show, I went looking for her.

The woods at the rear first. There was a gate in the fence back there . . . through it seemed the most likely way for her to have gone. On the other side was what looked like a deer trail, and I followed that to where it split in two. Damn! I went a little ways along each fork, looking for some sign of recent passage and not finding any. She could have gone in either direction—the timber ran all along the rear of the property and down on both sides. If she'd come in here at all.

I took the left fork first, followed it until it petered out against a deadfall. You could get around it, but not without making a detour through fern groves on either side. None of the ferns appeared to have been trampled.

Back to the other fork and along its winding course. Broken twigs, scuffed-through needles . . . somebody had been this way recently. Kerry? It could also have been a deer; in one place, I came on a little pile of black pellet droppings. I was not enough of a woodsman to make the distinction.

The trail led me out of the trees, across a shallow streambed and a rock-strewn brown meadow. No sign of Kerry. No sign that she'd ever been here. What was discernible of the path ended at the far end of the clearing, beyond which was a moderately steep incline through trees and underbrush. I thought about climbing up there, but I didn't do it. The muscles in my legs were already tight-drawn from the exertion.

I couldn't keep searching blind like this. The dusky light was deepening, which made the footing even more uncertain; in my tired and edgy state, I was liable to be the one to suffer a harmful fall. My watch told me I'd been chasing around in these woods for nearly an hour. Kerry might have returned to the cabin by now, be there waiting and wondering where I'd gone. If she had, I'd feel like a fool for all this frantic activity—a relieved fool.

I made my way back through the trees, and even with my eyes cast downward, I stumbled a couple of times over hidden obstacles. Once I thought I'd managed to get myself lost, then located the trail again and finally emerged at the gate in the boundary fence. I half ran around to the front of the cabin.

The door was still locked.

Kerry wasn't there.

Now I really was scared. I hurried down to the graveled parking area, drove to Ridge Hill Road. The shortest route to the main valley road was to the north; I turned in that direction. No Kerry. There was a good-sized public park on the west side of the valley road intersection, a campground a short distance away on the east side; I made looping passes through both. No Kerry. Back along Ridge Hill in the opposite direction. No Kerry. Another secondary road branched upward to the left; the signpost there gave its name as Skyview Drive and warned that there was *No Outlet*. I swung up there. No Kerry.

Ahead was another intersection, this one on the left. When I neared it, I saw that the branch was unpaved and heavily rutted—an old logging road probably, that angled up through the woods. I sleeved sweat off my face as I slowed to make the turn. Follow the logging road as far as it goes, I thought, and if I still didn't find her, go back to Ridge Hill and start knocking on doors in the vicinity and asking if anyone had seen her.

The explosion happened just as I swung onto the logging road.

Booming concussion, somewhere nearby. A fireball inside a cloud of oily black smoke boiled up above the timber to my right—very close. My frayed nerve endings sparked like live wires; reflexively, I jammed on the brakes. The flames were no longer visible, but the smoke kept pumping upward in great gouts, putting a black filter across the fading blue of the sky.

I don't believe in the kind of ambulance chasing mindset that draws people to accident scenes, but with Kerry missing and the nearness of the blast, I wasn't about to ignore it. Christ knew what had happened over there. I slammed the gear shift into reverse, backed out in a sideways slide onto Skyview Drive pointing south. The blacktop climbed up over a rise, and when it dropped down out of the pines into several hundred yards of rolling open space, I had a clear view of the source and aftermath of the explosion.

There was a house in a pocket backed by a humpbacked hill . . . what had been a house. Now it was a pulsing, squared-off sheet of flame, the oily smoke still pouring out of it and blackening the sky above. A car in the yard had been blown onto its side by the force of the blast, its blue paint scorched and blistered. Which meant at least one person had been inside the house when the place went up. Dead . . . no way anybody could have survived that kind of fiery eruption.

Not Kerry. Of course, not Kerry. *Not Kerry!*

I was the first person on the scene: no other cars on the road or on the drive leading up to the burning house. I accelerated to the bottom of the rise, pulled up in a shallow ditch on the far side of the driveway. There was no good reason for me to run up into the yard but I did it anyway, propelled by my half-panicked fear for Kerry. No sign of anybody inside or out, alive or dead. I couldn't get any closer to the conflagration than fifty yards. The radiating waves of heat were intense, the smoke thick enough to affect my breathing, start me choking and hacking.

Neither of the two outbuildings, a barn and a smaller structure, had caught fire yet, but falling embers had already ignited patches of grass in the yard and on the lower edges of the hill. The pine woods along the hilltop and on the near perimeter were untouched so far. If a fire got started in any part of them, as dry as some of the underbrush was, it would move fast enough to destroy acres of timberland and threaten any number of other homes.

Other vehicles were arriving now—a couple of private cars, a deputy sheriff's cruiser. In the distance, I heard the first wail of sirens. I was back on the access drive by then, away from the pulsing heat and roiling smoke, trying to suck in enough fresh air to clear my lungs.

A fresh-faced young deputy came running up. "What the hell happened here?"

"I don't know," I said between coughs. "Sudden explosion, that's all I know. Only been here a couple of minutes."

"Either of the Verrikers inside?"

Verriker. The name was vaguely familiar, but I didn't try to place it. "Car there says somebody was."

"Christ. Oh, Christ."

I had nothing to say to that. The roof of the barn was burning now, in crawling flames like napalm. Out on the road, the oncoming noise of sirens and rumbling engines overrode the thrum and crackle of the blaze.

The deputy said to me, "Go back to the road, stay out of the way," and hurried off without waiting for an answer.

I retreated down the driveway. People were still showing up; eight or nine cars were now strewn along both sides of Skyview Drive. Men and a few women had begun milling around in little groups, their faces reflecting shock and that avidity you always see in the watchers at disaster scenes—a mixture of dread, relief that it was somebody else's disaster, and a primitive eagerness for the horrors they might be confronted with. A fat man in a stained undershirt crowded up next to me as I came out onto the road, saying excitedly, "What was it? The furnace blow up?" I shook my head at him, moved over to stand next to my car. I didn't want to talk to anybody else. I felt bad for whoever had died in that house, but it was a distracted sympathy. All I could think about was Kerry.

A few seconds later, the fire trucks came rushing into view, three of them with *Green Valley VFD* written on their sides, the one in the middle a tanker; a paramedic unit made it a caravan of four. They barreled up the access drive, lights flashing and sirens dying, and veered off across the yard. Firefighters jumped out and scurried to unload hoses, axes, shovels, and other equipment. A pair of EMTs emerged, too, but there was nothing for them to do except stand around looking alert.

No other vehicles came down Skyview Drive; a roadblock must have been hastily set up to keep out any more gawkers. The two deputies on the scene had joined forces to disperse the ones that were already here. One of them had a bullhorn and was shouting through it, telling everyone to leave the area for their own safety. The small crowd broke up pretty fast, people heading for their cars but with their heads turned and their eyes fixed on what was happening on the property—firemen deploying with hoses that sprayed water and fire retardant foam, other volunteers swarming along the hill above and behind the burning house to dig firebreaks. I was anxious to leave, too, get back to the cabin to find out if Kerry had returned. At the same time, I was reluctant because I didn't know for sure that she hadn't been inside the house when it exploded. Crazy notion, the odds against it millions to one. What would she have been doing here? But I could not get it out of my head.

I had the driver's door open when a white van careened down over the rise, let through for a reason that soon became clear. Somebody near me called out, "Look! That's Ned Verriker's van." It raced up, slewed to a stop, and a wiry, dark-faced man in work clothes jumped out and started a splay-footed run up the driveway. I knew then why his name sounded familiar: he was one of the trio who'd occupied the booth behind Kerry's and mine in the Green Valley Café yesterday.

The deputies got in his way, held him back. "You don't want to go up there," one of them said. "Nothing you can do."

"She . . . she didn't get out? Alice?"

"Looks that way. I'm sorry, Ned."

"Oh God, that's her car in the yard, she must've just got home when . . . What happened? I don't understand—"

"Easy now. Easy."

"I had to work late or I'd've been in there, too. Alice . . . oh Jesus, Alice!"

I felt a little sick listening to Ned Verriker's outpouring of pain, but at the same time, his words brought a sense of relief. Must've just got home, he'd said. Then Kerry *couldn't* have been anywhere in the vicinity when it happened; there was no sensible reason for her to have hung around an empty house.

A sudden roaring, echoing crash drowned out the other sounds: the roof of the house collapsing into the black- and white-foamed shell. Flames and firebrands burst up and outward through fresh billows of smoke. The firefighters manning the retardant hoses continued to pour foam over the house while the water pumpers worked on saving the barn, putting out the grass fires. Keeping the blaze contained so it didn't spread into the surrounding timber was the important thing now.

All the onlookers were in their cars, backing and filling and jockeying into a stream that flowed uphill on Skyview Drive. I maneuvered into the middle of the pack. It crawled along; crawled along because the drivers up front were still rubbernecking. I had to resist a sharp impulse to lean on the horn, stick my head out the window, and howl at them to hurry the hell up.

Up over the hill at last, and then the line moved a little faster to the intersection with Ridge Hill Road. That was where they'd set up the roadblock: flares and another deputy, this one a woman, directing traffic from in front of her cruiser. Ridge Hill had become a parade route, only the big-eyed watchers were inside the passing cars. It took a couple more minutes before I was past the cruiser and able to turn northbound, but the driver of the car in front of me wouldn't go over twenty-five despite a couple of horn taps from close behind. By the time I got to the Murray property driveway, I was soaked in sweat and the blood beat in my ears was like an extended jazz drum riff.

I slid the car into the parking area, spewing gravel, and ran up onto the front deck. Empty. I yanked open the screen door, twisted the knob. Locked, as I'd left it.

Kerry was still missing.

6

PETE BALFOUR

Nothing ever seemed to go right for him, nothing important anyways. He had no damn luck at all. Sometimes it seemed like the gods or whoever had had it in for him even before he come squalling out of the old lady. Ugly face, head like moss growing on a fuckin' rock, no decent woman, no money except for what he could scrounge up by using his brains along with his muscles. And to top it off, Verriker's Mayor of Asshole Valley tag. Wasn't fair, dammit. Neither was what'd happened today. You couldn't get anymore unfair than that.

First the woman showing up where she had no business being, fooling around his pickup, and then calling him Mr. Balfour. Maybe he shouldn't of cut loose and choked her the way he had, but he couldn't just let her walk away knowing who he was. Yeah, and how the hell had she known? He'd never seen her before in his life.

And then, just as bad, finding out Verriker was still alive. Oh, that bitch Alice had got hers, all right, but she didn't matter half as much. Verriker had plenty of luck, that was for sure. Always quit work right at five-thirty, always got home before Alice did, but no, not tonight. Tonight of all nights, he'd had to get stuck working late at Builders Supply on account of a shipment of PVC pipe coming in delayed and needing to be unloaded. How could you plan against something like that happening? Something like the woman happening? You couldn't, nobody could. Just plain lousy luck.

Such a sweet plan, too. He couldn't of had it worked out any better.

He knew the Verriker place well enough because he'd done some repair work out there a couple of years ago. No other homes close by, the woods running up along the hill on one side, the old logging road that nobody hardly ever used in the daytime. And no worries about the house being empty in the afternoon. Verriker and Alice both worked in town, her in the beauty shop, which was a laugh with a horse face like hers. No kids, no live-in relatives.

Easy as pie getting down there with his toolkit, then getting inside through the side door under the carport. Door opened straight into the kitchen, a wall switch just inside that turned on the kitchen light. He'd rigged the switch first, so it'd be sure to arc, then exposed the wires in the ceiling light fixture for good measure. Then he'd loosened the gas line connection behind the stove just enough to let the gas bleed out slow. That was all there was to it. In and out in less than fifteen minutes. Figuring Verriker might hit the switch right away even though it'd still be daylight when he got home, but if he didn't, well, him or Alice would do it once it got on toward dark. Figuring either way, Verriker would be dead before nightfall.

Figuring wrong.

He'd found out Verriker was still alive and why when he walked into the Buckhorn. He wasn't supposed to be in there tonight, or anywhere near Six Pines when the house blew up. Supposed to be in Placerville. What he'd planned to do was drive down there after he rigged the Verrikers' kitchen and buy a few things at Home Depot so he'd have a good excuse for the trip in case he needed one. Eat an early supper and afterward hunt up a bar he'd never been in before, where nobody'd know him and he wouldn't have to listen to any of that mayor crap. Then drive back to Green Valley late, long after the house and Verriker and Alice blew sky high.

But the woman wandering around the woods had screwed that up. Screwed it up royal.

By the time Balfour got done with her, he was too shaky to do anything except go home and guzzle three boilermakers, fast, to calm himself down. The drinks put him about half in the bag, and that was why he hadn't gone to Placerville—he didn't want to risk getting stopped by a county cop or the highway patrol, couldn't afford to do anything that might call attention to himself. So he'd stayed put. Hell, why not? Didn't really make any difference if he was home alone when Verriker got his. Slow gas leak, an arcing light switch, nobody would think it was anything but a freak accident. Accidents happen all the time, right?

The Verriker place was a couple of miles from his, so

he hadn't heard the explosion. Just as well. If he'd known right when the house blew, he'd of had an urge to drive over there, try to get a squint at the wreckage with Verriker burning up inside, and that wouldn't of been smart with all the liquor in him. But he'd heard the siren on the fire truck from the up-valley VFD garage as it shot past, and it'd told him enough to put a smile on his face and give him half a boner. He'd waited an hour or so, and then drove slow and careful into town. Thinking on the way that he'd pretend not to know who or what had blown up because he'd been busy working at home; act real surprised and solemn when he heard the news.

They were talking about it in the Buckhorn, all right, Ramsey and Stivic and Alf the bartender, and Balfour cocked an ear and that was how he found out Verriker was still alive. Nobody said anything to him, not one word. They didn't want nothing to do with him unless they could rag on him. It was like he was some goddamn stranger walked in off the street.

He didn't have to act surprised. Hardest thing was trying not to show how frustrated and pissed off he was, not that it would of mattered if he'd clapped his hands and danced a jig. He had two more boilermakers because he needed them and because maybe it'd look funny if he rushed out without hoisting a couple. He was on his second when Ramsey said Verriker didn't have insurance or much savings, why didn't they take up a collection to help pay for poor Alice's funeral. Alf got a jar and passed it around. Balfour had to kick in, too—two bucks, all he had in his wallet except for twenties. Lucchesi gave him a dirty look and somebody else muttered, "Cheap bastard." Screw 'em all. He didn't care what they thought as long as they didn't start up with that mayor shit.

He was still pretty shook up when he got back to the house. More whiskey and beer didn't help, all it did was make him fuzzy-headed. He turned on the TV, turned it off again, then just sat in his chair, drinking and trying to think what he was going to do about Verriker.

Couldn't just back off, let him go on living and making Pete Balfour's life miserable. Had to find some other way to fix him.

And the woman on the logging road . . . real problem there, too. She'd said something about a husband before he jumped her. Staying at the Murray place with her husband, that was it. Husband would report her missing if he hadn't already. County cops'd be out looking for her sooner or later, combing the woods. Christ, what if they found her? No, they wouldn't find her, not where he'd stashed her. But he couldn't just leave her there. Had to find some permanent place to hide her body so they'd never be able to tie her to him. Body. Jesus. But what other choice did he have?

Maybe he should—

No, forget it. Deal with that tomorrow.

Verriker, too—tomorrow. Couldn't think straight now, couldn't plan.

He poured another drink, cracked another brew.

Why didn't nothing ever work out easy for him?

7

The sheriff's deputy in charge of the Six Pines substation was the fresh-faced young guy who'd come running up to me in the Verrikers' driveway. His name was Broxmeyer. I waited half an hour for him; the only person in the station when I walked in just before dusk was a gray-haired woman who worked the desk and the radio dispatch unit, and she wasn't in a position to help me. So I waited, alternately squirming on a wooden chair and pacing, sweating even though the air-conditioning was on, trying to adopt Jake Runyon's method of blanking his mind during a downtime period. It didn't work. All sorts of dark images kept spinning and sliding around inside my head, banging into one another. The knot that had formed in my stomach, cold and hard and acidic, kept funneling the sour taste of bile into the back of my throat.

Broxmeyer looked draggy and worn out when he finally showed. His uniform was rumpled and stained under the armpits; a smudge of something darkened one cheek. He smelled of smoke and sweat. So did I, probably; I hadn't even thought about changing clothes.

The woman asked him if the fire at the Verriker place was completely out and contained yet. He said yes, but there was still some concern about a flare-up that would endanger the surrounding timber; one of the VFD trucks would remain on watch all night. I made some noise getting up off the chair to remind the woman that I was there. She said to me, "This is Deputy Broxmeyer," and then to him, "Man's been waiting to see you, Greg."

Broxmeyer took a look at me. "You're the man I talked to at the fire scene."

"That's right." I told him my name.

"You're not local. What were you doing there?"

"Looking for my wife. She's missing. That's why I'm here."

"Missing? For how long?"

"Since sometime this afternoon. Six, seven hours." I was making an effort to keep my voice even, unemotional, but some of the fear leaked through and made it break a little here and there. "She went for a walk, just a short walk, and she hasn't come back. I can't find her anywhere."

Broxmeyer ruminated for a few seconds, chewing on a corner of his lower lip. Then he said, "Let's talk in my office."

He led me through a gate in the waist-high partition that cut the station into two uneven halves, then through another door into a glass-walled cubicle. He said, "Have a seat," and sat heavily behind a modular gray desk strewn with papers. I stayed on my feet; I was too jittery to do any more sitting.

He took off his cap, revealing a mop of lanky blond

hair, and pinched at his eyelids with thumb and forefinger before he was ready to talk. "Your wife went for a walk, you said. From where to where?"

"The Murray place on Ridge Hill Road. She may have gone into the woods nearby . . . I don't know for sure. I was away part of the day fishing."

"And when you came back, she was gone?"

"Yes. She left me a note about the walk. I waited until I got worried enough and then went out looking for her. In the woods first, on foot. Then in the car. I was up on Skyview Drive when the house exploded. That's the reason I was on the scene so quick."

"Uh-huh. I wondered about that."

"I talked to some of the neighbors before I came here, as many as were home. None of them had seen her."

Broxmeyer nodded and then asked, "Has your wife ever done anything like this before? Gone off someplace and not returned when she was supposed to?"

"No."

"Two of you have an argument, anything like that?"

"No."

"Was she upset or worried about anything?"

"Not that I know about. No."

"What was her frame of mind when you left her?"

"She was fine. Cheerful. We're enjoying . . . were enjoying the stay. Like the area, were thinking about making an offer on the Murray property."

"Retiring up here?"

"No. Second home."

"Where's your first home?"

"San Francisco."

"Uh-huh," Broxmeyer said. "Well. How long have you been here?"

"Since early Saturday."

"No, I don't mean Green Valley. I mean waiting here in the station."

"Better than half an hour."

"Could be your wife's come back in the meantime."

"She hasn't," I said. "I tried calling on my cell phone a couple of minutes before you came in."

"She have a cellular, too?"

"Yes, but she didn't take it with her. It's in her purse at the house."

Broxmeyer scrubbed at his face again, blew out his breath in a heavy sigh. "Well, I hate to say this, but there's not much I can do for you right now. Officially, I mean. A person has to be missing forty-eight hours before I can make a report, mount any kind of organized search."

"I know that. But at least you can put out a BOLO alert."

"BOLO alert. You seem to know a lot about it."

"I'm in the business myself."

"Is that right?" He was more alert now. "Police officer?"

"I used to be. Licensed private investigator since I left the SFPD twenty-five years ago."

I had my wallet out and opened it to the license photostat, laid it on the desk in front of Broxmeyer. He leaned forward to look at it, looked at me, looked at the license again before he shunted the wallet back across the desktop. Whatever he thought of my breed, he wasn't letting me see it; his lean face was expressionless.

"About that BOLO," I said.

"Sure," he said, "I'll do that for you. Least I can do. I'm married myself—I know how worried you must be."

No, you don't, I thought. You can't imagine how worried I am. Or how much I love Kerry. Or that I'd cut off my right arm, give up my life in a nanosecond, to save her from harm. Nobody can possibly know how I feel right now but me.

Broxmeyer rummaged around on his desk for a pad of paper and a pen. "Your wife's name?"

"Kerry. K-e-r-r-y. Kerry Wade. She kept her maiden name."

"Description?"

I gave it to him, in detail. Age: 55, but after her facelift, she could easily pass for ten years younger. Height: 5'4". Weight: 120. Body type: slender, willowy. Hair color: auburn. Hairstyle: medium short, with a kind of underflip on the sides. No visible distinguishing marks.

"What was she wearing?"

"White shorts, light blue blouse, white Reeboks with blue trim. And probably a wide-brimmed straw hat. She wouldn't go out in the bright sun without it."

"Okay," Broxmeyer said when he'd finished writing, "I'll have Marge put it on the air right away."

"Thank you."

"One more thing. Contact phone numbers—the house, your cellular. Your wife's, too, for the record."

I recited the cell numbers from memory. "I don't know the house number. Not even sure the phone's connected."

"Cellulars'll do. I'll call you, or somebody will, if there's anything to report. Your wife comes home on her own, let us hear from you right away."

I said okay.

He worked on his tired eyes some more. "Look," he said, "this kind of thing happens a fair amount up here in the summer. People wander off into the woods, get themselves lost. Usually, they find their own way out."

"Unless they have an accident—a bad fall so they can't walk."

"Well, that's possible. But she couldn't have gone too far on foot. She's still missing come morning, I'll get one of the other deputies to start combing the area. Or do it myself if I can free up the time. She'll turn up."

"Or I'll find her."

"Right." Then, as I took a step toward the door, "One thing you should know. Green Valley is a quiet place. Low crime rate. Very few assaults against women, and none against a nonlocal as far back as I can remember."

"I wasn't thinking along those lines," I said.

But I had been. After what had happened to me, the three months of hell at Deer Run, how could I not think along those lines?

The house was just as I'd left it: locked door, dark windows, empty silence.

Hurt to see it like that, but it didn't make me feel any less hopeful. Kerry had told me that she'd never given up hope the entire three months I was missing and presumed dead; never once lost faith. She'd lived on it, and so would I.

But I couldn't just sit around doing nothing. Still a

little daylight left. I unlocked the door, reached in just far enough to turn on the porch light, then locked it again, and put myself back into the car.

I don't know how long I drove the hillside and valley roads in the general vicinity, stopping at three lighted homes that had been unoccupied before, showing the portrait photo of Kerry I kept in my wallet, and watching heads shake and listening to voices saying the same words over and over: "No, sorry, haven't seen a woman looks like that. No, sorry. No, sorry." At least an hour, maybe two, until long past dark. A fat harvest moon made it easier to see what lay along the shadow-edged blacktops, but there was nothing to see. Every few minutes, I hit the redial button on my cell phone. Nothing to hear, either, except the empty ringing.

The only reason I gave it up was vision-blurring fatigue. I lost my bearings and spent five minutes roaming around in a maze of darkness and distant flickering house lights before I came upon a street sign with a name I recognized. Then I misjudged a turn and nearly slid off into a ditch. Danger to myself and to others. And this kind of aimless search wasn't going to find Kerry, no matter how long I kept it up. There were just too many places she could be, hidden by the night.

Back to the house. I still couldn't make myself go inside, wrap those unfamiliar walls around myself, so I sat out on the deck. The darkness was alive with the pulse of crickets, a soothing sound on previous nights, but one that had the opposite effect now. It had gotten cold, the kind of after-dark chill that descends on mountain country even in summer, but I noticed it only when the wind kicked up, and only then in a peripheral way. Same with a dull, throbbing headache.

The section of woods I could see on the north side was a clotted wall of black rising up against the moonlit sky. What if that was where Kerry was? I should have gone in there earlier. Checked the timber on the south side, too, and down along the far side of Ridge Hill Road. She couldn't have walked far from the house, Broxmeyer had said that himself. But there were so damn many copses and stands and wide stretches of timber within a radius of a couple of miles; she could be anywhere.

If she wasn't back by first light, I'd start combing the woods nearby and work my way outward and downward. As much ground as I could cover, by myself and with Broxmeyer or whoever he sent out to help search. If I couldn't find her by noon, I'd appeal to Broxmeyer again for an organized hunt; and if that didn't work, try to talk Sam Budlong into helping me prod the local politicians into it. Tourism was Green Valley's major industry and the powers that be couldn't afford the bad publicity that would come from letting too much time pass; a suddenly missing fifty-five-year-old ad agency executive and wife of a longtime San Francisco private investigator was sure media fodder.

Even so, it was bound to take time. Broxmeyer and his fellow deputies had other worries—last night's explosion, and people pouring into the valley for the holiday weekend among them. No matter how much pushing I did, it wasn't likely Kerry would become a priority until Wednesday morning at the earliest. And the longer she remained unaccounted for, the slimmer the odds she'd be found in good health.

Getting ahead of myself. Still a chance a law officer responding to the BOLO alert would find her tonight, or she'd make it back here on her own. Or that I'd find her in the morning. The rest of tomorrow and the day after were a long way off. One hour, one minute at a time.

The night chill sharpened, built a tingling in my hands and face, and started me shivering. That, and exhaustion drove me out of the chair, into the house. Get as much rest as possible, or I wouldn't be worth a damn in the morning.

I took one unshakable certainty to bed with me, let it carry me into a fitful sleep.

Kerry was alive.

I'd know it if she wasn't. The bond we shared was so deeply forged that if it had been broken, the knowledge, the loss, would be like a piece of steel thrust into my brain. I'd know it, all right.

Wherever she was, whatever had happened to her, she was *alive*.

8

KERRY

Lucky to be alive.

That had been her first thought when she regained consciousness on the floor of the pickup, her hands and ankles bound with duct tape. And when the crazy man, Pete Balfour, had carried her in here and dumped her on the floor and then left without hurting her anymore, she'd had it again. Lucky to be alive.

But for how long?

Terror swelled again in her mind. She beat it down with an effort of will. She'd never been more afraid in her life, but she'd learned long ago—and Bill had reinforced the knowledge through his experiences—that the only way to deal with fear was to take control of it, hold it at bay. Focus on other things, on Bill, who must be frantic by now, on rescue and safety. Dwell on the fear and it would overpower you, take away your ability to think and reason—and you'd be lost.

Oh, but how long could you hold out? Bill had done it

for three months chained to that cabin wall, and still managed to emerge sane. Unimaginable. She'd thought she understood what the ordeal had been like for him, how strong his will to survive had been, but she hadn't until now. Nobody could unless they found themselves in a similar situation, facing the same kind of horrors. Monstrous coincidence that each of them, husband and wife, could be taken and held captive separately in the same lifetime, no matter what the reasons. Random insanity, for God's sake. Yet it had happened. It was *happening*.

She'd had two other experiences with personal peril. The first time, shortly after she and Bill were married, when the serial rapist he'd been pursuing had caught her by surprise on what was supposed to have been their honeymoon getaway in Cazadero; she'd escaped serious harm through luck and guile and Bill's last-minute arrival. The second time was the breast cancer episode, the months of radiation therapy, the constant mind-numbing anxiety— but that had been a known quantity, the cancer a tangible enemy, and she'd had the support and medical knowledge of others. This was different from either of those menaces. Accidental blunder into a situation and an enemy she didn't understand; alone, bound, trapped, with few, if any, resources and only the slim hope of rescue. She was not sure how long she could keep the fear under control, just what the limits of her endurance were.

She kept trying to convince herself that Bill would find her somehow. He'd always been there when she needed him, always kept her safe, like that awful time in Cazadero. There was no better detective anywhere, she believed that with all her heart. But how could he know where

she'd been taken, and by whom? And where she was being held when she didn't know herself?

He'll find out. Clinging to the thought, repeating it in
her mind. Believing it and not believing it at the same
time.

The battle with terror was harder now that night had
come. Inside of her prison, it was pitch dark, not a glimmer
of light anywhere, the single window covered with some
kind of shutter and the only door tight in its frame top,
bottom, and sides. The blackness magnified the smells
of old wood, dust, linseed oil, paint, rodent droppings,
and God knew what else. Scurryings in the walls and sporadic night sounds outside seemed magnified, too, thick
with possible menace. Balfour had been back once while it
was still light, to check on her; she'd pretended to be unconscious and he'd stayed no more than a minute. If he
came back in the dark . . .

She rid her mind of that thought, shifted position in
an effort to ease the numbness in her hands and legs. She
could barely feel her fingers; pictured them swollen,
like the fingers on gloves inflated with helium. Bruises
throbbed on her arms, a blood-scabbed rip in one knee
gave off little twinges of pain. Her throat felt as if it she'd
swallowed hot sand. Once, a long time after Balfour had
left her the first time, she'd given in to the urge to scream,
but the only sounds she could make were painful squeaks
and she hadn't tried it again.

She could still feel the marks of his thick fingers on
both sides of her neck, as if they'd made permanent indentations in the skin. But he must have stopped choking
her right after she blacked out, otherwise she'd be dead

now. Assaulted by a wild-eyed stranger because she'd "screwed something up" for him. Senseless words, senseless attack . . . as if he'd had some sort of psychotic break. He hadn't said anything in the pickup or when he'd put her in here to give his actions a rational explanation. Hadn't said anything at all.

Stopped choking her. Stopped just in time.

Focus on that. If he wanted her dead, he'd have finished the job then and there, wouldn't he? Why bother to tie her up, bring her to his home, confine her in this storage shed, unless he had something else in mind?

Rape?

Torture?

Both?

Kerry shuddered at the thought of his hands on her bare flesh.

God, if he was that kind . . . But he wasn't, or he'd have done something by now. Unless he was savoring the anticipation. Fragments of atrocity stories she'd read or heard flickered across her mind and she shuddered again. She could bear sexual assault, no matter how brutal or how many times he repeated the act, if he let her go when he'd finally had enough—

He wouldn't let her go. She'd seen his face and knew his name, she could identify him. He was known and didn't seem to be liked in Six Pines, lived somewhere in Green Valley . . . his pickup had still been on the logging road when she regained consciousness and they hadn't driven far to this property, what must be his property. Crazy man, but not crazy enough to turn her loose, let her walk away . . .

The fear broke through her defenses again, a black wave of it that left her weak and shaking before she could lock her mind against it. The rumpled piece of old, dirty canvas she was lying on gave off a mixture of rank odors that made her suddenly nauseous. Her stomach convulsed; she twisted onto her side, head down, to keep from choking on the thin stream of vomit that came up.

She spat her mouth clear, wiggled backward away from the vomit odor. The stiff canvas rustled beneath her, cold and crawly on her bare arms and legs. Something touched her face, skittered across it. Bug. Spider. She recoiled, shook her head, and brushed it off against the curve of her shoulder.

Outside, the dog started barking at something.

The dog frightened her, too. Pit bull, as big and ugly as its owner. It had made a lot of noise, barking and snarling, when he carried her in here. Not allowed to roam free; tied by a long lead with a hook looped over a cable stretched across the yard, so that it could run back and forth. Guard dog. Patrol dog.

Her shoe scraped against a solid object. She knew what it was—one of the leg supports on the long bench below the window, the same support she'd propped herself against earlier. She squirmed over to it, rolling onto her buttocks, digging the heels of her shoes into the canvas, until she was again sitting with her back against the rough wooden edge. The position gave some relief to her cramped muscles, but not to her hands or feet. She didn't have the strength to lift herself upright.

She knew that because she'd tried, more than once, even though there was nothing on the bench she could use to free herself. Balfour had taken box cutters, a saw, a pair of hedge clippers, and a few other gardening tools away with him before leaving the first time—everything with a sharp edge. He might have overlooked something, but she couldn't stand, let alone search, with her hands and feet bound the way they were.

Kerry leaned against the support until her breathing eased and the last of the nausea went away. Then she wiggled around slightly so that its edge was in the middle of her back, leaned forward to bring the joining of her wrists up against it, and struggled to make up-and-down sawing motions. She'd done that before, too, thinking that the rough wood could be made to cut through the duct tape. But she hadn't been able to sustain the effort then, and she couldn't now. Almost immediately, pain began to radiate through both arms, across her shoulders, sharpening until she bit her tongue to keep from crying out. She had to quit then, change position to keep from crippling herself.

She let a little time creep away, working the muscles in her shoulders and upper arms to loosen them, then tried again. Same result. But the sawing was having some effect on the tape . . . or was it? She couldn't be sure. Not enough feeling in her hands. And there was no sense of separation when she sought to move her wrists apart. He'd used a lot of the tape, tying her hands crosswise at the wrists and winding it partway up both forearms—

Scuffling noises outside, close to the shed. She heard them clearly because the pit bull had stopped barking.

Footsteps? Balfour coming back?

She froze, holding her breath, listening.

The scuffling came again, but only once more and not as near; then the night was quiet. And it stayed quiet except for the singsong chatter of crickets and the irregular thumping of her heart.

Not him. The dog prowling around. Or bumps in the night.

The painful cramping forced her down onto her side again. She was sweating from the exertion, the tension, but the sweat had an icy feel. She shivered, shivered again, her skin crawling with gooseflesh. Cold in there . . . she hadn't realized just how cold until now. All she had on were the knee-length shorts, the thin summer blouse. She'd freeze in this godawful place before morning.

No, she wouldn't. The canvas . . . it was large enough to cover her. Filthy, bug-ridden, but it would keep her warm enough if she had to resort to rolling herself into one end of it. If she had to. Only if she had no other choice.

She worked her body upright, gritting her teeth, and began sawing again at the rough-edged wood.

9

Four A.M. Still an hour until first light, but I was all through sleeping. I hadn't slept much, anyway. Mostly just dozing, snapping awake whenever a noise intruded or there was a spasming in my mind. Waiting in a twilight world for the footsteps that hadn't sounded, the call that hadn't come.

The first thing I did was check my cell to make sure it was charged, and a good thing I did. Low battery. I got the charger and plugged it in.

I killed a few minutes with a hot-and-cold shower and a shave (cut myself twice, the hell with it), and then dressed in clean clothes. In the kitchen, I brewed coffee, poured orange juice, made toast. I had no appetite, but I hadn't eaten since yesterday noon—the sandwiches Kerry had made for me, alongside one of the trout streams. I had to put butter on a piece of toast to get it down. The coffee was too strong and the juice had a sticky, too-sweet taste; a couple of swallows of each was all I could manage.

The house's cold, silent emptiness had a charged atmosphere, like a place haunted by ghosts. Time seemed to have slowed down to a stutter. I kept staring at the darkness beyond the windows, willing it to fade into dawnlight. The need to get out of there, get moving, start the search was so strong it began to have a claustrophobic effect. Tension, strain, lack of sleep. There was some Xanax in Kerry's purse that she used occasionally as a sleep aid; I thought about taking one to calm myself down, but I didn't do it. I don't trust drugs, even prescription drugs. I was afraid even half a tablet might make me drowsy, impair my ability to function.

But I had to do something to take the edge off. Deep breathing and aerobic exercises . . . Kerry's methods to relieve stress. They helped some. And used up more dragging minutes.

Finally, the darkness beyond the kitchen window began to show a grayish tinge. I went outside. Chilly. And it would be chilly and damp in among the pines, too. Back inside to put on a light jacket, then down off the porch and around past the shed to where I could see the eastern sky above the pine and fir along the ridgetop. From there, I watched the gray spread and lighten, faint pinkish streaks appear. A few more minutes and it would be light enough to find my way around in the woods.

Into the house one more time. My cell phone wasn't completely charged, but the battery should have enough juice now to last most of the day. I thought about taking Kerry's cellular with me, too, just in case—she always made sure to keep hers fully charged—but it would be better to leave it here, with a voice message on it asking for an immediate callback. That way, I'd know if she returned on her own or with help from somebody else.

When I finished doing that, it was time to go.

The woods along the northern perimeter fence first. Down past the car, across the weedy yard. The fence was made of waist-high redwood stakes; no gate, but the stakes were old and there were gaps here and there large enough to pass through. I picked one, and a few seconds later, I was into the forest gloom.

The ground cover was damp with morning dew, the footing slick enough so that I had to be watchful of where I walked. Pretty soon I found what looked to be a deer trail, but it petered out after a short distance and if it continued at another point, I couldn't find it. It was slow going, the shadows still long in places, the uncertain footing and bushes, fern brakes, and deadfalls impeding my progress. At intervals of a minute or so I yelled Kerry's name at the top of my voice. The close-packed pines caught the shouts and threw them back at me in dull, empty echoes.

I plowed ahead, changing direction now and then, looking for other trails or some sign that Kerry might have passed this way—and still not finding any. Wasting my time . . . I accepted that, finally. She wouldn't have gone on into woods like these with no path to follow. I found my way back to the fence, turned uphill to the long section of timber that stretched from the property line all the way up and over the ridge.

An hour slogging along a barely discernible maze of animal trails to the north and east. No sign of her.

South and east then, over some of the same terrain I'd covered yesterday. When I reached the rocky meadow, I found another trail that skirted it on the uphill side and took that until it vanished in thick underbrush. No sign of her.

Across the grassy open space and into the trees on the other side. No sign of her.

Back over the far end of the meadow and up the slope beyond. I hadn't climbed up there yesterday and I should have, because partway up there were indications of recent passage—a trampled fern, a slide mark on the needled ground. The marks weren't distinct enough for me to tell if they'd been made by a human or a large animal like a deer. I hunted for more signs, didn't find any except for another unidentifiable ground scrape. I shouted Kerry's name until my voice began to go hoarse.

At the top of the slope was an unpaved, rutted road that appeared to be little used—the old logging road I'd been on yesterday when I heard the explosion, I thought. Yes: I walked down it to the right, and after a couple of hundred yards I was at the intersection with Skyview Drive. No sign of her.

I turned back to follow the logging road in the other direction. Fifty yards or so after I passed the place where I'd climbed onto it from the slope, I came to an area along the far verge that caught and held my attention. Broken branches, crushed vegetation, faint tire tracks in the soft earth that hadn't been there long. Kids parking for sex or drugs, maybe. I walked around, studying the ground. No other tracks. A slope fell away below the road on that side as well; I moved along the edge, looking down among the trees and underbrush.

A short distance from the tire tracks, there were more

signs of what seemed to be recent passage. But again, I couldn't tell who or what had made them. There was no trail, so I had to make my way down the incline using pine trunks and boughs for leverage. Toward the bottom were more marks in the soft, needled earth, one that might have been a footprint.

The terrain leveled out through heavy timber. A couple of faint scuffs in the carpeting of needles, then nothing. I kept going, winding through the trees until they thinned and the ground angled downward again. Another fifty yards and I could see through the trees to open daylight.

I could smell something, too, sharp odors that over-powered those of pine resin and leaf mold and moist earth.

Burnt wood. Smoke residue.

I groped ahead to where the treeline ended near the bottom of the slope. The open space I was looking at was the long, wide section spanning the bottom of Skyview Drive. And straight ahead, the burned-out remains of the Verriker house.

VFD firemen were still on watch, a single truck parked at the edge of the driveway. Quick action and luck had prevented the blaze from spreading into the surrounding timber. If there'd been any delay, a strong wind, they'd have had a holocaust on their hands. Scorched grassland extended partway up the rear hillside to where the fire-fighters had dug long, irregular firebreaks; half a dozen trees and the remains of the upended passenger car spread out like charred skeletons. The smaller outbuild-

ad been destroyed, the front wall and one side wall

barn blackened, and the roof burnt through.

Difficult looking at what was left of a home where a woman had been alive one minute, incinerated the next. I turned away, back into the trees.

As shaky as I was, the climb up to the logging road seemed interminable. Two steps forward, one sliding step back, like one of those slow-motion dream sequences where every step you take feels as if you have fifty-pound weights strapped to your legs.

But then, near the top of the rise to the logging road, I found the hat.

Spotted it out of the corner of my eye as I was climbing, a pale blob caught behind a moss-covered tangle of broken tree limbs. That was why I hadn't seen it on the way down. I veered over there, caught it up.

Wide-brimmed straw hat. Kerry's sun hat.

Recognition brought a rush of relief. If the hat was here, then she had to be somewhere close by.

But neither the deadfall nor the vegetation that stretched out around it had been disturbed. No marks in the grass, no trampled ferns, no torn boughs or trunk-bark scratches. Just the hat.

I plunged along the slope to the west, stumbling, sliding, pawing through the ground cover, shouting her name. A hundred yards, two hundred, until I could see Skyview Drive through a break in the trees. Nothing to indicate that she'd come this way. I dropped down lower, groped my way back past the faint animal trail to search and call in the other direction.

Still nothing.

I must have gone another four or five hundred yards, up and down the slope, before I gave it up and dragged myself onto the road. And then along the road to where it began a steep, curving climb up toward the ridge. And then back along the slope on the other side.

No Kerry, no other sign of her.

By then, my breathing was so labored I began to feel light-headed. Muscles quivered all through my body. If I didn't quit moving, rest a while, I was liable to keel over.

I found a rotting log, sat with my legs splayed out and my head lowered until I had control of my breathing again. The dial on my wristwatch swam into focus through a blur of sweat. Christ. Not even nine o'clock. It seemed as though I'd been out here half the day. Three-plus hours gone, and already I was low on stamina. Sixty-four years old, not in prime physical condition . . . I could not keep making unreasonable demands on my body, or I'd end up having a stroke or a coronary, and then what good would I be to Kerry?

The straw hat was still clenched in my hand. I turned it over and over again, staring at it. If her hat was here, she'd been here. So why hadn't I found her? Lost the hat, then somehow got herself lost? No. If the hat had fallen or been knocked off and she wasn't hurt, she'd have been sure to retrieve it. Favorite of hers, she wouldn't just abandon it.

Hurt somehow . . . but please, God, not too badly? She might have managed to walk or hobble a distance away from here, trying to get back the house, looking for help or shelter. Maybe she had made that trail I'd followed down to the Verriker property after all—

No, no, you couldn't see the property from up here; she wouldn't go downhill through heavy timber to an unknown destination. She hadn't been anywhere near the Verrikers' house when it exploded, or somebody would have found her by this time. I'd already settled that in my mind.

If she had been hurt, it had to've been up here on the trail—there'd been no evidence of a fall down the slope anywhere near where I found the hat. In that case, logic said she'd have stayed on the road until she reached Skyview Drive. Made no sense she'd have gone the other direction, up that long steep incline toward the ridge. Besides, there was no evidence on the road to support that explanation, either.

Something else had happened here.

The grassy place across the road, where a vehicle had been parked recently . . . suppose the vehicle had been there when Kerry came along, suppose whoever owned it had been there. The spot wasn't far from where the hat had lain.

I went over there, walked around carefully so as not to disturb any of the signs. Look closely, and you could see the tire indentations in the grass, the slide marks on the needle-covered earth that had been left when the vehicle backed up and turned around. One of the indentations was clear enough and deep enough to indicate that the vehicle had been heavy and broad-beamed—SUV, van, pickup. I could make out other marks, too, less distinct, that might have been made by shuffling feet.

A coldness moved through me, tightening my gut, stiffening the hairs on the nape of my neck. Negative vibes, hypersensitivity, sixth sense—call it whatever you wanted to. I'd had it before and I'd learned to trust it, and in this place, it scared the hell out of me.

Something had happened here, all right.

Something bad.

10

PETE BALFOUR

First thing, before he did much of anything else, he went out to check on the woman.

He felt snake mean this morning. She was one reason, and his pounding head and sour gut from all the booze he'd sucked down last night was another. But Verriker still alive was the main one. Nobody better give him any shit today, or they'd regret it.

The shed was up on a little rise next to the garage. Built it and fixed up the whole place himself, with the only help a couple of spic illegals he'd hired for the grunt work. Good with his hands, the best carpenter, best builder, best repairman in the valley. But did anybody appreciate what he could do? Hell, no, they didn't. Carped at him about cutting corners, doing shoddy work, that was all they ever did. Miserable bastards.

Balfour unlocked the shed door, toed it open, and clicked on the overheads to see where she was before he went in. Still on the canvas where he'd put her, but rolled up in it now, lying on her side, staring at him with round, scared eyes. Part of one bare leg was out where he could see it. Pretty nice leg for an old broad. She must be more than fifty, but well preserved. Good body, slender, the way he liked them.

He had the notion again, looking at that bare leg, same one he'd had after he stopped himself from strangling her yesterday. That was part of the reason he'd stopped—a small part. Just a notion that slipped into his mind and slipped out again pretty quick. He liked his women young, the younger the better. Never had a whore over twenty-five. Never had any woman over twenty-five except for Charlotte, and she hadn't been much more than that when he married her. Pigs, all of 'em. Never had a good-looking woman in his life, not old ugly Pete Balfour. This redhead, she must've been some sweet piece when she was young. Now she was just too damn old to bother with.

He moved over to her, reached down to unwrap the canvas from around her body. She cringed back away from him. Scared, all right, but not so scared she wasn't looking him square in the eyes. Hell, most women would've peed all over themselves by this time.

"You . . . untie me now?" The words came out sounding funny, half whisper and half croak. The bruises on her throat . . . he'd come damn close to crushing her windpipe yesterday.

"No way, lady."

"Please. I can't . . . feel my . . . hands."

"No."

Balfour bent down again, pushed her over on her side. Whimper came out when he touched her, the sound like an ass-kicked dog made. But all he wanted to do was check the duct tape. It was okay around her feet, but there was a couple of tears and some up-and-down scratch marks where it was wrapped around her hands and wrists. Been scraping it on something, trying to get loose. Good luck with that. He thought about putting on a few more loops, but why bother? She wasn't going nowhere even if she freed herself and managed to find a way through the locked door. Bruno would see to that. Chew her up into dog food if she tried to get past him.

"Why?" she said.

"Huh? Why what?"

"Why are you . . . doing this?"

"Shouldn't of been in those woods, that's why. Your fault, not mine."

"I don't understand."

"Don't need to. None of your business."

"What are you going to do to me?"

Didn't have an answer for her. He shook his head, looked at her a little longer—notion in, notion out—and then turned for the door. Went on outside and locked up again.

What the hell *was* he gonna do with her?

He didn't know yet, couldn't decide. Should've finished what he'd started on the logging road, but somehow, he just couldn't do it. Smacking a woman around when she deserved it, that was one thing; choking the life out of her with your bare hands, that was a whole different bag of cats.

He might not of grabbed her at all if she'd hadn't called him by his name. Might've kept his cool, let her go her way while he went his. So she'd seen his truck up there, seen him with his toolkit, so what? Real good chance she'd never have tied him to the Verriker place blowing up later on. But calling him Mr. Balfour, knowing who he was . . . this black rage had come over him and the next thing he knew, he was choking her.

Well, one thing for sure: he couldn't just let her go. Maybe he ought to let Bruno have her. No, Jesus, he couldn't do a thing like that, not to any woman. Crazy idea and he wasn't crazy, except like a fox. Besides, then he'd have to clean up the bloody mess afterward.

Some other way. Had to be some other way . . .

The dog was yammering for food. Balfour stopped to move the chain on the cable strung along the yard so Bruno could roam closer to the shed. That'd make sure the woman stayed put until he figured things out.

In the house, he scooped up a bowlful of kibble and took it outside to the pit bull. Needed to put food into his empty gut, too, but he didn't like to cook, never was no good at it, and he didn't keep much in the house except snack stuff, potato chips and salted peanuts. Which reminded him—he was almost out of beer. Have to remember to stop on the way home tonight and pick up a couple more six-packs.

He didn't feel like doing any work today, but there wasn't no way around it. It was already the first of July, the big Independence Day celebration at the fairgrounds just three days off. Concession repairs were mostly done, but there was still a lot of work left to do on the men's and women's crappers. He'd have to push Eladio and the half-wit and himself to get the job finished on time.

Balfour drove into Six Pines, stopped at the café for a quick breakfast. Goddamn Jolene gave him a "Good morning, Mr. Mayor" look when he sat down—made him feel even meaner. Why couldn't everybody just leave him the hell alone?

He cocked an ear to the conversations around him. Couple of guys talking about the explosion, but all they were saying was what a terrible accident it'd been, and what a shame Alice had to die like that. Yeah, shame. Nothing about where Verriker was. Nothing about the tourist woman, either. Husband must've reported her missing last night sometime. But the law wouldn't be out looking yet. Took time to get a search organized, and anyhow, they wouldn't have no reason to go looking around his place a long way from where he'd grabbed her.

When Jolene served him his eggs, Balfour got her talking about the explosion by pretending to be sorry himself about Alice. Then he asked, "What's Ned gonna do now?" real solemn, like he gave a fat crap. "I mean, where's he gonna be living? Anybody know?"

"Well, he spent last night with Frank Ramsey and his wife. But they don't have enough room for him to stay on there."

"Got relatives down in El Dorado Hills, don't he?"

"A brother. But they don't get along."

"Somebody'll find a place for him here, then."

"Sure. He's got a lot of friends in Six Pines. There's talk Jim Jensen might let him stay at his house for a while."

"That right?" Wasn't what he wanted to hear. Jensen

was the owner of Builders Supply, had the biggest house in town. Full of people as it was—Jensen had a wife and three kids. Verriker'd be hard to get at there.

Jolene flashed him the mayor look again. "If that don't work out, why'n't you offer to take him in? You got plenty of room at your place."

"Comes to that, maybe I will."

He finished his eggs, paid the bill without leaving a tip. On his way to the fairgrounds, he played around with the idea of doing what Jolene'd suggested, offering to let Verriker stay at his place. Get him there and then set up something to take care of him and the woman at the same time, some other kind of accident. Seemed like a pretty good notion at first, but then he knew it wouldn't work. Verriker accept an invitation from him? No way. They'd never been friends, couldn't stand each other; Verriker'd know something was fishy soon as the offer was made. The accident idea was no good, either. Two fatals coming one on top of the other, both involving Verriker . . . make people suspicious, maybe start the county law looking his way. Besides, what kind of accident could he rig with Verriker and a missing tourist woman? And keep himself out of it with an alibi at the same time? No kind he could think of.

Okay, another accident was out. What other way was there to finish Verriker? Never mind the woman, he'd worry about her later. Couldn't just shoot the bastard . . . yeah, he could, blow his head off and then make the body disappear. No, that was too risky. He had to come up with something foolproof. And soon. He wouldn't have no peace as long as Verriker was still alive.

Eladio's rattletrap Dodge was parked between the fairgrounds' restrooms and the portable storage unit where he kept his power tools and other job-site materials locked up. The unit's door was open, Eladio and the half-wit already working. You couldn't trust most Mexs, but Eladio had worked for him off and on for years—Balfour hadn't had any qualms about letting him have a key.

He was still feeling mean, so he ragged on them some, told them to quit dogging it even though they weren't. The kid showed his smarmy grin, but kept his mouth shut—good thing for him he did. Two of them were doing the last of the fixes on the two big booths that sold beer, inside out of the sun, so he got his hand tools and a couple of sheets of already-sized and cut plywood, and went to work on the partitions between the toilets in the women's can. Already hot closed up in there; he was sweating like a pig before long.

Some days he could work off a hangover. Not today. His head ached like a bitch and his gut felt as if it was boiling, getting ready to toss up his breakfast any minute. Couldn't keep this up all day, not without a break and a little hair of the dog—two or three beers and a double shot of Jack. Take an early lunch, go on over to the bar at Freedom Lanes. The bowling alley was closer than the Miners Club, and he'd had his fill of the Buckhorn.

He was thinking about that, outside using his table saw to cut another section of plywood, when Tarboe showed up.

The faggot went to check on the concession booths first, so he finished the cut and took the piece back into the women's can. He was fitting it into place when Tarboe came prancing in. Not a drop of sweat on him, not a wrinkle in his clothes. Suit and tie in the middle of summer, for chrissake. Like he was somebody important . . . a lousy small-town fairgrounds manager.

"You and your men don't seem to be making much progress, Balfour."

"Then why don't you pick up a hammer and some nails and give us a hand?"

Tarboe's nose twitched like he was smelling something bad. "Why do you always have to be so disagreeable?"

"Why do you always have to come around biting my ass when I'm trying to work?"

"The mayor—"

"Don't start with that mayor shit!"

"If you'd just *listen* before flying off the handle. I was about to say the mayor, Mayor Donaldson, called me this morning. He's concerned that the work won't be done by the Fourth."

"How many times I got to tell you it will be?"

"Well, it doesn't look that way to me," Tarboe said. "If you'd started this project when you were supposed to, and worked a full, forty-hour week instead of whenever you felt like it, it would have been done long since."

"So you said maybe fifty times already."

"You know we're expecting between fifteen hundred and two thousand people on Friday. The rows of portable toilets won't be enough, we need *all* the facilities to be available."

Balfour gritted his teeth, banged a nail into place.

"And *all* the refreshment booths open for business. Do you have any idea how much money we'll lose if—"

Lost it then. "No, and I don't give a flying fuck!" Spitting the words.

"You have a foul mouth, Balfour. If it had been up to me, you would never have been hired for this project."

"Yeah, and if it was up to me, the county wouldn't hire fags to tell people what to do."

Tarboe's mouth got thin and tight. "You'll regret that," he said. "I'll see to it that you do."

"Yeah, yeah. Why don't you go find somebody to bugger and let me get back to work?"

Big glare. Tarboe turned away, then turned back and said before stomping out, "You know, what everyone's saying about you is right. You really *are* the biggest asshole in Green Valley."

Balfour stood there with the sweat running on him and it felt like the top of his head was ready to come off. Nothing going right anymore, pressure from every direction. Verriker, the woman, the Buckhorn crowd, Charlotte, Tarboe, Donaldson, snotnose kids and half-wits and people he hardly knew . . . seemed like everybody in the valley was his enemy. Looking at him like he was a pile of dog turds, wrinkling their noses like they couldn't stand his smell. Ragging on him, laughing at him to his face and behind his back, screwing him over, pulling the noose so tight he couldn't breathe. Man could only take so much. Some of the pressure didn't get released quick, he was liable to blow like a boiler with a busted safety valve.

He couldn't work anymore today. Just didn't give a shit anymore. He bulled out of the restroom, yanked off his toolbelt and threw it into the storage unit, then got into his truck and roared out of there. Didn't bother to tell Eladio and the half-wit he was leaving and not coming back; screw them, too.

He drove over to Freedom Lanes, went into the bar, and threw down two double shots and a bottle of Bud before some of the pounding in his head and boiling in his gut eased off. But he could still feel the pressure like a hundred-pound sack of cement sitting on his shoulders, weighing him down.

Out on the alleys, balls thudded on hardwood and pins crashed, and the sounds all seemed to come together into one steady beating noise that got inside his head like a voice talking, shouting. Verriker's voice, saying the same things over and over.

Biggest asshole I know, maybe the biggest one in these parts. I bet somebody'd nominate you for mayor, I bet you'd win hands down. Pete Balfour, the first mayor of Asshole Valley . . . mayor of Asshole Valley . . . mayor of Asshole Valley . . .

11

Broxmeyer was at the substation to take my call and showed up on the logging road, alone in his cruiser, within fifteen minutes. He examined Kerry's sun hat, looked over the area where I'd found it, looked at the marks on the ground where the vehicle had been parked, poked around elsewhere in the vicinity. Accommodating, professional, sympathetic up to a point, his expression carefully neutral the entire time. But he was too young, too inexperienced, too detached to share my place sensitivity, or my fears. None of it seemed to add up for him the way it did for me.

"Well, those tire impressions don't necessarily mean anything," he said when he was finished looking. We were standing next to his cruiser, me leaning against the rear door because my legs were still a little shaky. "Kids park up here sometimes. One of the other deputies caught a couple last year . . . you wouldn't believe what they were doing—"

"I don't *care* what they were doing. All I care about is finding my wife."

"I understand that. But I think you're jumping to conclusions. There's no evidence here to support the idea that she was abducted."

"What about the other marks on the ground?"

"Anything could've made them. No clear signs of a struggle."

"The hat," I said.

"Not damaged in any way. Nothing on it but some pine needles stuck in the straw."

"That doesn't mean it wasn't forcibly knocked off her head."

"It indicates she was here, but—"

"Indicates? The hat wouldn't have been if she wasn't."

"On this road, yes. She could have lost it walking along."

"No," I said. "I told you, it's her favorite. If she'd been able to go get it, she would have."

"Maybe she tried, and couldn't find it. You said so yourself you missed seeing it the first time you went down the slope."

"I wasn't looking for it. It wouldn't've been all that hard to spot if I had been. Besides, there wasn't any sign that she'd been down there. I told you that, too."

"There might've been some that you missed. You were excited, you moved around down there calling her name. You could've accidentally covered up any she made."

"Except that I didn't. There was no sign. I'd've found it if there was. I'm not an amateur when it comes to situations like this, Deputy."

"But you are the woman's husband. Concerned, upset—"

"There was no goddamn sign." Frustration made me snap the words at him. "Not down there, not anywhere else around here. Just what I showed you."

"All right, take it easy," Broxmeyer said. "I'm not saying it's not possible somebody else was here when she came along. Just that it isn't likely there was . . . an encounter. We've never had anything like that happen in Green Valley. Not a single incident along those lines."

"That doesn't mean it couldn't happen."

"No, but all I have to go by is what I see and what evidence tells me."

I said between my teeth, "So what are you going to do?"

"The only thing I can do under the circumstances. Get a search team out here, enough volunteers to scour the entire ridge, if necessary. If your wife is still somewhere in the area, they'll find her."

"When? How soon?"

"ASAP. Meanwhile, I'll run you back to the Murray place."

"No. I want to be part of the search."

"Not a good idea. You're unfamiliar with these woods, the terrain gets pretty rugged higher up—"

"She wouldn't've gone that far."

"—and you've worked yourself pretty hard already. The best thing you can do is wait at the house and let us do the job we're trained for."

Distraught old man, tired old man—I could almost see the thoughts reflected in the deputy's steady gaze. Other thoughts, too, the speculative kind I might be having myself if our positions were reversed. I resented what he was thinking, but I couldn't blame him for it. Stubborn argument meant delay, and it wouldn't do any good anyway. He had that ridged-jaw look law officers get when they've made up their minds to go by the book.

"All right," I said. "Your way."

In his cruiser as we rode, Broxmeyer radioed his dispatcher to contact the list of search team volunteers. Neither of us had anything to say to each other until we pulled up in front of the house. One look was enough to tell me it was as deserted as I'd left it. I'd expected it would be, but I felt an inner wrenching just the same.

He switched off the engine, turned toward me, and said with his eyes fixed on mine, "Mind if I come inside with you, have a look around?"

I'd expected that. Good at his job, but not very subtle and pretty easy to read. It wasn't that he necessarily disbelieved what I'd told him about Kerry's disappearance or finding her sun hat; but even if he'd run a check on me, and he probably had, he didn't know me or what I might be capable of. Without anything concrete to back up my story, he was inclined to be just a little suspicious, and careful, thorough, as a result. When a husband or wife goes missing under unexplained circumstances, there's always the chance domestic foul play is involved. There'd been any number of high profile cases to make even a rural cop aware of the possibility. The bitter irony here was that Broxmeyer had retained that false suspicion and dismissed the much more likely one I'd given him.

I didn't call him on it. Or question him. Counterproductive; I needed him on my side. All I said was, "Come ahead," and swung out. He was right behind me as I climbed onto the porch and used my key.

Already muggy inside the house. I left the door standing wide, went to open a couple of windows while Broxmeyer poked around the living room. Kerry's purse was on a burl wood coffee table; he stopped when he saw it, then glanced at me.

I came close to telling him no, he couldn't look through it. I'd have been within my rights if I had—invasion of privacy. But there was nothing in the purse he shouldn't see, and the more cooperative I was, the sooner he'd get the hell out of here.

"Help yourself," I said. "Just don't make a mess."

"Women's purses are always a mess." Trying to keep things friendly, but it didn't come off. I just looked at him. "Well, my wife's is, anyway."

He got Kerry's wallet out, opened it to her driver's license, read what was on the license, and to his credit closed it again without examining any of the other contents. Her cell phone next. He turned it over a couple of times in his fingers, aimed another glance at me; I took it from him, opened up voice mail so he could listen to the string of frantic messages I'd left on it. He seemed almost embarrassed when the last of them played out. A quick sifting through the rest of the items, and he was done with the purse.

He made a fast tour through the other rooms, lingering only in the bedroom and then for just a minute or so, all without touching anything. Back in the living room, he said, "Sorry about this. But I guess you understand my reasons."

"I'd've done the same in your place."

"Situations like this . . ."

"Just find her, okay? That's all that matters."

"Do our best. Might take most of the day to cover all the timber up along the ridge. You'll be here?"

"I don't know where I'll be. You've got my number."

"You look pretty worn out. Better get some rest."

"Sure. Rest."

Broxmeyer seemed to want to say something else, chewed his lip instead, and finally turned on his heel and left me alone. I stayed put until I heard the sound of his cruiser heading down the driveway. Then I went into the kitchen, slaked my thirst with a couple of glasses of ice water from the fridge. From there into the bathroom, where I washed my hands and splashed cold water on my face. The image that stared back at me from the mirror was that of a lookalike stranger: drawn, hollow-eyed, tattooed with an assortment of nicks and scratches. A face to scare little children with.

Children. Emily.

Thank God she wasn't here to go through what I was going through. What would I say to her if Kerry wasn't found or wasn't found alive? So much tragedy in her young life already. Birth father and mother both victims of violent deaths. And the time in Daly City, shortly after she'd come to live with us, when a jammed pistol was all that had saved me from a violent end . . . she'd been there that night, and the narrow escape had freaked her out for weeks afterward. No telling how devastating an effect losing her adoptive mother would have on her.

Yes, and there was Cybil, too. Pushing ninety, fragile

health, the two of them so reliant on each other. Lose
her daughter, her only child, and the shock was liable to
end her life—

*For God's sake, what's the matter with you? Cut out that
kind of thinking!*

I went back into the bedroom. The burbling ringtone
on my phone brought me up short, started my heart racing. But it was only the real estate agent, Sam Budlong.
He'd just heard the news, he was so sorry, was there anything he could do? I asked him if he knew of anybody
who had reason to be hanging out afternoons on the old
logging road off Skyview Drive; there was a little silence
before he said no in a puzzled voice, but he didn't ask
why I wanted to know. Instead, he said he hoped my wife
would be found safe, and paused, and added another
hope—that this unfortunate incident wouldn't change
our feelings about buying a second home in Green Valley.
I hung up on him. Bastard. That had been the real reason
for his call, not to offer aid or express sympathy.

What I wanted to do then was to get in the car and
start another canvass of area residents, this time to ask
the same question I'd asked Budlong, and one more:
Had anybody seen a vehicle in the vicinity of the logging
road yesterday afternoon? The search party was not going to find Kerry anywhere in the woods up there. No
matter how hard I tried to convince myself they would, I
couldn't make myself believe it. What I'd felt on that road
was neither an irrational fear nor a figment of an over-
wrought imagination.

But weariness held me in the house. I was in no shape
to go anywhere without some rest first.

Dark in the bedroom with the curtains closed over the windows. I stripped off torn and dirty and sweat-soiled clothing, stretched out with an arm draped over my eyes. I felt so damn alone. And plagued, too, by a feeling that Kerry and I must be the victims of some monstrous, long-term cosmic conspiracy. Paranoid reaction, but justified. How else to explain that both of us now, husband and wife, had been subjected to separate kinds of kidnap horror in the same general part of the state? Crazy coincidence? What were the odds?

Eventually, the warmth and the darkness dragged me into the kind of sleep that lies just below the surface of awareness. Kerry's face haunted a ragged series of drug-like dreams, so vivid that I once jerked awake, thinking for a few heart-pounding seconds that she'd come back, she was in the room with me. I tried to keep awake, but my eyes wouldn't stay open. And I drifted back into the half-world of peripheral consciousness and streaming dream images.

A burning thirst and a swollen bladder pulled me out of it. Another dousing with cold water chased away the sleep fuzz. My body ached and there were itching red rashes on both arms—poison oak, probably—but I didn't feel quite so beat. My watch told me how long I'd been down and out: more than three hours. Almost one-thirty now.

The silence in the house seemed deafening.

I checked the voice mail on my cell, even though I was sure the ringtone would have wakened me if there'd been a call. Then I put on clean clothes—I couldn't talk to people looking like a refugee from a hobo camp—and ran a comb through my hair and hurried out into the midday heat.

For more than four hours I drove around and around and around, showing Kerry's photograph and asking my questions. Residents of a dozen or more houses on Ridge Hill Road and Skyview Drive. Campers and RVers at the campsite. Picnickers in the park down on the valley road. Shopkeepers and customers in the stores in Six Pines. Men and women stopped at random on the sidewalks.

Nobody had anything to tell me.

Sorry, can't help you. Sorry, sorry, sorry.

The only part of the valley I avoided was the logging road. If the search team had found anything, I'd have been notified right away. And the entire time, the phone was a silent weight in my shirt pocket.

The heat, the constant frustration finally took their toll. I drove back to the house, where I sat limp and listless on one of the chaise lounges in the porch shade, nursing a cold beer and fending off mosquitoes. Trying not to think too much, worry too much—like trying not to breathe.

Broxmeyer showed up at 6:55.

It was cooler then with a light breeze, the tops of the nearby pines gold-lit and the shadows among their trunks as black as ink. Fading sunlight threw glints like mica particles off the cruiser's top as it turned in off Ridge Hill Road and climbed up into the parking area below. Going slow, which confirmed what the cell phone silence had already told me. The deputy's grave expression and his first words when he joined me on the porch were an anticlimax.

"I wish I had good news," he said, "but I'm afraid I don't. The searchers didn't find her."

"Or any sign of her."

"Not yet. I'm sorry."

Sorry again. But sorry was a meaningless word. As Kerry had said to me once, quoting one of her agency's clients, sorry don't feed the bulldog.

I said, "What now?"

"The search will go on tomorrow morning."

"In other wooded areas, you mean."

"Everywhere within a three- to four-mile radius."

"You're not going to find her that way."

Broxmeyer took off his cap, sleeved sweat from his forehead, and ran fingers through his lanky blond hair. Delaying his response so he could frame it in his mind first. "You still think she was in the wrong place at the wrong time. Up there on the logging road."

"That's what I think. What do *you* think now?"

"The same as before. Possible, but unlikely."

"So you don't intend to investigate."

He was uncomfortable now. I hadn't invited him to sit down, and he didn't take the liberty on his own; instead, he moved over to the railing, leaned a hip against it. "What would you have me do?" he asked. "Those tire impressions are too faint to make identifiable casts. There's just no way to determine what kind of vehicle made them, let alone who it belongs to."

"You could check on known sex offenders in the general area."

"I could, and if I had reason to, I would. But there

aren't many, and as far as I know, none has a violent history."

"As far as you know."

"Look," Broxmeyer said, "nobody guilty of the type of crime you're suggesting is going to admit it. I'd have to have some kind of strong evidence to do anything more than ask a few polite questions. You were a cop once, you know how the system works."

Or doesn't work. "It isn't the questions you ask," I said, "it's the kind of answers you get. Most felons aren't very smart—they make little slips, show their guilt in other ways."

His mouth tightened a little; he didn't like being lectured. "Let's say your idea has some validity. The person or persons responsible don't necessarily have to be sex offenders, or have a record of any kind. Could be anyone who lives in the valley or is here on a visit, somebody who acted on a crazy impulse. How do you propose I go about finding a needle in a haystack?"

"By doing what I did this afternoon. Legwork. Look for somebody who saw something, knows something, and move on from there."

"But you didn't find anybody, did you?"

"No, but I'm only one man."

"That's right," Broxmeyer said, "and I'm only one deputy. We're short-staffed in Six Pines and the rest of the sheriff's department . . . damn budget cuts. Fourth of July weekend coming up and that means drunks, fights, idiots misusing fireworks—extra work for everybody. Even if I wanted to, I couldn't spare the time or the manpower to mount an investigation based on a distraught husband's unsubstantiated theory about his missing wife."

"And you don't want to."

"I didn't say that. Don't put words in my mouth." He pushed off the railing, slapped his hat back on and straightened the brim. "All I can do is what I said I would . . . keep a team of volunteers out searching for as long as it takes to find your wife. You'll just have to rely on us, be patient. Okay?"

I kept silent.

He said "Okay" to himself this time, then moved on down the steps and got into his cruiser and drove off with a little more speed than he'd used arriving.

Rely on us, be patient. Bullshit. The danger to Kerry was real, her life in jeopardy, and urgent action was necessary.

I thought about calling the FBI. Yeah, sure—another exercise in futility. I had no contacts in the Bureau, and contrary to a television show like *Without a Trace*, the FBI has no task force that deals with missing persons cases unless there is substantial evidence that a kidnapping has taken place and federal laws violated. The chances that I could convince an agent to come up from Sacramento were slim and none; with the threats of homegrown, as well as foreign, terrorism and the social and political unrest that seemed to be amping up, manpower in the Bureau was stretched thin, and low-priority cases received short shrift as a result. What I'd get was a polite listen on the phone and the same kind of brush-off I'd gotten from Broxmeyer.

Forget the FBI for now, forget the county law. But the conversation with the deputy had convinced me that I could not go on depending on hope, strangers, myself alone. I needed help, which meant it had to come from a known quarter I could rely on. And I needed it fast.

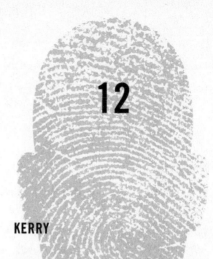

12

KERRY

Sometime during the morning or afternoon, she managed to free her hands.

She no longer had any sense of time. At intervals it seemed compressed, sluggish, and then it would expand in jumps like a defective clock. The light that filtered in through chinks in the wall boarding, at the edges of the shutter over the single window, was no help: there wasn't enough of it to do more than put a faint sheen on the murkiness. Objects in the shed, the low ceiling, were shrouded in shadow. The gathering heat was the only indicator that the day was moving forward at all. Smotheringly hot in this prison, but it didn't bring an ooze of sweat from her pores the way it had yesterday. So dried out now, she could no longer produce enough saliva to ease the burning in her mouth and throat. Her thirst was almost unbearable.

But none of that kept her from sawing at the duct tape binding her wrists. She'd squirmed her body painfully from one end of the long bench to the other, in the hope that the other support leg would have a rougher edge. If it did, she couldn't tell; she had almost no feeling left in her hands or arms. The sensors in her back told her when she had herself positioned, then she'd begun the long, arduous process. Rock forward and back, slowly, scraping the tape against the wood until she could no longer stand the strain; rest for a while and then start in again.

The task seemed impossible. More than once, she came close to abandoning it. But what else could she do, trapped in here, helpless? Wait passively for her captor to return and try to talk him out of killing her? No. She wasn't made that way. All her life she'd been a doer, a fighter: never give in, never give up. The more difficult the task, the more determined she became. That wasn't going to change now. Her outrage was greater than her frustration; so was her will to survive.

Now and then she prayed. She'd never been particularly religious, but she did believe in God; and if others believed in the power of prayer, then maybe there was something to it. She'd led a reasonably moral life, a more Christian life than so many of the self-important, hate-preaching hypocrites on the Far Right; maybe God, if He was merciful after all, would take pity on her.

The rest of the time she focused her mind on freeing herself. Her thoughts had grown sluggish anyway, and thinking only led to anxiety, a return of fear, and the crimping edges of panic.

The heavy rasp of her breathing kept her from hearing the duct tape finally rip and split. She didn't realize she was free, or almost free, until she leaned forward to rest again, flexing her back muscles forward to ease the strain, and her arms bowed outward slightly and she had just enough feeling left in her wrists for an awareness of the tape's pull on her skin.

A kind of dull elation moved through her. She didn't have enough strength to tear loose the rest of the tape, and her fingers were useless. All she could do was keep flexing her back muscles, try to work enough feeling down through her arms so she could widen the spread of hands and wrists. It took a long time . . . bunches of minutes broken up by rest periods, an hour or more for all she knew. Slowly, slowly, the tape pulled and scraped, and there was another ripping sound and a faint stinging sensation on the back of her left hand. And both hands dropped apart and she was free.

Kerry wiggled away from the support, then over onto her side, and then her stomach with arms now splayed out on either side of her body. Still no feeling in either of them or in her hands except a residue of the stinging. She lay there breathing in the stifling air, willing her blood to circulate. More passing minutes strung together like links in an extended chain. Then the pain came, tiny prickles of it at first, gradually increasing until it began to radiate up and down both arms and in her fingers.

The pain brought on an impulse to weep, but her tear ducts were as dry as her mouth and throat. She rolled over onto her back, attempted to lift her arms. Not enough strength yet. She lay still, looking up at the shadowed ceiling where a huge cobweb hung from one of the beams, working now to flex her fingers. One twitched and moved and ached, then another and another, until she could feel them all, clumsy things as useless as sausages.

When the tingling and throbbing began to modulate from sharp pain to dull ache, she was able to raise her arms off the canvas and onto her bare thighs. She struggled into a sitting position, sat staring at her hands. God. They looked, as well as felt, swollen. Torn strips of duct tape still clung to both; blood streaks dried and fresh marked cuts, scrapes, welts all along her wrists and forearms. Again she felt the impulse to cry, but it lasted no more than a few seconds.

She made an effort to strip off the tape binding her ankles. No good. Fingers still too sore, too tender to grasp and pull. She lay flat again to ease the cramped hurt in her back. Flexed the fingers, chafed her wrists as circulation gradually improved—

Thrumming noise from outside: the link on the pit bull's lead sliding along the ground cable as the animal broke into a sudden run away from the shed. A couple of seconds later, the dog began a furious barking.

Balfour, coming back?

Oh, God, no! Not yet, not while her hands were still useless, her feet still bound.

She sat up again, managed to catch hold of a corner of the canvas, hang on and pull it up over her legs. Lost the grip, regained it, dragged the canvas to her waist.

The dog's barking tapered off into sporadic yips and whines. Kerry sat motionless, straining to hear. The animal wasn't running anymore, either.

She clutched at the heavy canvas, her weight on one hip

and her eyes on the door. If Balfour had returned, she'd hear him in time to roll herself into the canvas before he unlocked the door and came inside. And then pray he wouldn't uncover her the way he had this morning.

Quiet outside now. She held her breath.

Silence.

Not Balfour, not yet. Something had spooked the dog, that was all—a wild animal or stray cat, a phantom sound or movement. It didn't take much to set off a beast like that.

Kerry twisted free of the canvas. The tingling in her fingers was pins and needles now, a good sign. They still felt big and clumsy when she set to picking at the tape around her ankles; it took patience, concentration to scratch an edge loose, pinch it between thumb and forefinger. She didn't have enough strength yet to tear it, but she found she could unwind it in little jerks—an agonizingly slow process that left her weak and a little dizzy when she finally stripped the last of it off.

Her hands were better by then; she sat rubbing the numbness out of her ankles, her swollen feet. Another long, slow process before returning circulation brought shoots of pain, then the tingling and the pins-and-needles prickling.

She had no idea how long she worked before she was ready to try standing. Stop time, lost time. Awareness of nothing but the task of restoring her body to a functional state, and the occasional sound from outside that froze her until she was sure it had no meaning.

Onto her knees first. Crawl over next to the bench. One hand on a storage door padlock, the other stretched up to the edge of the bench. Raise up, lift up onto her feet. The first time her legs refused to support her weight, even with her body braced against the bench, and she slid down hard to her knees. The jolts of pain increased her determination. She stayed upright the second time, held herself in place while she rested.

All right. Now walk.

Shuffling baby steps, both hands clutching the bench, trying to keep her weight braced and evenly distributed. Good. Another baby step. Another. Buckling knee that time; too much weight on the sliding foot. Rest. Go slow. Another step. Another. Turn at the end of the bench, walk back along it at the same slow pace to the far end. Turn again, come back. Four times, five times, until she could walk with minimal support. Every step had its measure of agony, but it was the kind of endurable, satisfying hurt you felt after a long run.

Ready then to explore the confines of her prison, look for a weapon she could use against her captor.

The switch for the overhead lights was next to the door. Risk putting them on? She'd have to; she couldn't see much in the gloom, and with the canvas bunched up on the floor, there was a greater risk of stumbling, falling. Still daylight outside. Even if Balfour came back before she was done, he wouldn't be able to tell from a distance that the lights were on.

Kerry felt her way to the end of the bench, around the end to the wall, then along the wall to the corner and from there over to the door. The sudden glare from the naked ceiling bulbs hurt her eyes; she narrowed them to slits until her vision adjusted.

The storage room seemed even smaller from an upright perspective—a twelve-by-twelve box, cramped, dusty. Across the back wall was a row of metal storage lockers, each door fitted with a heavy padlock. No help there. Nor from whatever was in the cabinets built in under the bench; the same kind of padlocks closed those off. The bench top was empty except for another piece of folded canvas and a thick-bodied television set. The rest of the enclosed space held rolls of insulating material, a pyramid of three one-gallon cans of paint, an old-fashioned standing ice chest, a brass-studded armchair bleeding stuffing from one dirty arm, some stacked cardboard cartons, not much else.

Could she use one of the paint cans as a weapon, hide behind the door and clout him with it when he came in? She tried to lift the top can with both hands . . . and couldn't do it. Full, not empty. Too unwieldy anyway to swing with any accuracy, even if she could manage to lift it. The TV set? No good, either. It was at least twenty years old and looked as if it would weigh thirty or forty pounds.

The cartons were the kind with lids, none of them taped down. Old clothes, drop cloths, rags, more canvas . . . nothing she could use. In frustration, she yanked on a couple of the padlocks on the row of lockers, not thinking about the rattling noise until the pit bull's lead ratcheted on the cable outside and the animal started barking again. How close to the door could the damn dog get? She couldn't tell even when she went over to stand close to it; the wood was thick, solid, and the keyhole too small to see through. She moved sideways along the wall, looking for a peephole chink between the boards. There wasn't one.

The window? Wire mesh screen bolted to the wall. Even if there were a way to pry it loose, the outer shutter, made of green-painted metal, was sure to be locked or bolted as well.

Still trapped, after all that effort to shed her bonds. No way out and nothing she could use to defend herself.

The fear rose in her again, a surge of it that came close to panic. Fighting it, controlling it, left her weak and shaky again. She hobbled to the door to switch off the lights, then sank down onto the canvas. Exhausted, pain-riddled, dehydrated, hungry. But her determination and her will to survive remained unshaken. As long as there was breath in her body, she would not give up.

She made a blank screen of her mind, sitting humped forward in the near-darkness, massaging wrists, ankles, feet to keep the blood flowing.

It was still daylight when Balfour came back.

The dog's barking alerted her far enough in advance so that she was able to roll onto her side and wrap the canvas around her before his key scratched in the lock and the door opened. Again he put on the lights by reaching in from outside. Kerry had her eyes slitted so the glare wouldn't blind her, saw him stand there looking in at her for a few seconds before he entered. Crazy, but not stupid. Even if she'd been able to lift one of the paint cans and tried to hide with it behind the door, she wouldn't have taken him by surprise. Not that way.

She watched him move to within a few paces of where

she lay, stop at the edge of the canvas. If he got close enough, bent down to check on her as he had that morning, she might just catch him off guard. Claw his face, kick or punch him in the groin, disable him long enough to scramble outside, then try to get past the pit bull and make a dash for freedom. She could see the dog through the open door, sitting on its haunches fifty or sixty yards away—far enough so that there might just be enough time to elude him. Desperate plan, with little chance of succeeding, but what else could she do?

Not even that. Balfour didn't come any closer, just stood looking down at her with a funny little smile flicking at the corners of his mouth.

He looked different somehow. Red-faced and not a little drunk—she could smell the alcohol fumes leaking out of him—but not as grim or as tense. That smile . . . the secret kind, as if he were pleased about something. Or had made up his mind about something.

"How you doing there, lady?"

Maybe she could entice him into checking on her. She had the words, but it took three tries before she could force them out through the arid caverns of her throat and mouth. "How do you . . . think I'm doing, tied up like . . . piece of meat?"

"Your own fault. Should've stayed away from my truck."

"Untie me, please." The "please" tasted like camphor on her tongue.

"Uh-uh. Not yet."

"When?"

"Won't be too long."

"Then what?"

"You'll find out when the time comes."

A dry cough made her say, "At least . . . some water."

"Thirsty, huh? Yeah, sure, why not some water. You hungry, too?"

"No."

"Sure you are. Tell you what. I got some beef stew cooking—Dinty Moore's, best there is. How about I bring you some along with the water?"

"And what? Feed it to me?"

Balfour laughed, closed one eye—a wink, for God's sake—and turned for the door. Went out and locked it behind him, leaving the lights on.

Kerry sat waiting, planning. He'd have to come close, squat or kneel down, to feed her the food and water. If she acted quickly enough, she could grab hold of his privates and twist them hard enough to hurt him, really hurt him. She repositioned her body, arranged the canvas over her hands and legs so that she could free herself with a quick flip and then strike with her right hand. Tried it three times to make sure. Then she was ready.

The dog didn't announce Balfour's approach this time. Her pulse rate increased when she heard the shuffle of his steps, the key in the door again. Adrenaline rush, with the added fuel of her anger. Her fingers, pressed together behind her, tensed and tingled.

The door opened and she saw him look in, then lean down to pick up two bowls from the ground in front of him and carry them inside. Not ordinary bowls, she saw then. Round metal dishes, old and scratched.

Dog dishes.

He came no closer than the edge of the canvas, where

he set the dishes down again. "There you go," he said. "Water in one, stew in the other. Help yourself."

". . . How?" It was all she could manage.

"Same way Bruno out there eats and drinks. Stick your face in the bowls and slurp it right up."

Balfour laughed again, went away again, locked her up in darkness again.

And left her, for the first time in her life, with enough seething hatred to want to kill another human being.

13

JAKE RUNYON

He was at Bryn's, playing a science fiction video game with Bobby while she cooked dinner, when the call came in on his cell.

Nice little domestic scene, the sort he'd missed out on all his life. He and Andrea had fought most of the short time they were together, usually over her drinking, and Joshua had been a toddler when he'd left them and filed for divorce. Plenty of good evenings with Colleen over the twenty years they'd been married, but it'd been just the two of them—she hadn't been able to conceive a child. These recent get-togethers with Bryn and Bobby were comfortable enough, but they were infrequent and had a temporary feel. He wasn't married to her, or living with her, and the boy was her son, not his. But that was only part of the reason.

Since a family court judge had reversed the earlier court decision manipulated by her lawyer ex and awarded her primary custody, her focus was all on Bobby. On re-cementing a bond two years broken by her stroke, the messy divorce that followed, and severely restricted visiting privileges. The boy was what she lived for, always had been. Now that she had him back, she no longer needed Runyon to lean on; they saw each other half as often as they had before Bobby came to live with her three weeks out of every four. She seemed to want him in her son's life—Bobby liked him, and they got along fine—but as a friend, not a father figure. And with restrictions.

He wasn't allowed to spend the night when Bobby was in the house. The boy was nearly ten and no stranger to adult intimacy—most of the time he'd lived with his father, Robert Darby had had an out-of-wedlock, live-in affair with a woman named Francine Whalen—but Bryn felt a mother should set a better example, especially while Bobby was still healing from the effects of the physical abuse Whalen had inflicted on him, the woman's violent murder and its aftermath. He had no problem with that. Sex was not a central part of their relationship; from the beginning, the connection between them had been built on loneliness and their damage control service to each other. Still, it added to his sense of being an outsider.

For a while, he'd thought that the kind of dependence they'd shared might eventually evolve into something more. But it was unlikely that either of them would ever be ready for that kind of commitment. What they had was still viable, so it would be status quo for a while yet; sooner or later, though, it would morph into a more casual friendship, one that would remain supportive, but no longer intimate. There'd be some sadness when that happened, but no regrets. His mental health was much improved from their time together, and so was Bryn's. You couldn't ask more than that from any relationship.

When his cell vibrated, Runyon left Bobby's room and stepped into the hall to answer it. Figured to be Tamara, who seemed always to be working late these days, with some sort of agency business. No. The screen showed him Bill's name. Back early from his vacation? No on that, too.

"Jake, how heavy is your caseload? Working on anything that can't be put on hold or turned over to Alex?"

The sound of his voice, as much as the abrupt questions, put Runyon on alert. Tense, with a strong emotional undercurrent.

"Nothing pressing," he said. "Why? Something wrong?"

"It's Kerry. She's missing."

"Missing?"

"Since yesterday afternoon. Went out for a walk somewhere while I was off trout fishing, didn't come back. Nobody's seen her since."

"Christ. You're still up in . . . where is it?"

"Green Valley, in the Sierras. I got the local sheriff's deputy to put out a BOLO alert last night, and a search team in a section of woods where I found her sun hat this morning. No sign of her."

"Lost? Some kind of accident?"

"That's what I thought at first. Now . . . I'm afraid it might be something worse."

"Worse?"

"I think she might've stumbled into a situation."

"What kind of situation?"

"You know what kind. Wrong place at the wrong time.

Damn world's full of predators, even in remote places like this."

Torn-out words that tightened Runyon's fingers around the phone. He didn't say anything. There was nothing to say except to ask for details, and Bill would provide those when he was ready.

"The deputy, Broxmeyer, doesn't agree with me," Bill said. "Doesn't have enough manpower for an investigation even he did. Jake . . . I'm about half out of my head here, and I can't handle this alone. I need your help."

"You've got it. I can leave right away . . . ."

"No need for that. Three-hour drive to Green Valley, and I wouldn't be in any shape for talking by the time you got here. Half dead on my feet right now. Get some sleep yourself, come up early in the morning, we'll start fresh."

"How early do you want me there? Seven, eight?"

"Make it eight," Bill said. "Little town at the south end of the valley, Six Pines . . . coffee shop called the Green Valley Café on the main drag. I'll meet you there. Easier to find than the place where we're staying, and I'll need to get out of here in the morning anyway."

"Right. Does Tamara know yet?"

"No. I wanted to talk to you first."

"I can call her, fill her in—"

"Better if she hears it from me. I want her to compile a list of known sex offenders and violent felons living in this general area, recent unsolved rapes and missing persons cases involving women. Broxmeyer won't do it, doesn't think it's necessary. I'll have her call with any hot leads, e-mail the rest of what she gets to you. Bring your laptop along—Kerry left hers at home."

Runyon said okay, but he wouldn't need it; the agency had bought him an iPhone a while back and he could use it to access his e-mail. "Anything else?"

"Not until you get here. Thanks, Jake."

Runyon started to say "We'll find her," but there was no benefit in offering up hollow reassurances. He settled for, "Eight o'clock, Green Valley Café," and let Bill break the connection.

He went down the hall, through the dining room into the kitchen. Bryn was at the sink draining pasta into a colander; steam plastered wisps of her ash blonde hair to her forehead, dampened the lower edges of the scarf she wore tied under her chin to hide the crippled left side of her face. The only time she removed the scarf in his presence was under the cover of darkness. He'd had only one clear look at the stroke damage, and that was on the night they'd met, when a couple of rowdy teenage idiots yanked her scarf off in a Safeway parking lot. As far as he knew, she'd never allowed Bobby or anyone other than her doctor to see it, either.

The uninjured side of her mouth curved in a smile. "Dinner's almost ready. There's a bottle of red wine on the counter."

He said, "No wine for me tonight. I'm going to have to eat and run."

"Oh? Why?"

He told her why. "I'm driving up there early tomorrow. Don't know when I'll be back—I'll call you."

"God, I hope she's okay."

"So do I."

"Poor Bill. He must be frantic."

Frantic was the word for it. He knew too damn well what Bill was going through. Kerry was the love of the man's life. Her breast cancer diagnosis and the long months of treatment, and now this. If he lost her, it'd be as if part of him had been ripped out, leaving a bloody, gaping wound—the same as it had been for Runyon when the cancer tore Colleen, the love of his life, away from him.

But all he said was "He is," and moved to help her get dinner on the table.

He was up and on the road at five o'clock. Early riser anyway, and six hours' sleep was all he ever needed. A three-hour drive was nothing to him; he'd logged thousands of miles in the Ford since moving to the Bay Area, using up downtime and familiarizing himself with his new home turf. Driving satisfied his restless need for movement, activity; the longer he was behind the wheel, the better for him. When he stepped out of the car after a long drive, he was calm, focused, ready for whatever needed to be done.

Getting out of the city was no problem because he was traveling against the flow of early commute traffic on the Bay Bridge, and except for a quick stop in Vacaville for gas, he made good time on Highway 80 all the way to Sacramento. Middle of the commute rush there; he crawled for a while through the city and its eastern outskirts. But once he was on 50 passing through the long stretch of suburban towns, traffic thinned down considerably, and he was able to hold his speed at a steady ten miles per hour over the limit all the way to the turnoff that led him to Green Valley.

A two-lane county road took him on a winding route through a couple of hamlets at the northern end of the valley. Nice enough area, he supposed. Scenic. Good spot for a vacation or a second home. But a bad place for a missing-person hunt, with all the pine and fir woods. That was as much notice as he took of the surroundings. Colleen had had a keen awareness of the environment, talked him into periodic trips to wilderness regions in Washington and Oregon, and some of her enthusiasm had rubbed off on him to the point where he looked forward to those getaways with her. But after her death, he'd lost interest. Rural settings, urban and suburban places . . . they were all the same to him then and now, colorless, devoid of any real distinction. Bay Area neighborhoods, roads, landmarks had all been filed away in a corner of his mind, but only for necessary business-related purposes. Until he was given specific reference points within a locale like Green Valley, the surroundings registered as little more than visual blips.

It was ten minutes shy of eight o'clock when he reached Six Pines. The Green Valley Café was easy to spot: painted bright green with a big sign, in the second block on the main drag. Bill was already there; his car was parked out front. The café was moderately crowded with breakfast trade, but Runyon spotted him at once, bent over a cup of coffee in a corner booth at the rear.

Bill's head jerked up when Runyon slid in opposite;

he'd been lost inside himself. "Jake," he said in a scratchy voice. "Good."

"Still no word?"

"No. I'd've called you."

"You holding up okay?"

"So far. Didn't sleep much last night."

Runyon hadn't needed to be told. Bill was a robust man, vigorous for his age, but the strain had had a corrosive effect on him already. Runyon had never thought of him as old, but he looked old now in the bright café lights. Faint grayish tinge to his skin, eyes muddy from lack of sleep, the lines in his cheeks and around his mouth deep-cut, as if by the same razor that had made a couple of scabbed-over nicks on his chin. The kind of face that had stared back from the mirror at Runyon in the weeks and months after he buried Colleen.

"How long's it been since you ate anything?"

"What? Oh. Part of a sandwich last night."

"Good idea if we have some breakfast while we talk."

"I'm not hungry."

"Long day ahead. Make yourself sick if you don't eat."

". . . Okay. You're right."

Runyon summoned the waitress, ordered scrambled eggs and toast for both of them, and a cup of tea for himself. When they were alone again, Bill said, "Kerry and I ate here on Sunday. Sunday. Seems like weeks ago."

Nothing to say to that.

"Nice little town. Nice peaceful valley. We liked it so much we were thinking of making an offer on the place we're staying. Jesus."

Or to that. Runyon said, "Let's talk about what happened. Fill me in on the details."

Bill sipped a little coffee, began to talk in that low, scratchy voice. It took a while, with Runyon interrupting now and then to ask questions and the arrival of their breakfast.

"So now you see why I'm so damn scared."

"Yeah, I see."

"Broxmeyer thinks I'm overreacting, jumping to conclusions. I wish to God he was right, Jake, but he's not. Somebody took Kerry, somebody's holding her somewhere."

Runyon said nothing, just nodded.

"Wherever she is, she's alive," Bill said. "I'm sure of that. I'd know it if she wasn't."

Hope and bravado talking, but that was all right. If the man let himself believe otherwise, he'd be a basket case by now. Runyon nodded again.

Bill grimaced at what was left on his plate, pushed it away, then ran hooked fingers over his face in a kind of self-punishing massage. "I keep thinking whatever happened, it's my fault. If I hadn't left her alone all day, I'd've been with her up on that logging trail."

"Would you? You like hiking in the woods?"

"I don't know. Sometimes."

"Maybe you wouldn't have felt like it yesterday. Maybe she'd have gone by herself anyway."

"Yeah. Maybe."

"Why beat yourself up? You're not to blame for circumstances beyond your control."

Wry mouth. "Standard message to a worried or grieving client. But all right. I know it's true, I just have to wrap my head around it."

Runyon said, "This logging road where the vehicle was parked and you found Kerry's hat. How far from the place where you're staying?"

"Half a mile or so."

"And how far from here?"

"About three miles up-valley."

"Let's go take a look at it."

14

There wasn't much left to see on the logging road. The searchers yesterday hadn't exercised any care in preserving the area as it had been; they'd obliterated the tire marks and trampled the underbrush along both sides. Maybe it didn't matter—there hadn't been much evidence to begin with—but it angered me just the same.

I pointed out the spot to Runyon where the mystery vehicle had been parked, the place where I'd found Kerry's hat. I didn't expect him to feel the same negative vibes I had; if he did, he didn't say anything about it and I didn't mention it. But I had the crawly, gut-wrenching sensations again, just as strong, if not stronger. They built a loathing in me for this damn road. Too much time spent here the past two days.

Jake prowled around for a time, not looking for anything specific, just getting a feel for the area. Then he went back to stand on the grassy verge. When I joined him, he said, "Where does this road lead?"

"Up over the ridge someplace."

"Outlet on the other end?"

"According to the deputy, no."

"Any homes along it?"

"No. Couple of homes nearby."

"Funny. If Kerry was taken by somebody parked here, what he was doing here on a Monday afternoon?"

"Same thing she was doing, maybe. Hiking in the woods."

"Doesn't seem too likely if he's local. Unless he had a reason."

"Like what? There's a *Hunting Prohibited* sign down at the intersection, and no poacher's stupid enough to fire a rifle in the middle of the day."

Runyon said, "The explosion you told me about. You were on this road when it happened?"

"Just turning onto it."

"What time?"

"Not sure. Five-thirty or so."

"And the house that blew up is close by?"

"Less than half a mile."

He gestured at the woods below. "The partial trail you followed yesterday morning leads straight down there to the edge of the property, right?"

"Yes, but I told you, Kerry couldn't have been anywhere near the Verriker place when it blew. She didn't make that trail."

"But somebody else could have that day. Was it fresh?"

"I couldn't tell. What're you thinking?"

"Pretty big coincidence that Kerry went missing not long before a nearby house suddenly blew up. What caused the explosion?"

"I don't know. Broxmeyer didn't say."

"How sure are they it was an accident?"

"Jesus, Jake. Rigged? By somebody with a grudge against the Verrikers?"

"There're ways to do it. Wouldn't be the first time."

"And what? Kerry happened by and saw the guy coming back out of the woods and he's the one who took her? Why? She wouldn't have any way of knowing what he'd done."

"I know it's a reach, but still possible, isn't it?"

Yeah, it was, and it should have occurred to me, too. Would have if my thought processes weren't so sluggish from anxiety and lack of sleep. And I was not about to discount it out of hand any more than Jake was. First rule of detective work: Take nothing for granted, pro or con, probable or improbable.

I said, "Broxmeyer won't like it any better than the other one, but we'll put it to him. He needs to meet you anyway, know we're working together."

We got into Jake's car; he'd insisted on driving and I hadn't argued. We detoured down Skyview Drive so he could get a look at the Verriker property. The VFD fire truck was gone, but the place wasn't deserted; an SUV with a caved-in side door was parked at the edge of the driveway, and a man and woman were poking around near the entrance to the barn. They stopped and stood staring as we drove by. Morbid curiosity seekers or scavengers.

Runyon said, "Must've been a pretty hot fire."

"It was. Big bang, too."

"Figures to be gas, then. Stove, furnace, water heater."

"My guess, too."

We went on a ways until Runyon found a place to turn around. When we came back past the Verriker property, the man and woman were still standing in the same motionless postures like a couple of scarecrows in a burned-out cornfield.

Halfway up the hill beyond, my cell phone went off. I grabbed it quick, but the call wasn't news about Kerry. Tamara.

"Any word yet?" she asked.

"No. Nothing."

"Damn! Jake make it there okay?"

"With me now."

"How about you? You doing all right?"

"Hanging in."

She'd been pretty upset when I talked to her last night. Still was, but trying to mask it by using her brisk professional voice. "I e-mailed the info you asked for to Jake," she said. "Twelve names, but only two with histories of violence against women. Nastiest dude lives in Green Valley, the other one in a hamlet called Rock Creek about twenty miles east. Thought you'd want the particulars on those two right away."

"Start with the one here."

"Donald Fechaya. F-e-c-h-a-y-a. Address: Sixteen hundred Old Mountain Road, Six Pines. Arrested twice for forcible rape, first time in Reno twelve years ago, second time in Auburn eleven years ago. Convicted on the second offense, served four and a half years in Folsom. Suspect in one other rape case, but no charges filed. One arrest after his release from Folsom, on suspicion of aggravated assault, charges dropped for lack of evidence."

I repeated the Six Pines address to myself twice to fix it in my memory. "The one in Rock Creek?"

"Jason Hooper. Owns the Roadside Garage and Towing Service there. Arrested and convicted of rape and attempted murder in Sonora ten years ago, paroled after serving six years in San Quentin. Nothing since except for one reckless driving violation."

"No possibles in the other ten?"

"Didn't look like it to me. Seven registered child molesters, their own kids or the children of family members in all but one case. Two with priors for statutory rape, one for weenie-wagging in public, the other for soliciting a minor for sex in a park restroom. None live in Green Valley."

"Missing persons cases involving women?"

"Several, but mostly teenage runaways. No woman over the age of forty in the past six years."

Which meant nothing one way or the other. "What about unsolved rapes and abductions?"

"Not much there, either," Tamara said. "Two unsolved rapes in the county, the most recent eight years ago, neither one in Green Valley. The only reported abduction still open is a child custody case—father snatched his son from his ex-wife and disappeared."

Another statistic that didn't have to mean anything. Most rapes go unreported even in this supposedly enlightened age. I said, "Okay. One more thing you can check on. An apparently accidental explosion up here the evening Kerry disappeared, destroyed the home of a couple named Verriker. I'm not sure of the spelling. See what you can find out about them."

"You think there might be some connection?"

"Too soon to tell. Covering the bases."

"Get back to you right away if there's anything you should know."

After we rang off, I conveyed the gist of the conversation to Runyon. He said, "I wonder if the deputy knows anything about this Fechaya?"

"One more thing to talk to him about."

We drove on into Six Pines. Broxmeyer was at the substation when we entered, talking on the phone in his cubicle. He frowned when he saw us through the glass, gestured for us to wait until he finished his conversation, and then took his time doing it. When he finally came out, he looked tired and harried. And none too happy to see me again so soon. He tried to cover it with a pasted-on half smile, but the first words out of his mouth were underscored with irritation.

"No need for you to come by. You'd've been informed right away if there were any developments."

"Some things we wanted to talk to you about." I introduced him to Runyon, watched him struggle not to lose the half smile as they shook hands.

"Another city private detective won't be of much help, I'm afraid."

That didn't sit well with either of us. Runyon said, "You'd be surprised how many missing persons we've found, some in more remote places than this."

"I'm sure you're a competent investigator, but in a case like this—"

I cut that off by saying, "Mr. Runyon's here at my request. You mind if we continue this in your office?"

He minded, but he didn't refuse. "It'll have to be quick. I'm busy as the devil right now . . . search for your wife, people pouring into town for the Fourth, a dozen other things." He opened the gate for us, led us into the cubicle, shut the door. But he didn't invite us to sit down or sit down himself.

I said, "Do you know a local resident named Fechaya, Donald Fechaya?"

"Fechaya? Why?"

"You do know him?"

"I know who he is, yes."

"Do you also know he's a convicted rapist?"

"What does that have to do with— Oh, I get it. That's why you brought your man here up from 'Frisco. You still haven't let go of the abduction idea."

"No, I haven't. You told me none of the registered sex offenders in this area had histories of violence against women. What about Fechaya?"

"I didn't see any reason to mention him."

"Why not? You already talk to him, find out where he was Monday afternoon?"

"I don't have to talk to him. He had nothing to do with your wife's disappearance."

"How do you know he didn't? He a friend of yours?"

"Hardly."

"Then how do you know?"

"Because he's not capable of committing another rape."

"Why isn't he?"

"Well, for one thing, he's a born-again Christian."

"So? Doesn't mean he's lost his violent urges against women. Not even castration can do that."

"All right, that's enough," Broxmeyer said. "I know you're upset, but I don't appreciate having my word or my authority questioned. Fechaya is not guilty of anything except being an ex-felon, and you're not going to find your wife by hassling him or anybody else in Six Pines. Now if we're done here, I need to be on my way."

I wanted to hit him. Stupid impulse, but powerful enough to put heat in my face and make me clench my fists.

Runyon said quickly, "We're trying to be thorough, that's all. Covering every possibility. You're a law officer, you understand how that is."

"Not when it amounts to interference in the performance of my duty."

Interference. Duty. Christ!

"We have no intention of stepping on your toes," Jake said. "But we have the right to investigate alternative possibilites as long as we stay within the boundaries of the law. That's right, isn't it?"

Broxmeyer admitted it, but not without hesitation or reluctance.

"Until Ms. Wade is found or we know differently, kidnapping is still a possibility. There's another one, too, maybe unlikely, but we think it needs to be addressed if only to put it out of the running."

"And what would that be?"

"The explosion Monday evening. At the Verriker place."

"What about it?"

"How sure are you it was accidental?"

That almost set Broxmeyer off again. He said, scowling, "What kind of question is that? Of course it was accidental."

"What caused it?"

"Gas leak, ignited by a spark."

"Gas lines can be tampered with."

"For God's sake, are you suggesting somebody *planned* to blow up the Verrikers' house? That's ridiculous!"

"Is it?" I said. I was all right now, my control buttoned up tight again. "I told you about the trail I followed from the logging road that came out on the hillside above the Verriker property. It started near those tire marks I showed you, and it could've been made by whoever owned the parked vehicle. Wouldn't have been difficult to slip down to the house, get inside with nobody home, loosen a fitting to fill the house with gas. Somebody who had it in for the Verrikers."

Broxmeyer was looking at me as if he thought I'd taken leave of my senses.

"My wife could have been on the road when he came back up," I said.

"And then I suppose he grabbed her and made her another victim?"

"She's not dead."

"I hope not. But she's not in the clutches of some phantom killer, either. In the first place, the explosion was an accident, plain and simple. No question of that. In the second place, Ned and Alice Verriker were and are good people . . . no enemies, no reason anybody would want to harm either of them."

"All right."

"Another thing. Even if it had happened that way, why would this phantom think your wife was a threat? She'd be a stranger to him and he'd be a stranger to her. All he'd've had to do was drive off and leave her there to finish her walk and she wouldn't have thought twice about it."

"I said all right."

The deputy shifted his gaze to Runyon. "Possibility out of the running for you now?"

Jake had nothing to say.

"It better be," Broxmeyer said. "What happened on Monday was a real tragedy, and I won't have you going around cutting into Ned Verriker's grief and stirring people up with a lot of unfounded nonsense."

Still nothing to say, either of us.

"So okay then. My advice is to stop trying to make something sinister out of a simple disappearance and join one of the search teams . . . two now, by the way, working separate sections east and west of Ridge Hill Road. But if you insist on conducting a private investigation, I won't try to stop you, only keep it quiet and don't make waves. Are we clear on that?"

I said, "We're clear," and he nodded and waved us out.

The midmorning heat and sun glare smacked me a little as we came outside. That, and my elevated blood pressure brought on a touch of vertigo. I took a couple of faltering steps on the way to the car, had to lean against an old-fashioned lamppost to steady myself.

"You okay?" Runyon asked.

"Just a little woozy. Give me half a minute."

He knew better than to try to help me. The dizziness passed, and I walked ahead to the car. When we were both inside with the windows rolled down, I said, "The sheriff's department isn't going to be any help, and you know

there's not enough kidnap evidence to bring the FBI into it. It's up to us."

"Looks that way."

"Thirty hours, Jake."

He knew what I meant. Anybody who has ever worked in law enforcement knows that if an abduction victim isn't found within seventy-two hours, the odds jump against the person ever being found alive. And Kerry had been missing more than forty hours now.

"More than that, maybe," he said.

"But not a lot more."

"Where do you want to start?"

"With Fechaya," I said. "Where else?"

15

PETE BALFOUR

He had plans now. Oh, baby, did he have plans *now*!

Felt real fine when he got up Wednesday morning, no hangover even though he'd put away pretty near a fifth of Jack Daniel's yesterday and last night. Slept like a baby. Rarin' to go, full of piss and vinegar, blood and fire.

Fed Bruno, thought about feeding the woman again, but why bother, just be a waste of time now that he knew what he was gonna do with her, and left the house at seven. Stopped off at the Green Valley Café for a quick breakfast and just grinned and shrugged when fat-ass Jolene threw her mayor look at him. Nothing and nobody could get his goat today or ever again. Then he drove straight to the fairgrounds, got there just as Eladio was opening up the storage unit. The Mex seemed surprised to see him, but he knew better than to say anything. Thing was, meeting the deadline was important now— keep Tarboe and Donaldson off his back. Ought to be able to get all the major repairs done on time if he worked

Eladio and the half-wit and himself bitch-hard for ten or eleven hours today and part of tomorrow, until it was time to run his errand in Stockton, then promise them double overtime pay to finish up.

He'd be tired as hell the next couple of days, but not too tired to take care of business. No siree, not with what he had brewing.

Luke Penny'd helped give him the first plan yesterday afternoon. He'd pulled into the Shell station for gas on his way back from Freedom Lanes, and Penny come out of the garage and wandered over, wiping his hands on a piece of waste. Pete Balfour wasn't the only ugly dude in the valley—Luke was no prize, either, and the slather of grease across his chin hadn't helped his looks none.

"Hell of a thing about Alice Verriker."

"Yeah. Hell of a thing."

"Guess you ain't the sorriest person around, though. Huh, Pete?"

As mean as he'd felt then, he'd of liked to punch the greasy bastard's lights out. Or tell him to go fuck himself, like he had that faggot Tarboe. But going off on Tarboe had been a mistake—he'd realized it sitting there in the Freedom bar with Verriker's voice pounding away inside his head. He couldn't afford to call any more attention to himself, not if he didn't want people getting suspicious of him when he finally fixed Verriker.

So he'd swallowed his rage and said, "Me and Ned had our differences, but that don't mean I'm not sorry for his losses. I feel real sorry for him, you want to know the truth. Real sorry."

"Sure you do."

"The truth, Luke. Some of the guys in the Buckhorn last night, they started a collection to help pay for Alice's funeral and I kicked in more'n my share. Plenty more'n my share."

Penny didn't look like he believed it. But then he shrugged and said, "Well, Ned can use the help, that's for sure."

"Might want to kick in a few bucks yourself."

"I'll do that. Tonight, after work."

"What I heard, Ned spent the night with the Ramseys, but they don't have enough room to let him stay on there. Jolene, over at the café, said Jim Jensen might fix him up at his place."

"That's old news," Penny said. "Jensen offered, but Ned said no thanks."

"That right? How come?"

"Don't care to be a burden to anybody. He's pretty tore up, just wants to be alone for a while. So Frank's brother's letting him stay in his cabin up at Eagle Rock Lake until he pulls himself together."

Oh, man, he'd near whooped when he heard that. "Might be best at that. When's he moving up there?"

"Later today sometime. Joe Ramsey's going up with him, get him settled."

Once Balfour was out of the station, he'd smacked the steering wheel and let out the whoop he'd been holding back. That cabin up on the lake . . . fishing cabin, sat by its lonesome on the east shore. He'd never been there, never been invited, oh hell no not him, but he knew where it was and how to get to it. Verriker and Stivic and Ramsey and some of the others had batted their gums often enough about what a perfect getaway place it was.

Yeah, perfect. They'd never know how perfect.

By the time he got home, he knew just what he was gonna do. Thinking about it made him feel real good for a while. Good enough to let the woman out there in the shed have some food and water. The look on her face when he'd plunked the dog dishes down in front of her and told her to slurp it up the way Bruno did . . . worth a chuckle all the way back to the house.

But then Mayor Donaldson called up, and for a while he wasn't feeling good anymore. Just for a while.

Where had he been all day? Why had his cell phone been out of service? Then the miserable old fart started in on him for insulting Tarboe and walking off the job. Said his behavior was inexcusable, said he had a foul mouth and a poor work ethic and no community spirit, whatever the fuck that meant. Said if he didn't have the fairgrounds work completed by midnight on the third, he wouldn't be paid the rest of the money due him on the county contract, and he might well have his construction license revoked for malfeasance, besides. Malfeasance. Jesus! Threatened him and ragged on him for three or four minutes until he was furious enough to slam the phone down, hard enough to bust the bugger's eardrum.

Ramsey and Stivic and the rest of them wanted an ass-hole mayor, well, they already had one. You couldn't find a bigger asshole politician in the county than Fred Donaldson. Matter of fact, they didn't have to go looking for another valley to collect assholes in, because they had this one right here. Donaldson, Tarboe, every one of 'em who got a kick out of making Pete Balfour's life miserable, they were the real assholes, not him, and they'd taken over and turned the whole valley and everybody else in it brown. Green Valley wasn't Green Valley anymore, it was Asshole Valley.

Pretty soon the poison had started eating away at him again, and his hate was as big and hot as ever. He'd poured himself a double Jack and followed it quick with another, trying to take himself down from a boil to a simmer. But what the whiskey did, it made everything real clear in his mind, and he'd seen what he should of seen a lot sooner. Seen it clear as looking through a pane of new glass.

Killing Verriker would be sweet, but it wouldn't change anything. Not one damn thing. The rest would go right on calling him mayor, pretending he was the one with "A for Asshole" tattooed on his forehead. Making a fool out of him, persecuting him, never giving him a minute's peace.

Well, he wasn't gonna let that happen. Wouldn't let them drive him out, neither, with his tail between his legs like a whipped dog. He'd had as much as he could take. It was payback time again.

And that was when the second plan come to him.

Real quick, too, as if it'd been percolating in the back of his mind all along. Well, maybe it had been. Maybe it was what he'd been heading toward from that first night in the Buckhorn, when Verriker and the rest of them turned his life into a living hell.

Seemed pretty far out at first. And scared him some

because it was Payback with a capital P, the kind that'd have every cop in the country after him. If he went ahead with it, how was he gonna save his ass afterward? But then the answer to that part of it come to him, too, how he could get away clean, and just where he'd go. The more he thought about it, the less scared and the more excited he got. They hadn't shown him any mercy, why should he show them any? And the timing . . . oh, man, the timing couldn't be more perfect.

So then he'd put in a call to Rosnikov's legit business number in Stockton. The Russian was there, late as it was, and when Balfour told him what he wanted, not in so many words because you had to be careful on the phone, Rosnikov said he could supply the package by Thursday night, and quoted a whorehouse price. Real cool, that Russian, like they were talking about apples and oranges. Didn't even ask what he wanted it for. Not that that was any surprise. Rosnikov didn't care what you did with the black market stuff he sold.

That cemented it for Balfour. He had the cash, with plenty enough left over. He had the time and the place all worked out. He was gonna do it, and no backing out at the last minute. Once his mind was made up, it stayed made up.

Oh, he was gonna raise some hell, all right.

Pure, sweet hell.

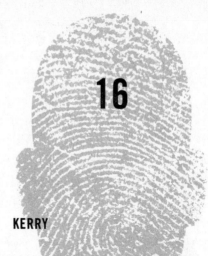

16

KERRY

Enough daylight filtered in to let her know it was morning. She'd been awake for some time, lying in the darkness, thinking about Bill out there somewhere, doing everything humanly possible to find her. Faith in him was all she had to hold onto now. There just didn't seem to be any way for her to get out of here on her own, not that she wasn't going to keep looking for one. Never give up, never give in. She kept repeating the words to herself, a kind of self-hynoptic chant to maintain calm.

For a long time she waited, expecting Balfour to show up again, praying he wouldn't. And he didn't. Outside, the dog barked a couple of times, but they were meaningless sounds. Then she heard the distant noise of an automobile engine starting up. Balfour's pickup truck? Must be: the engine noise increased once, twice, the way it did when you goosed the throttle.

Kerry waited a while longer, then threw off the filthy canvas and crawled over to the door, used the knob to lift her cramped body upright so she could switch on the lights. The first things she saw when her eyes adjusted were the two dog dishes next to the bench. Disgust tightened her throat again; the memory of the greasy stew made her stomach churn. What an inhuman piece of garbage Pete Balfour was. *Stick your face in the bowls and slurp it right up.* She'd have done that, too, if she'd still been bound, just like a dog. Humiliating enough scooping up the stew with her fingers, all but wiping the dirty dish clean. It had taken an effort of will not to drink all the water, to save about a third. She'd need it today to stave off the dehydrating effects of the heat.

If she lived through today. If Bill didn't find her, or she didn't find a way out of here herself before Balfour came back and did whatever he was planning to do to her . . .

Fear thoughts again. Don't!

She paced her prison for a time, working some of the painful stiffness out of her legs. Did a series of aerobic exercises to loosen the cramped muscles in the rest of her body. All the while, listening and hearing nothing from outside. Then she went back to the door, bent to peer at the lock.

Bill had taught her some things about locks, even showed her once how to use a set of lock picks. Could this lock be picked? It looked to be a simple deadbolt, not new, with no interior locking lever; you'd need a key to open it from either side. The key slot was small, too small to see through, but if you had the right tools— slender pieces of metal a few inches long—you might be able to manipulate the tumblers and spring the bolt.

Metal. Nails, a coat hanger, even a couple of large paper clips. Was there anything like that in here?

The handles on the gallon cans of paint . . . they were fairly thin, one of them might work. But that hope died quickly. The handles were firmly attached, and she didn't have the strength to twist off even one end, nor any kind of tool to pry it loose.

She investigated the cartons next. Emptied each one, shuffling through the contents. Nothing.

The TV set. She moved over to examine it both front and back. Plastic case, inset controls, its electrical cord taped to the back panel. She had no idea what was inside one of these older models other than a picture tube. Dump it on the floor, break it open on the chance there might be some piece she could use? Not until she'd looked everywhere else, and maybe not even then. If she couldn't get the door open, couldn't get away, Balfour would see the wreckage when he came back and know she had gotten loose and she'd have lost her one last desperate chance.

She pulled the spread canvas into the middle of the floor and folded it together, then got down on all fours and crawled along the walls and the row of storage lockers, felt along the locked cabinets beneath the bench. No loose nails that had been dropped and forgotten; there wasn't even a driven nail anywhere that hadn't been hammered flush to the wood.

On her feet again. The ice chest? The latch handles and plates were tightly fitted. The door opened easily enough, but all it revealed was a smooth-walled emptiness.

The armchair? She felt the brass studs, found one that wiggled a little; she managed to work it free. Damn! Too short. What about the underside, the springs? She tilted the chair up from the back, over onto its arms. Torn cloth covered the inner parts. She ripped it all the way off, coughing from the dust that plumed into her face. Springs, yes, but they were thick, coiled together . . . useless.

An involuntary sound vibrated in her throat, half grunt, half growl. Her hate for Balfour flared hot again; he hadn't only treated her like an animal, made her eat like an animal, now he had her sounding like one.

She started to pull the chair back into its upright position. Stopped when her eye caught and held on the edge of the frame where what was left of the cloth hung in tatters. The cloth had been fastened with tacks—thin, square-shaped, and two-pronged, the heads about half an inch wide and the thickness of a large paper clip. How long were the points that had been driven into the wood? If both were the same length as the head, that would make each an inch and a half when straightened out. Long enough and sturdy enough?

Kerry dumped the chair forward again, yanked and twisted at the remaining tatters. None of the tacks pulled out, but two were no longer flush against the wood. She tried wiggling one of them free, succeeded only in tearing a fingernail. What she needed was something to pry it loose. Yes, but what?

There wasn't anything. She'd been over every inch of this hellhole . . . no tools of any kind, nothing, nothing.

The dust in the hot, stale air brought on another coughing attack. She stepped away from the chair, went to lean against the bench until the fit passed. Her mouth was like a wasteland again . . . a little of the water that was left? Just a sip. The temperature in here would be sauna hot by midday, whenever midday was; she'd need fluid more then.

She pushed away from the bench, leaned down to where the dog dishes were—and she was looking straight at the TV set.

The electrical cord, the two-pronged plug!

Kerry almost kicked over the water dish in her haste to get to the television. She dragged the TV around, tore off the tape holding the cord to the casing. Half a dozen yanks on the cord convinced her that she couldn't disconnect it, and there was nothing she could use to pry open the back of the cabinet. The only way she could make use of the plug was to carry the set over to the up-ended chair.

Bulky, difficult to wrap her arms around so she could take firm handholds. She maneuvered it to the edge of the bench, slid one hand underneath, the other around to grip a back corner, set her feet, and eased it off against her chest. The set's weight buckled her knees and she almost dropped it. Then when she turned, she nearly tripped over the dangling cord. She managed to hold on, her fingers slipping on the smooth plastic casing, just long enough to stagger to within a few feet of the chair. Thrust her body into a low, forward arch just in time: the TV was only a foot above the floor when it fell.

Even so, the crash on impact seemed as loud as a gunshot. Immediately, the dog began barking outside. Between yaps, Kerry heard the animal come running toward the shed, but she couldn't tell how close it came to the door. She stood still, catching her breath as quietly as she could, until the barking subsided. Whirring sound then: the pit bull's leash ring sliding over the ground cable. Moving away again.

Part of the cord was caught under the television; she pulled it free, saw with relief that the plug had escaped damage. So had the TV itself, except for a crack on one corner of the casing. She sank to her knees in front of it, worked it over close to the back of the chair, trying to make as little noise as possible. Still, the dog's acute hearing set off another round of barking. But it didn't last long this time, only until she had the set close enough so that it no longer scraped on the rough floor—close enough to reach the tacks with the plug.

The prongs were too wide and too thick to slip beneath tack and wood; she had to use the edge of one prong to work each tack up from the corners. When the first one finally came free, she saw that the spike ends weren't quite as long as she'd hoped. The metal was fairly malleable; she was able to pry the ends apart. Good. With the help of the prongs, she straightened the tack out. If she could twist two of them together to make a longer, sturdier probe . . .

She tried it as soon as she had a second tack loose, again with the aid of the plug. It could be managed, another slow task hampered by arthritic cramping in her fingers, but when she had the two tacks wound together, the piece didn't look or feel tensile enough to manipulate the lock tumblers and snap the deadbolt. She'd have to twist a third tack onto these two, and even then, it might not do the job. There were four more in the chair, enough to make two probes.

It would take time to pry them up, time to fit them together, time to work with them on the lock. Time, enemy time. She prayed as she worked that Balfour wouldn't show up before she was finished, before she could at least try to get herself out of here.

17

Donald Fechaya was not the man we were after. We knew that five minutes after we found our way to 1600 Old Mountain Road.

The address was an old farmstead, not too well kept up. Green clapboard house, its near sidewall and part of the roof repaired with unpainted sheets of plywood. Vegetable garden, fenced in with chicken wire on one side, and a tumbledown henhouse on the other; a row of fruit trees and a small, dry-looking cornfield at the rear. Chickens and a fat red rooster pecked and clucked among the weeds and dirt in the front yard.

A thin, straw-hatted woman was picking green beans in the garden when we pulled in behind a twenty-year-old Ford pickup. She gave us a long look, put her basket down, and came out through a gate in the fence as Runyon and I quit the car. She looked to be about fifty, stringy and juiceless in a man's faded shirt and Levi's, her face a deep-seamed corduroy brown like old leather left too long in the sun. Up close, her pale eyes, steady and direct, told you that she'd had a hard, painful life, but that she'd made peace with it. Probably through her religion.

"Something you men want?"

"We're looking for Donald Fechaya," I said. "Is he here?"

"In the house. What you want with him?"

"Are you Mrs. Fechaya?"

"I am. Didn't answer my question."

"Was your husband here on Monday afternoon?"

"Why?"

"Please answer the question. It's important."

"Important to who? Who are you?"

Runyon said, "We're looking for a missing woman. We thought your husband might have seen her."

A mirthless smile twitched at the corners of her mouth. "He didn't see nobody on Monday."

"He might have if he was in the vicinity of the old logging road off Skyview Drive."

"He wasn't. We didn't go nowheres on Monday."

I said, "No offense, but we'd like to ask him."

Over at the house, the screen door banged open and a man rolled out onto the porch—a shrunken gray man in a wheelchair. "Martha, who's that you're talking to out there?"

"There he is," Mrs. Fechaya said. "Go on over and ask him."

"How long has he been in a wheelchair?"

"Ever since the good Lord seen fit to put him there six years ago. Tractor rolled on him and broke his back. Changed his life, changed mine."

"Martha!"

Damn Broxmeyer. He could have told us about the broken back and the wheelchair, kept us from wasting our time coming here.

"Well?" she said to me. The nonsmile flickered again; her voice was wise and weary. "You still want to ask him about that missing woman?"

Runyon said no, sorry to have bothered her, and we got into the car and left her standing there with her crippled husband still querulously calling her name.

Tamara called again as we were making our way through thickening traffic in downtown Six Pines. Wanting to know if there was any news, if either of the two names she'd given me earlier might be the person responsible for Kerry's disappearance. I told her Donald Fechaya was out, and why, and that we were on our way to Rock Creek to check on Jason Hooper.

She said then, "Well, there wasn't much I could find out about the Monday night explosion up there. Official verdict is accidental, not a whisper it could be anything else."

"Anything on the Verrikers?" I asked.

"Not much there, either, and I went down as deep as I could. Ned Verriker, age forty-two. Married to Alice Verriker in 1996, no children. Employed as a clerk and forklift driver at Builders Supply Company, Six Pines, the past nineteen years. No criminal record. Two DUIs, most recent four years ago."

"Injury accidents involved in either of the DUIs?"

"No."

"Financial troubles, unpaid personal loan, anything like that?"

"Not that I could find. No outstanding debts other than the usual mortgage and car loan. No recorded problems with coworkers or anybody else. Seems to be a pretty average citizen otherwise. Belongs to the Methodist Church, Elks, Six Pines Rotary Club—"

"Never mind all that. Mrs. Verriker?"

"Her slate's even cleaner. No criminal or arrest record of any kind. Only blot, if you want to call it that, an illegitimate daughter when she was eighteen."

"Ned Verriker the father?"

"No. Name on the birth certificate is Randolph Stevens."

"What'd you find out about him?"

"Enlisted in the army the same year the kid was born. Killed in action in Afghanistan in 2002."

"And the baby? You said the Verrikers are childless."

"Given up for adoption at birth."

And adoption records are sealed. The daughter would be sixteen now. Any chance she could hold a festering grudge against her birth mother for giving her up? Or that a member of her adoptive family did for some reason?

Tamara said, "It'll take some time, but I might be able to hack up the info if you think it's worth the risk."

It wasn't. What kind of grudge, real or presumed, could prod the daughter or anybody connected to her into turning the Verriker home into a time bomb? The possibility of a tie between the explosion and Kerry's disappearance was enough of a reach as it was.

"No, forget it. It won't help us find Kerry." In time, I thought, but didn't add. In time.

. . .

Jason Hooper was another bust. Forty-mile round-trip over twisty mountain roads to Rock Creek, a wide spot surrounded by wilderness—two and a half hours wasted.

We found Hooper working at his Roadside Garage and Towing Service. He was sullen and belligerent at first, but Runyon and I convinced him to cooperate. We didn't exactly muscle or threaten him, but we made it plain through choice of words, gestures, and body language that we were willing to do whatever was necessary to get straight answers.

He didn't know nothing about no missing woman, he said. He'd served his time on "that phony rape charge," he'd never been in trouble over a woman since, he didn't want no trouble now. Hell, no, he hadn't been down in Six Pines Monday afternoon. Hadn't been there in years, didn't know nobody lived in Green Valley, why the hell would he go there? He'd been right here working on Monday, same as always. Rush repair job on a Dodge Caravan, his brother-in-law'd come over to help with the job, go ask him and he'd tell us. Had a couple of towing calls, one around three to haul a tourist family's wagon out of a ditch, the other about five when Ed Larsen's pickup quit on him on the Hamblin Grade. Check his logbook, the calls and the times were written down in black and white. We checked. He was telling the truth.

Whoever had Kerry, it wasn't Jason Hooper.

Midafternoon by the time we got back to Six Pines. The town seemed even more crowded now, people gathering and preparing for the holiday weekend. At the high school football field, members of a marching band were practicing for Friday's parade. The crashing cymbals and bombastic brass notes of a Souza march grated in my ears, set my teeth on edge.

The frustration and the heat had taken their toll. I'd drifted into a half doze for part of the long ride back, but it had done more harm than good. I'd had one of the fever dreams, almost but not quite a flashback, that had plagued me after the time at Deer Run. Only in this one, it had been Kerry who was chained to the cabin wall, and I was outside looking in and couldn't get to her, and she couldn't see me because the wall was made of thick, one-way glass. I jerked out of the dream with such sudden violence that Runyon almost swerved off the road.

Now, I felt drugged—the sunlight too bright even with sunglasses on, the shadows too dark, buildings and cars and strangers' faces fuzzy at the edges. My thoughts fuzzy at the edges, too, so that I had to make a little effort to keep them focused. But I didn't say anything to Runyon about it. Now that he was here, I could afford to keep pushing myself. If my body rebelled at some point, I knew he'd go on doing everything he could, that he wouldn't give up. Where Kerry was concerned, he and Tamara were the only people on this earth I had that kind of faith in.

We hunted around for a place that had a Wi-Fi hookup. You can find one just about anywhere these days, and Six Pines was no exception. A pizzeria just off Main Street had a sign in front that advertised it for free. We went in there and slaked our thirst with Cokes while Runyon accessed his e-mail and we waded through the pages of info Tamara had forwarded, looking for another possible lead.

There wasn't one. None of the other registered sex offenders on her county list lived in Green Valley—the closest was in a small town near Placerville, thirty miles away. The perps in the two statutory rape cases had been nineteen and twenty, the girls fifteen and sixteen, the sex consensual and violence-free. All the other sexual violations had involved the molestation of minors, the oldest child a boy aged ten, or public decency laws. The victims of the two unsolved rapes had both been young women in their early twenties, a waitress assaulted on her way home from work, and a hitchhiker picked up and attacked by two men she'd ID'd as Latinos. One of the female missing persons cases concerned a fifteen-year-old runaway from Six Pines, but that had been seven years ago and the girl had been found six months later living in the Haight in San Francisco.

So what now?

Neither of us addressed the question until we were back in Runyon's Ford. I said then, "Somebody has to've seen the vehicle, whatever it was, going in or out of that logging road. You can't drive the valley roads without passing another car somewhere along the line."

"You pretty much covered all the locals in the vicinity. Maybe a tourist roaming around? We could try canvassing the motels, the B and Bs, that campground out in the valley."

"Long shot. I worked the campground yesterday . . . nothing. But okay. I don't see any other option."

Runyon reached for the ignition key, but he didn't

start the engine. He said, "One just occurred to me. There's one person out on those hillside roads every weekday—the man or woman who delivers the mail."

"Right, good thought."

"If his route puts him in the area afternoons."

"We'll find out."

The post office was housed in an old brick building down one of the side streets. The local postmaster was a woman in her fifties who'd "heard about the missing tourist lady" and was both sympathetic and cooperative when I told her who I was. Frank Ramsey was the mail delivery person for that part of the valley, she said, and yes, his route generally put him in the vicinity of Skyview Drive in the afternoon. He was usually finished and back between four-thirty and a quarter to five.

Ten minutes shy of four o'clock now. The better part of an hour to kill—not enough time to start canvassing the tourist accomodations.

We went back to the air-conditioned pizzeria. The sign in front gave me another idea, slim but worth checking while we waited to talk to Frank Ramsey. Below the *Free Wi-Fi* was another line that said *Free Delivery*. Inside, I asked the kid taking orders if any pizza deliveries had been made in the Skyview Drive area on Monday afternoon. No. They didn't deliver until after five o'clock. He was willing to let us look at their copy of the local phone directory, so we sat with another Coke each and looked through the Yellow Page listings for other Six Pines' businesses that offered delivery service of one kind or another. There were only a handful. Runyon called each one, asked the same question and got the same answer. No Monday afternoon deliveries.

Almost time to head back to the post office. We sat clock-watching in silence; there was nothing to say until after we talked to Frank Ramsey. I'd been thirsty enough to get most of the first Coke down earlier, but one swallow of this one had been all I could manage. Gaggingly sweet. What I'd really wanted was a cold beer, but in my keyed-up state, it would have been a bad idea.

At four-twenty, we were back at the P.O. The postmistress told us we could wait for Ramsey on the rear dock, and described him so we'd know him when he came in. Four-thirty. Four-thirty-five. Four-forty. Come on, Ramsey, come on. Four-forty-five . . . six . . . seven . . .

A postal van finally turned into the yard, rolled to a stop alongside half a dozen others. The man who hopped out was tall, skinny, knobby-kneed in a pair of uniform shorts—Ramsey. He looked vaguely familiar, but I couldn't place where I'd seen him before. We told him our names and asked our questions, and he was as cooperative as the postmistress. Only he had nothing to tell us.

"Sure, I know that old logging road," he said. "I'm usually up around there about two, two-thirty. Delivered mail to the Verrikers that afternoon. I guess you heard about their house blowing up, terrible thing, poor Alice. But I don't remember seeing any cars on the logging road that day or any other day. I mean, I pass a lot of vehicles coming and going on my route every day, and I don't pay much attention unless folks I know honk or wave at me. . . ."

Another bust.

So now it was the motels and bed and breakfasts and campground, and if we didn't get anything out of them, either, then what?

18

KERRY

She couldn't pick the lock.

The twisted-together tacks weren't strong enough to hold and snap the tumblers, she didn't have the necessary skill, and her fingers and wrists became too crabbed from the effort to maintain pressure. All of that, and the debilitating heat forced her to quit after . . . what, one, two, three hours? Her sense of time had become nonexistent. She could no longer even remember how long she'd been imprisoned.

All that work with the chair and the TV set and the tacks, all for nothing. Futile time-passers. False hope. Even if she'd been able to spring the deadbolt, she wouldn't have gotten away. She accepted that now. The pit bull would have torn her apart the instant she tried to slip through the door. The sounds she'd made with her makeshift picks had alerted the animal again, started it barking, brought it close. Very close. When the racket ceased, she'd heard the dog just beyond the door, snuffling and growling. That convinced her its lead reached all the way to the shed. And of just how vicious it must be.

Now, she sat limp with her back against the door, her legs splayed out. She knew she should try to put the room back in order before Balfour came again, right the arm-chair, somehow get the television back up onto the bench, but she couldn't make herself do it. Didn't have the strength or the will. Apathy had set in. In a little while, maybe she'd be able to overcome it. And maybe not.

The near-darkness coiled around her, sticky, stifling. She had shut off the lights before she started work on the lock. Didn't need light for that kind of chore; it had to be done by feel.

Done, she thought dully. But not the chore—her. All done.

She would never get out of here. Never be rescued—if Bill were going to track her down, he'd have done it by now. Completely at Balfour's mercy, and he would show her none. His acts of cruelty so far proved that. Sooner or later, one way or another, in this shed or somewhere else, he was going to kill her.

Dying had never particularly frightened her. She'd had too much experience with the concept—the deaths of her father and Emily's birth parents, the times Bill's life had nearly been lost, the cancerous cells in her breast. Death was natural and inevitable, you couldn't escape it. But the way your life ended . . . that was what terrified her. The cancer had been bad enough, the thought of wasting away in a sick room, dying by degrees the way Jake Run-yon's wife had. But this was worse. This was the ultimate horror. Suffering death at the hands of a madman. Alone, with loved ones far away and no knowledge of her fate, facing years of not knowing in the event her body was never found.

Bill, Emily, Cybil. Their faces swam dimly across through her consciousness. She wouldn't see any of them, hold any of them in her arms again. Gone from her. And she gone from them. Alone.

Emotion overwhelmed her. Not fear, she was beyond fear, but a kind of terrible grief. She didn't try to fight it, simply gave in to it. Dry, wracking sobs shook her body; she heard herself mewling like a child. The breakdown lasted a long time, or seemed to, finally ending in a series of heaving hiccoughs that left her drained and exhausted. Gradually, then, her mind shut down and let her escape into a sleep so deep it was unbroken by nightmares.

It was late in the day when she awoke. Not dark yet— fragments of daylight still filtered in through the chinks in the wall boards—but late enough so that her prison wasn't quite as suffocatingly hot. A sharp breeze had begun to blow; she could hear it whistling, flapping a loose shingle on the roof.

She sat listening for a little time. The dog, wherever it was, was quiet, and there were no other identifiable sounds.

The sleep had had a cleansing effect on her mind. More alert now, more in control of her feelings. But her body was a mass of grinding aches, her throat so dry her tongue seemed fused with the roof of her mouth. Water . . . the last of the water. She rolled onto one hip, then onto her side, groaning at the pain from stiffened muscles, and used the doorknob to lift herself upright. Slitted her eyes and switched the lights on. Held herself braced against the door until she was sure she was steady enough to walk, then moved slowly to the bench.

With one hand on its edge for support, she leaned down to pick up the dog dish with the water in it, straightened slowly, and used both hands to raise it to her mouth. A crack in her chapped lower lip broke open and began to bleed when she pressed her mouth against the metal rim. The water was as warm as bathwater; she couldn't swallow the first sip, moved it around in her mouth until it dissolved some of the dry cake and freed her tongue. Then, when she tilted her head back, her throat muscles unlocked and let the wetness trickle down.

Three more sips, swirled and swallowed the same as the first, and the dish was empty. Kerry set it on the bench, turned to survey the room. Put things back together or not? Yes. The apathy was mostly gone now; she was *not* going to just sit and wait passively to die.

She moved across to the armchair, struggled to shove it into an upright position. A piece of the torn cloth showed along one edge; she toed it out of sight. Now the television. Foolish to try to pick it up and carry it to the bench. Push it over there, close, and then summon enough strength to lift it up—

Outside, the pit bull resumed its barking. The sounds had a different cadence than before, the loud rumbles interspersed with little yips. Eager sounds. Welcoming sounds.

Balfour was out there in the yard.

She knew it even before she heard him call out the animal's name, tell it to shut the hell up.

Panic spiraled in her. He might not have been able to tell at a distance that the lights were on, there was still time to turn them off. But when he opened the door, he'd put them on himself, he'd see the TV set, he'd see her—

Eyes, his *eyes*!

The panic gave way to fury. She staggered ahead to the door. The twisted-together tacks were on the floor where she'd dropped them, their sharp points gleaming faintly in the glare. She snatched them up, then flipped off the lights. Stood with her arms raised, one slender piece like a miniature dagger in each clenched fist.

He was at the door now. His key scraped in the lock.

As soon as he opened it, she'd hurl herself at him, plunge the tacks into his eyes. Even if the dog tore her apart afterward, dying in agony would be worth it because he'd be dead, too.

19

JAKE RUNYON

There were four motels and six B&Bs in and around Six Pines. He and Bill divvied them up to save time, agreed to rendezvous at the campground if neither of them found out anything worth a summoning phone call. Tiny hope at best, but it was all they had left.

Until a few minutes past seven o'clock. And then they didn't have it anymore.

All of the accommodations were booked solid. The method in a canvass like this was to talk to clerks, managers, hostesses first to find out which guests had been staying since Sunday night, then take those individuals room by room. There weren't many in the places on Runyon's list; most of the visitors were late arrivals, in town for the Independence Day weekend. Some of the doors he knocked on stayed shut, the occupants out somewhere. The people who were in, most obliging, a few not, had nothing to tell him: either they hadn't been driving in the valley hills, or if they had, they didn't know anything about an old logging road, and they'd never seen the woman in the photograph Bill had given him. The silent cell phone in his shirt pocket said Bill was getting the same negative responses.

Runyon had been at the campground for fifteen minutes and had already spoken to several of the campers when Bill showed up. Together, they covered the rest, with the same lack of results.

Bill wanted to go back and start over, to see if any of the tourists they missed had returned to their rooms, but Runyon talked him out of it. The man was in no shape to do any more interviewing—a couple of the campers had reacted warily to his disheveled and hollow-eyed appearance, and they might not have been the first to shy away. He knew it, too; he didn't put up an argument when Runyon offered to go back into town and make the rounds again by himself.

"All right," he said. "The rental house isn't far from here. Follow me up there first so you'll know where it is."

Bill's driving was a little erratic, another sign of how strung out he was. Runyon followed at a safe distance, memorizing the route from the valley road. He'd packed an overnight bag before leaving the city; he got it out of the trunk while Bill opened up the house, took it into the spare bedroom he was pointed to.

When he came out again, Bill was sprawled on the couch in the living room with a piece of notepaper in his hand. Wordlessly, he extended it to Runyon. List of motels and B&Bs, names, room numbers; all but three of the names had lines through them. A similar list in Runyon's

pocket contained four names left to check. Seven alto-
gether. Chances a couple of points above zero.

"One other thing," Bill said. "The mailman, Ramsey."

"What about him?"

"He looked familiar and I just remembered where I'd
seen him before. Sunday, Green Valley Café, while Kerry
and I were in there having lunch. He and two other guys
were in the booth behind us—I think one of them was
Ned Verriker. They got into a verbal wrangle with another customer, an ugly little guy they called the mayor."

"What was the wrangle about?"

"That mayor name. Little guy seemed offended by it,
made some noise and stomped out."

"Why was he offended?"

"No idea. Some sort of local joke."

"Anybody say his name?"

"Yeah. Balmer, Baldor, something like that . . . I just
can't remember for sure. First name Pete."

"You think he noticed you and Kerry?"

"Can't say. He looked around, but the place was
crowded."

"Talk to him or see him since?"

"No. But the connection to Verriker . . . worth checking him out."

"I'll try to find him," Runyon said. "Don't know when
I'll be back. Might be quite a while."

"Call me if you get even a whisper."

"You know I will. Try to get some rest."

"Yeah."

"Something to eat, too. Food in the house?"

"Enough. Don't worry about me. I'll be okay."

Runyon left him, drove down to the valley road and back into Six Pines. Four of the seven remaining tourist possibles were in their rooms; three had nothing to tell him, the fourth wouldn't even talk to him through the door. Three to go. Chances now one point above zero.

Next option: a round of the watering holes, the ones that catered to the locals. Even though the people didn't know you, you could pick up information if you asked the right questions the right way. Runyon had developed a knack for that kind of thing. Or maybe it just came naturally. In Seattle, before his life got turned upside down, he'd been one of the regular guys—good listener, easy rapport with strangers.

Barely possible somebody'd be drinking in one of taverns that they'd missed talking to, somebody who had seen something or had some idea of who might've been parked on that logging road Monday afternoon. There was still the Verriker angle, too. Broxmeyer's judgment that Ned Verriker and his wife had no enemies, were well liked by everyone, wasn't necessarily true; what Bill had told him about Sunday's incident in the Green Valley Café indicated that. If nothing else, making the rounds should net the full identity of the Pete Something who didn't like being called mayor.

The first place he went to was the Bank Shot, a block off the south end of Main Street. No different than every other small-town bar he'd been in, except that there was a pool tournament going on in the back room and the place was jammed to capacity. The noise level was such that you couldn't hold a normal conversation. He wasn't going to find out anything here, at least not until the tournament ended and the crowd thinned out.

His next stop, a couple of blocks away, was a place called the Miners Club. Pretty much a carbon copy of the Bank Shot, but without the pool tournament, the heavy crowd, and the ear-slamming noise. He found a place at the bar, ordered a light beer, and helped himself to a handful of pretzels to appease the mutterings in his belly. The bartender was too busy at the moment for conversation, and the couple on Runyon's left were busy discussing the screwed-up love life of the woman's sister. He made an effort with the middle-aged man on his right, but it didn't buy him anything except a half glare and a couple of grunts.

He picked up his glass, moved to the other end of the bar where a fat man in a Hawaiian shirt sat alone shaking dice. Liar's dice, from the number of die and the way each turnover was scrutinized. Runyon slid onto the stool next to him, watched him shake out another hand, then asked conversationally if he were practicing his game. The fat man glanced at him, grinned faintly, shrugged, and said he needed all the practice he could get because every two out of three times he shook Mel the bartender for a beer, he lost. There was a state law against shaking dice for drinks in taverns, but if you didn't pay any attention to it, it made you one of the guys. Runyon asked the fat man if he wanted to shake for a new round, got an affirmative nod, made sure he lost the match, and thereby established a casual bar bond.

The fat man's name was Harve and he was talkative enough. Runyon told him he was a salesman from Modesto, that he and the wife had come into town on Tuesday and were staying through the weekend. Then he said, "I hear you had some excitement here Monday night. Somebody's house blew up and a woman was killed?"

"That's right," Harve said. "One of them freak accidents. Bad enough, but it could've been worse."

"You mean the woman's husband might've been home, too."

"That's one thing. Ned Verriker was real lucky. Explosion almost caused a forest fire, that's another. VFD just got it contained in time."

"Must've been some blaze. You in the neighborhood when it happened?"

"Not me," Harve said. He sounded disappointed. "Working on a road crew the other end of the valley."

"The man . . . what's his name, Verriker? . . . must be taking it pretty hard."

"Wouldn't you if it was your house, your wife?"

"Hell, yes. Never be the same again."

"Ned probably won't, neither."

Runyon took a sip of his beer before he said, "Pretty well liked in the community, Verriker and his wife, weren't they?"

"Guess you could say that."

"Not friends of yours?"

"No. Never met her, but I know him a little from where he works. He don't come in here much. The Buckhorn's his hangout. Keeps everybody in stitches over there, they tell me."

"Is that right?"

"One of them guys with a wicked sense of humor. Well, the poor bastard's not laughing now, that's for sure."

"Wicked?"

"Always making jokes about other people. You know, if they don't hurt, they ain't funny."

The bartender, Mel, had come down to this end and was standing within earshot. He said a little sourly, "Like that mayor business."

"Yeah, like that."

"Pete sure didn't think it was funny, and I don't blame him."

"Guess I don't, either. But you got to admit, Verriker nailed him pretty good."

"Better not tell Pete that."

"Not me. He throws a fit every time anybody even looks at him cross-eyed these days."

Runyon said, "Mayor business? What's that about?"

"The Mayor of Asshole Valley," Harve said. "Guy hung that name on me, I'd be pissed, too."

"How'd it come about?"

"Him and Pete never got along, that's how. Almost come to blows a couple of times, didn't they, Mel?"

"So I heard," the bartender said.

"How long ago'd it happen, the name-calling?"

Harve said, "Few weeks. At the Buckhorn one night."

"Wouldn't've happened in here," Mel said, "not on my shift."

"Dunno how it got started, different versions floating around. Something about too many assholes in the world these days. Verriker said what they ought to do was round 'em all up and put 'em in a valley somewhere, armed guards all around to keep 'em there. Pete didn't like that and said so, and Verriker said that was because he was the biggest asshole in *this* valley, and if he was put in with the rest, they'd probably elect him mayor. The Mayor of Asshole Valley."

"And the name stuck?"

"Oh, it stuck all right. Or at least Pete thinks so."

Runyon asked, "Who is Pete anyway?"

"Good customer," the bartender said. "You wouldn't know him."

"Curious, that's all. He's not here tonight, I take it?"

"He was, we wouldn't be talking about him like this. Talked about him enough as it is." He glanced meaningfully at the fat man before he moved away.

"Yeah, Mel's right," Harve said. "Oughtn't to be spreading local stuff around to out-of-towners." He picked up the dice box, rattled it a couple of times. "Shake for another beer?"

Runyon declined; said his wife was a fit-thrower, too, and if he didn't get back to her, she was liable to throw one tonight. He'd gotten all he was going to get out of Harve and the bartender. Time to move on.

The Buckhorn Tavern was on a side street at the north end of town. From the name, you expected walls decorated with deer antlers, animal heads, hunting paraphernalia, and that was what you got. Macho place. The two dozen or so patrons were mostly male and from the look of them, regulars. Every eye fixed on Runyon when he walked in, watched him ease onto a bar stool and spend four dollars on another light beer.

The glances weren't unfriendly, just openly curious. But he couldn't get anybody to talk to him. Tried three times, with two men and a woman, and either got the cold shoulder or a quick brush-off. He took his beer over near an antiquated shuffleboard game for a better look at the rest of the patrons. He'd been there less than thirty seconds when one of them slid out of a booth and came sidling over to him.

The man was about forty, rangy and hollow-cheeked, dressed in Levi's and a sport shirt. He nodded and offered a "How's it going?" greeting. Then, "Aren't you one of the guys been asking about the woman went missing a few days ago?"

"That's right. Runyon's my name."

"Ernie Stivic."

"Sorry, but I don't remember talking to you."

"You didn't. Saw you with Frank Ramsey this afternoon."

"The mailman?"

"Yep. He's a friend of mine, he told me about it after you left. Any luck finding the woman?"

"Not so far."

"Frank said her husband's pretty shook up. I would be, too, if I was married." Stivic took a swig from the bottle of Bud he was holding. "You and him really private detectives down in 'Frisco?"

"Yes."

"Can't do much in a thing like this, can you? Woman wanders off into the woods and you don't know the area?"

"Is that what you think happened? She just wandered off and got lost?"

"What else? Happens all the time up here. Well, not all the time, but often enough in the summer."

"You wouldn't happen to've been in the vicinity of Skyview Drive on Monday afternoon, would you, Mr. Stivic?"

"Not me. I was at work."

"Know anybody who might've been?"

Stivic shook his head. "Sorry. Mind if I ask you a question?"

"Go ahead."

"How come you're here? In the Buckhorn, I mean. You looking for somebody or just taking a break?"

It was curiosity, nothing more, that had brought Stivic over. But he was friendly and talkative enough, the type open to being probed. You wouldn't be able to get much from a man like this about one of his friends, but you could pry out some information if the subject was somebody he didn't like.

Runyon said, "I thought the mayor might be here. Is he?"

"Fred Donaldson? Why'd you think he'd be here? He don't drink."

"I meant the man they call the mayor. Pete something."

"Oh, hell, him," Stivic said, and his mouth bent into a lopsided grin. "The mayor. Yeah, and it fits him like a glove, too. You know why we call him that?"

"I've been told. *Is* he here?"

"Not tonight. How come you're looking for him?"

"Just trying to cover all the bases. What's his last name?"

"Balfour. Pete Balfour."

"What's he do for a living?"

"Construction. Balfour Construction."

"Big outfit?"

"Nah. Just him and a couple of helpers. Works out of his house."

"Any idea where I can find him tonight?"

"Miners Club, over on Third. That's where he usually hangs out."

"I was just there and he wasn't."

"Probably out at his place then."

"Where would that be?"

"Up-valley, five, six miles."

"Wife, kids?"

"Not Pete. He don't have any friends, neither."

"Sounds like you don't much like the man."

"Ain't much to like. He didn't get that mayor name for nothing."

"I understand Ned Verriker hung it on him."

"That's right. Poor Ned. You heard about what happened to his wife?"

"I heard. Verriker and Balfour don't get along, I take it?"

"You take it right." Stivic sucked on his beer again. A dark frown had replaced the crooked grin. "Balfour come in here Monday night, pretended to be tore up over Alice dying horrible like that, but he don't really care. Not about her or any woman."

"Why do you say that?"

"Beat up on his wife until she walked out on him a few years ago. No other woman around here's had anything to do with him since."

"Did Balfour ever threaten the Verrikers?"

"Threaten? Why'd you ask that?"

"No particular reason. Just wondering."

"Well, not that I know of. Ned would've kicked the crap out of him if he had." Stivic seemed to have realized he was being a little too frank with a stranger. He said, "Listen, you talk to Balfour, don't tell him what I said about him, all right? He don't scare me none, but I don't want him hassling me."

"I won't mention you at all, Mr. Stivic. Thanks for your help."

"Okay. Good luck finding your friend's wife."

Stivic moved across to the booth he'd vacated. Runyon carried his unfinished beer to the bar, left it there, and went down a corridor near the front entrance where the restrooms were. The Buckhorn was old-fashioned enough to still have a public wall telephone with a battered local directory hanging underneath. There was a small ad for Balfour Construction in the Yellow Pages, with an address on Crooked Creek Road, Six Pines. He memorized the name and number. On his way out of the tavern, he glanced up at an illuminated beer company clock on the wall between two racks of antlers. Almost nine-thirty.

In the car, he sat mulling for a couple of minutes. Judging from what he'd learned so far, Pete Balfour was a definite maybe: didn't get along with the Verrikers, history of violence at least against one woman, loner with a nasty temper. The best lead they'd had so far, but still tenuous without more information. No reason yet to get Bill's hopes up with a phone call. How to handle it then? Talk to Balfour tonight or wait until morning? Almost full dark now, late to be bracing somebody. But not too late, not with the time factor working against them.

Runyon programmed the Crooked Creek Road address into the Ford's GPS. Five point eight miles north of Six Pines, zero point four off the main valley road. Shouldn't take him more than ten minutes to get there.

Crooked Creek Road lived up to its name: a narrow, twisty lane that followed the watercourse up into the hills. In the purple dusk, the Ford's headlights picked out two unpaved driveways before a third loomed ahead on his left and the GPS unit told him he'd reached his destination. He put the side window down, slowing, as he neared the drive. It angled in across a short wooden bridge, on the other side of which was a closed gate in a chain-link fence that stretched out into the trees along both sides of the creek. A half moon was coming up, and in its pale light he could make out a house and two or three outbuildings on a flattish section of ground inside. From out here, all of the structures appeared dark—no lights anywhere.

He drove uphill until he came to another property, turned around in the driveway there, rolled back down to Balfour's, and turned in so that the headlights illuminated the gate and some of the property beyond. Leaving the engine running, he stepped out into a night breeze that now held a mountain chill.

The two gate halves were padlocked together. No intercom device that would allow you to announce yourself from out here. Runyon peered through the opening between the two upright bars. The house was small, plain, well maintained. The largest and closest outbuilding, set at an angle to the left, was almost as large and probably housed Balfour's workshop. The other, smaller buildings were shadow shapes outlined against the pine woods that walled off the rear of the property. There was a stake-bed truck slanted in near the workshop, but the open-ended carport along one side of the house was empty.

Somewhere out back, a dog had begun yammering, deep-throated barks that had an echoing effect in the light-splashed darkness. Tied up, because between yaps, even at this distance, he could hear the dog lunging at the end of the chain or rope or whatever was holding it back there. If Balfour was in the house, the animal racket and the bright headlight beams should have alerted him by now. But the front door stayed shut, the windows and porch light stayed dark.

Runyon turned to look at his watch in the headlight glare. Nine-twenty. No choice now but to hold off until morning. He couldn't just sit out on the road and wait; no telling how long it would be before Balfour came home, if he wasn't already forted up in there. Hanging around a stranger's property after dark was a fool's gambit anyway, unless you had damn good cause or a desire to spook the subject. And he had neither.

20

PETE BALFOUR

The road around the east end of Eagle Rock Lake was in lousy shape—ruts, potholes, crumbled edges. Leave it to the goddamn county. Not that he gave a crap what the county did or didn't do, not anymore. Off on his right as he jounced along, the lake looked like the big oil slick they'd had down in the Gulf—smooth and shiny black, skimmed here and there with reflections of moonlight. It was a mile and a half wide, maybe a mile long, supposed to be a lot of fish in it on account of it was fed by a bunch of mountain streams. Couldn't prove it by him. His sport wasn't fishing, it was hunting.

Going hunting tonight. Big-game hunting—Verriker hunting.

Balfour could feel the weight of the revolver in his jacket pocket. Charter 2000 Off Duty .38 special, two-inch barrel. Serial number filed off like on all the guns in his collection. Had it for years, couldn't be traced back to him—not that that mattered anymore. Perfect piece for this kind of hunt.

He was pretty juiced now that he was close to settling the score with Neddy boy, but he'd of been more juiced if he wasn't so pissed at that tourist woman. He'd swabbed the cut under his right eye with iodine, but it still burned like hell. Missed sticking them twisted-together tacks through his eye by about two inches. Bitch. Lunging at him like a freaking ninja soon as he opened the shed door, surprised the hell out of him, he'd just managed to get his head snapped back in time. She'd worked herself out of the duct tape in there, okay, he'd figured she might, she'd had plenty of time, but what he hadn't figured on was her getting her hands on something she could use as a weapon to attack him. Where the hell had those tacks come from? For sure not the old TV set she'd pulled down on the floor.

Two inches higher, and he wouldn't be out here with Verriker in his sights. He'd be back at the house or on his way to the hospital—Pete One-Eye. Or maybe Pete Dead.

Well, he'd make her pay for it. Just like he'd make the rest of them pay for what they'd done to him.

The truck bounced around a bend past a long lime-stone shelf. And in the distance, then, he could see lights through the trees at the edge of the lake. That'd be the Ramsey cabin. He'd been over this road before on other hunting trips, seen the cabin squatting down there with its little T-dock poking out into the water.

So Verriker hadn't gone to bed yet. He'd hoped the bugger would be sound asleep, all the lights off, so he could slip on up to the cabin and maybe a door or window'd be unlocked and he could surprise Verriker in the sack. But now what he'd do, he'd just knock on the door and when Verriker opened it, stick the .38 in his face, look him square in the eye, and tell him why he should of died along with Alice. Then laugh the way he'd been laughed at that night in the Buckhorn, let Verriker know before he blew him away that the last big joke was on him and it was Pete Balfour who was getting the last laugh.

Better not drive any farther. The pickup's engine was quiet, the muffler in good shape, but sounds carried a long way at night in country like this. He looked for a place to park the truck, found one in the trees on the inland side. He hadn't seen any other cars since he'd turned in, but that didn't mean somebody wouldn't come along. There were only a few cabins and cottages out here, spaced wide apart, but at least half had people in them this time of year. He'd seen other lights on the way in, could make out a few now glimmering over on the south shore.

He walked along the edge of the road, ready to jump off into the trees at the first sight of headlights. But the road and the night stayed dark, except for the cabin lights winking ahead. Moonlight let him see so he didn't stumble over something. Took him six, seven minutes to get near the turnoff to the cabin. Then he angled down through the pines, moving slow and quiet in the underbrush, until he could see the front of the cabin.

Verriker's Dodge van was parked there, dirty white in the moonshine. Yeah, but it had company. Jeep Cherokee sitting there, too—Joe Ramsey's Jeep.

Shit!

Verriker was supposed to be alone in the cabin, licking his wounds. What was Ramsey doing here?

Balfour edged down farther through the trees, until he was about fifty yards from the cabin. From there, he could see a light in a screened-in rear porch, and that somebody was standing on the dock looking out over the lake. Verriker? Ramsey? The red eye of a cigarette glowed sudden in the dark. Hell, it wasn't neither of them. Verriker didn't smoke, Ramsey'd made a big deal about quitting a couple of years back . . . but Ramsey's scrawny wife, Connie, lit up every chance she had. Well, it was no big surprise she'd come out here with her old man— mother hen type, make sure poor Ned baby was okay, change his diapers for him.

Cold in among the pines with a night wind blowing in off the lake. He pulled the collar of his jacket up and stuffed his hands in the pockets, watching. The cold got to Connie Ramsey, too. She finished her smoke, tossed the butt into the lake, turned back toward the cabin. Damn woman waddled like a duck when she walked.

The screen door slammed, and when the porch light went out, Balfour moved up toward the front again. Stood there waiting for the Ramseys to come out and get in their Jeep and drive the hell away so he could finish the hunt. He could already feel it bubbling up inside him, taste it sweet like candy on the back of his tongue.

Only they didn't come out.

Ten minutes, fifteen, twenty. What was taking them so long?

A light come on behind one of the windows on this side, probably a bedroom. Then the front room lights and the bedroom light went out. And the whole damn cabin was dark. Dark!

What the hell?

Took Balfour a few seconds to get it, and when he did, the rage went boiling through him like hot oil. The Ramseys weren't going home, they were spending the night here. That bitch Connie's doing, didn't want poor Neddy Boy to be alone, and gutless pussy-whipped Joe Ramsey had let her have her way like he always did.

Another monkey wrench in the plans. The tourist woman twice, the explosion not getting Verriker, now this. And none of it Pete Balfour's fault, none of it he could've seen ahead of time. As if it wasn't just Asshole Valley that was out to get him, but the whole damn world, everything and everybody working against him, laughing at him, letting him think he was in control and then spinning him around and around like a bug on a pin.

He leaned against a tree trunk, shaking with fury. Blood pounded in his ears. The cut under his eye burned like fire. Inside his head, the voices started up again, saying the same like always, over and over, over and over. *Biggest asshole I know, maybe the biggest one in these parts. I bet somebody'd nominate you for mayor, I bet you'd win hands down. Pete Balfour, the first mayor of Asshole Valley . . . mayor of Asshole Valley . . . mayor of Asshole Valley . . .*

An urge came over him to bust into the cabin, blow all three of them away, *wham! wham! wham!* Almost gave in to it. Yanked the .38 out, shoved off the tree, and took a couple of steps toward the cabin. But then he come to his senses. He stopped, breathing hard, and pretty soon the thunder in his ears eased, the voices faded into a low mutter. He put the revolver away, wiped cold sweat off his forehead.

Too much risk. He might be able to take all three of them out, but then again, he might not. For all he knew, Verriker or Ramsey had a piece, too, and would use it to shoot him before he finished the job. And even if he did get them all, they'd be missed come tomorrow and somebody'd drive out and find the bodies. If it'd just been Verriker, no problem, because he'd of made it look like a suicide, like poor Ned couldn't deal with losing his precious Alice and took the quick way out—that'd been the plan. But three bodies . . . plain murder, the kind that could raise a stink and maybe throw a monkey wrench into his other plan, the big one. He had to be careful. He had to have all of tomorrow to himself, no hassles, because of all he had to do to set things up just right. He wasn't gonna let anything screw *that* up.

But what about Verriker? Still had to watch him die, still had to have his last laugh. Tomorrow night maybe, depending on what time he got back from Stockton, and whether or not the Ramseys stayed over again. If that didn't work out, well, then he'd come out here and do it early Friday morning. Bring the Sterling semi-auto with him, make sure he had plenty of firepower in case the Ramseys were still hanging around. Wouldn't make no difference then how many dead bodies there were in that cabin. No difference at all.

Better get on home, get a good night's sleep. Big day tomorrow. He pumped both middle fingers at the dark cabin, then turned and headed back through the trees to the road.

21

Balfour. Pete Balfour.

Was he the one?

Best lead yet, thanks to Runyon, but only because of his connection with the Verrikers; there was nothing to tie him directly to the logging road or Kerry's disappearance, nothing we could take to Broxmeyer, or direct to the county sheriff, or act on ourselves. Two things we could do. One was to have Tamara run a deep backgrounder on Balfour; I called her after Runyon came back with his news and we'd talked over the situation, and she was on it right away. The other thing was for Jake and me to talk to the man, see if we could squeeze anything out of him.

Tamara worked fast, called back in a little more than an hour. Nothing much, no red flags except for an arrest six years ago on a spousal battery charge. But Balfour's ex-wife had dropped the charge the next day. Two other brushes with the law: a DUI three years ago and a charge of poaching deer out of season, fines and probation on both. There'd also been two complaints against his construction business, one by a private individual for overcharges on a house remodel, the other by the owners of a restaurant in one of the hamlets at the north end of the valley for use of inferior building materials; the second complaint got him a modest fine by the county licensing board. Those were the only blemishes on his record. Lived alone, no dependents, paid his bills more or less on time. Probably worthy of the mayor tag, but being an asshole didn't necessarily make him a felon.

But God, I wanted it to be him. I ached for it to be him. If it wasn't, then we were as much in the dark as before.

I'd been able to sleep some while Runyon was making his rounds—sheer exhaustion had knocked me out for a while—but I didn't get much more that night. Fits and starts, the dozes interrupted by running dreams and one nightmare that woke me up in a cold sweat but I couldn't remember afterward. I was in fair shape come dawn, my tank partially refilled. I'd be okay for part of the day, but if it went on like the last two, full of frustration and overexposure to the sweltering heat, I was not sure how long I could hold up.

I was up and dressed at five-thirty, a few minutes ahead of Runyon. As much as I wanted to head out to Balfour's place right away, I knew it was too early. It wouldn't matter whether or not he was up at this hour if his front gate was still locked. In that case, with no communication device, the only ways to let him know we wanted to talk to him were a phone call or blasts on the car horn. Guilty or innocent, he'd either refuse to see us or be closed off and hostile if he did. We had to handle this right. If Balfour was the man, Kerry's life depended on it.

I made coffee, toast, boiled a couple eggs—disposing of time, not because I had any appetite. Runyon didn't seem to have much, either, but we both choked the food down for sustenance. Not talking much; we'd hashed it all out the night before. He looked a lot more clear-eyed and rested than I did. Plenty of stamina in him, and why not? He was twenty years younger, in better physical shape, and he had no abiding personal stake in this—the woman he loved was not in the hands of Christ knew what brand of maniac.

No, that wasn't fair. The woman Jake had loved as desperately as I loved Kerry was already dead, the victim of a different kind of horror.

We left the house a few minutes before seven, Runyon driving again. I sat leaning forward, tense, as we wound up Crooked Creek Road to Balfour's property. And when we got there . . . gate in the chain-link fence closed, padlocked.

Runyon parked in the driveway and I got out, crossed a short platform bridge, and went up to peer through the gate. House, barn/workshop, another outbuilding at the rear whose roofline I could just make out between the other two. There was no chimney smoke or other sign of life in or around the buildings.

Jake came up beside me. "Looks deserted."

"Yeah."

The dog had started barking and snarling somewhere behind the house. From the noise it was making, Jake's guess of a guard dog, big and vicious, was the right one.

I'd had a run-in with another animal like that, a kill-trained Rottweiler, only a few months ago and it had come close, very close, to ripping my throat out. I had no desire for a repeat of that incident. But I'd stand up against this one, too, if it came to that.

I said, "Was that stake-bed truck parked over there last night?"

"Same place."

"And the carport was empty?"

"As empty as it is now. Up and gone early, maybe."

"Or he didn't come home at all last night."

Neither of us put voice to the possibility that Balfour had closed up shop and left the valley for the holiday weekend.

Silent drive into Six Pines. The Green Valley Café was open, and busy with breakfast trade. I scanned the room, but none of the customers was the ugly little guy I'd seen on Sunday. I shook my head at Jake, led the way to where a couple of stools stood vacant at the counter. When the plump blond waitress got around to us, I asked her if she knew Pete Balfour.

"Oh, yeah, I know him."

"He been in this morning?"

"No. Usually is, but not today so far."

"Any idea where we can find him?"

"Fairgrounds, probably. Supposed to be finishing up a remodel job in time for the Fourth."

We drove down there, through the open front gates to where the construction work was going on at a row of concession booths behind the grandstand. Two vehicles parked next to a metal storage shed, two men working—a sixtyish, gray-haired Latino and a young guy with red hair under a turned-around Giants baseball cap. There was no sign of Pete Balfour.

We approached the Latino, who stopped hammering a section of countertop into place inside one of the booths. He wore a sweat-stained, blue chambray workshirt with the name Eladio Perez home-stitched over one pocket. I asked him if Balfour had come to work today.

"*Sí*. Yes. Very early."

"But he's not here now?"

"He go out to buy something he needs."

"So he'll be back pretty soon."

"Pretty soon."

Runyon asked, "Were you working here on Monday afternoon?"

"Monday afternoon, *sí*. Every day."

"Was your boss here, too?"

Frown lines crosshatched Perez's forehead. Trying to remember.

I said, "The day the house blew up on Skyview Drive."

"Oh, Monday. Yes."

"*Was* Balfour here that afternoon?"

"No. He leave early that day."

"How early? What time?"

"After lunch. One o'clock."

"And he didn't come back?"

"No."

"Do you know where he went?"

Shrug. "*¿Quién sabe?* He don't tell me much." Perez's

expression was more or less stoic, but he had sad, expressive eyes, and the impression they conveyed was that he didn't much like his employer.

"Have you worked for Balfour long?"

"Six years." Six years too long, the sad eyes said.

"So, you must know him pretty well?"

"No, *señor*. I work, he pays me, that's all." Then, "*Excúseme, por favor*. I must be finish here when he come back."

Jake had parked in the shade of a big oak; we went to sit in the car and wait. I said, "Some other business on Monday. Like maybe setting a gas-line boobytrap to murder the Verrikers."

"Maybe. Let's see what he has to say."

The voice of reason. But I was tensed up again, fidgety; I couldn't hold my hands still, kept running them back and forth across my thighs.

The wait lasted ten minutes. Then a dirty white Dodge pickup came rattling along the blacktop and angled to a stop near the shed. The driver hopped out, went around to take material out of the pickup's bed. Balfour.

He was still unloading when Runyon and I approached him. Pear-shaped, stubby-legged, chinless; bullet head topped with a couple of tufts of colorless hair. And a dirty Band-Aid under one eye that gave him a faintly piratical look. He scowled when he spotted us, then seemed to make an effort to shift his expression into neutral. I don't normally judge people by their appearance; I've spent a personal and professional lifetime letting actions and personalities dictate my opinions. But even though I warned myself to keep an open mind, I took an immediate dislike to the man.

"What you guys want?" Flat, with an undercurrent of irritation.

"Few minutes of your time," Runyon said. "You're Pete Balfour?"

"That's right. Who're you?"

Jake told him. Names, professions. The last deliberately, so we could gauge his reaction.

There wasn't much. A couple of eyeblinks, a little twitch along one side of his mouth. He didn't look particularly bright, but you sensed the kind of self-protective shrewdness that keeps some men from revealing much about themselves when you catch them by surprise.

"Detectives? Yeah? What the hell you want with me?"

I said, keeping my voice even, "We're trying to find my wife. She's been missing since Monday."

"Oh, yeah, I heard about that. Hope you find her." Sure he did. "But I didn't know you was a detective."

"Does it matter?"

"No. Hell, no. But I can't help you none. Why come to me?"

"We're talking to everybody we can," Runyon said, "looking for someone who might've seen Mrs. Wade Monday afternoon. You didn't happen to be anywhere near the old logging road off Skyview Drive that day, did you?"

"Me? No. I wasn't nowhere near the valley that day."

"Mind telling us where you were?"

"Right here, working."

"All afternoon?"

"Sure. All day. We got to finish these repairs by tonight. Big holiday doings tomorrow, you probably heard about that."

Lying through his stained-yellow teeth. I had an irrational impulse to grab him, shake him like a dog shakes a bone. I shoved my hands into my pockets to keep them still. Being a liar didn't necessarily make him a kidnapper. Not necessarily. Not enough evidence yet. Innocent until proven guilty.

"Know of anyone else who might've been out that way on Monday?" Runyon asked him.

"No. Wish I did."

"Well, if you hear of anyone who was, let the deputy sheriff, Broxmeyer, know, will you?"

"I sure will."

I said as he started to turn away, "What happened to your face?"

"Huh?"

"Under your eye. The Band-Aid."

His mouth twitched again. He lifted a hand, let it drop without touching the adhesive. "Oh, that. Splinter from a piece of wood I was cutting. Couple of inches higher and they'd be calling me One-Eye."

Another lie. The hell he was innocent.

Back to the car. When we were inside, I said, "He's the one, Jake. I can feel it in my gut."

"He's a damn liar, that's for sure."

"I'm thinking we ought to go back out to his place, climb the gate and look around, and to hell with the dog."

"If we get caught, then what? If we don't find Kerry, then what?"

I didn't argue. Voice of reason again.

We were moving now, heading for the gates. In the side-view mirror, I could see Balfour standing alongside his pickup, pretending to rummage around in the bed while he watched us drive away.

Runyon said, "What we need is more information on Balfour. His life, his habits, if he owns any other property where he could be keeping a prisoner."

"There's one person who can tell us. Plenty."

"Ned Verriker."

"Yeah," I said. "Ned Verriker."

22

PETE BALFOUR

Detectives!

He hadn't had any idea the woman was married to a damn private cop. How the hell could he? She hadn't said nothing, nobody else'd said nothing. Probably all over the valley by now, everybody knew it but him. The last to know anything, that was how it'd always been for him, unless he pried it out of somebody like he'd pried Verriker's whereabouts out of Jolene and Luke Penny. Asshole Valley didn't want nothing to do with Pete Balfour, wouldn't give him the time of day, just laughed at him and called him mayor and wouldn't give him any peace.

Them two nosing around, asking where he was on Monday afternoon—one more threat to him and his plans. Just making the rounds, asking everybody, like they'd said? Or did they suspect him somehow? Come into the fairgrounds, private property, you couldn't see the construction work from out on the road . . . maybe they did suspect him. But that didn't make any sense. How could

225

they? Unless somebody'd pointed them at him, said go talk to the mayor, he's a schmuck nobody likes, he could be the one has the woman locked up somewhere.

No, hell, that didn't make sense, neither. Everybody figured she was lost in the woods, they couldn't have any idea she'd been grabbed. Sure. Sure. It was all right. Those city dicks didn't suspect anything. Getting himself all worked up for no good reason.

But why the questions about the old logging road, Skyview Drive? They couldn't of put it together that that was where he'd snatched the woman or what he was doing up there in the first place. They didn't live in the valley, they didn't know how much he hated the Verrikers. Guys like the Ramseys and Stivic and Lucchesi knew him and Verriker didn't get along, sure, but that was all they knew. Couldn't tie Pete Balfour to the explosion. Nobody could. Tragic accident, everybody thought so, everybody said so. Wasn't no way to prove otherwise.

Yeah, but still . . . the way the old guy, the husband, had looked at him. Eyes boring into his like he was trying to see inside his head. Hard eyes. Suspicious eyes. Tight mouth, too, and it'd got tighter when he said he hadn't been nowhere near that logging road, that he'd been right here working all day Monday—

Shit! They'd been waiting when he come back from Builders Supply, they could of been here long enough to ask the Mex or the half-wit the same questions they'd asked him.

He went quick to where Eladio was working in the beer concession. "Them two guys that was just here. You talk to them while I was gone?"

"*Sí.*"

"What'd you tell them about Monday? You say I was here all day?"

"That would be a lie. I tell them the truth."

"You stupid son of a bitch! That I left early, didn't come back?"

Eladio nodded, looking at him with those big sad eyes of his. Then he shrugged, half smiled, and started banging away again at the countertop.

Balfour came close to jumping in there, smashing his face in. But it wouldn't of done no good, the damage was already done. He jerked away, went around to lean against the wall of the men's crapper. Sweat ran like grease on his face; he rubbed it off on the sleeve of his shirt.

Those detectives suspected him now, all right, if they hadn't before. But they didn't *know* anything yet. He could of had some other reason for lying about Monday, right? Off doing something illegal, buying drugs, banging somebody's wife, people had all kinds of reasons for telling lies. No, they couldn't know anything for sure, but that wouldn't stop them from nosing around.

Suppose they went nosing around his place?

They could get in if they wanted to, the gates and the fence wouldn't keep them out. Bruno wouldn't let them get near the shed, but if they had guns . . . Jesus, if they found the woman . . .

His plans, his revenge, finished right then and there. He couldn't let that happen. Couldn't, wouldn't!

What if they were out there right now?

The thought turned his sweat to ice. Then he thought, no, that wasn't the way cops operated, even private cops.

They'd try to get something else against him before they went busting onto his property, shooting his dog. Wouldn't they? Sure they would. They might go ahead and do it later anyway, whether they found out something or not, but not yet, not for a while. There was still time to make it all work the way he'd worked it out. What he had to do was shift the timetable, get everything ready as fast as he could, move out *now*.

The only problem was the woman. Couldn't leave her where she was, too much chance of her being found. Couldn't put her where he'd planned to until tonight, either. What the hell was he gonna do with her?

Well, there was one thing. No, two things. Both risky, but he'd have to do one or the other. Didn't have to figure out which now. First things first. Get on your horse, man, get moving before it's too late!

Balfour hurried back to the beer concession. "Eladio, listen, I'm sorry I jumped on you. Having a lousy day, that's all."

Another shrug, another half smile.

"I got to go out again for a while, some other business to take care of. I should be back sometime this afternoon, but if I'm not . . . repairs are almost done, all the major ones anyway. You and the kid can finish up the men's restroom."

"*Sí, jefe.*"

"One more thing. Those two guys come back, you tell them you made a mistake about Monday. Tell 'em I was here all day working with you and the kid. You understand?"

That half smile again. Fucking stupid Mex!

Balfour unbuckled his toolbelt on the way to the pickup, tossed it into the front seat. He didn't need to take anything else from the job site. Everything he was gonna need was in his workshop at home.

He drove out of there to the south, took back roads to get to his place so he wouldn't have to go through town—the private cops might spot him and the last thing he wanted was them following him home. He was careful when he neared his driveway, but it was all right. Nobody around, the gates locked tight. Bruno started barking up a storm when he unlocked them, drove into the yard. Okay, good, everything just the way he'd left it.

Still time. Make it fast, but don't forget anything.

First thing was the camper shell. He locked the gates again, drove over to the workshop, opened the double doors, then backed the pickup in close to the rear wall where he had the shell drawn up on pulleys. He lowered it, swung it into place, released the pulleys, and locked it down.

Work supplies next. Didn't take him long—his toolkit was already in the truck. Double-bitted ax, shovels, a pick, some other hand tools and hardware. Nothing electric or battery-operated except for his B&D drill, a grinder, and a small Skil saw. Nothing big or bulky. He hated to leave his big power tools, the circular saw and jigsaw and lathe and router, but there just wasn't enough room. Wouldn't be needing them anyway, where he was going.

Plenty of space left once he had it all stored. Plenty. When he drove out, he took a long look at Crooked Creek Road to make sure he didn't have company, then went on up to the house. Inside, he unlocked and emptied his gun cabinet. Took two trips to load the Bushmaster, the MK7, one of his deer rifles, an over-and-under shotgun, the Glock .380 auto, and all the ammo he had on hand. His hunting knives, too, the 16-inch Bowie and the skinner and the gut-hook. The .38 he'd use on Verriker was already locked inside the glove box.

Bedroom. That was where he kept his laptop, and when he saw it sitting on the desk, he thought again about taking it along. But it just wouldn't be smart. They had ways of finding you when you used your computer. Cut all his ties, don't leave any traces—that was the only way to do it. And don't take anything along that wasn't absolutely necessary.

He got his suitcase out of the closet, the big one Charlotte had bought him right after they were married so they could travel around, see the country, as if he'd cared to take any kind of trip with that fat cow. He packed it up with pants, shirts, two heavy sweaters, underwear, and shaving gear and a few other things from the bathroom. Stored that in the camper shell, then went and got his hiking boots, both pairs, the old Marlboro Man jacket he'd bought secondhand in Placerville, the rolled-up camp bed and two wool blankets.

What else?

Food, right. Not too much, just enough to hold him for a few days so he wouldn't have to stop at restaurants or fast-food places. Do his eating and sleeping at rest stops or campgrounds, no other stops except for gas. Straight on through.

He filled a flour sack, added his last two bottles of Jack Daniel's, and took that to the truck. Then he went and got a frying pan, a couple of cook pots, the old tin coffee pot he took on his hunting trips, a few other things. All of that pretty much filled up the camper. Just enough room left.

Bruno was yapping again, but it wasn't because anybody'd showed up. Yeah, he'd figured the detectives right. Dog was just barking because he was a dumb mutt that liked to hear himself make a lot of noise. Or maybe he was hungry, but the hell with that. No time to feed him. Didn't make no difference what happened to Bruno now anyway.

Back inside, he used a screwdriver to pop off the baseboard on one bathroom wall. The hole he'd cut out behind it was just large enough for the two cigar boxes he kept in there. His stash. All the cash he'd been paid for construction work and never reported to the IRS; screw the IRS. A little over seven thousand, mostly tens and twenties, nothing larger than a fifty—he'd counted it two nights ago, after he had his plans all worked out. Last him a long time if he was real careful. He put three hundred in his wallet, stuffed the rest into one cigar box, took that out to the pickup, and hid it under the floorboards on the passenger side. Somebody'd have to be looking for it, strip-searching, otherwise they'd never find it.

Just about done. He quick-checked his list to make sure. No, he hadn't forgotten anything.

One last thing to do and he'd be loaded and ready to roll.

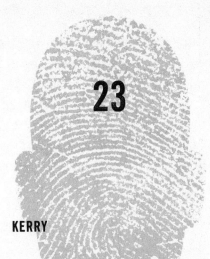

23

KERRY

She lay marinating in heat and the stench from her soiled body. Drifting in and out of consciousness now, a floating limbo. Wrapped in tape from neck to feet this time, a gray mummy stretched out on its back on the dirty floor, unable to move even a little because more tape held her immobile against one of the bench stanchions. For a long time, there had been agony—cramped muscles, sensations of suffocation, shoots of pain in her jaw where Balfour had hit her after she missed stabbing his eye with the tack weapon. Fear and hate, too, rising like tides, receding, rising again, receding again. Then resignation had set in, followed by a return of the apathy, followed by a numbness both physical and mental.

Now, she felt as if her mind had become detached from her body, her spirit already hovering just outside her body. The spirit withering, losing sentience, drifting for long periods in a trancelike state where nonfrightening images swam and darted like creatures beneath the surface of a calm sea. Then it would stir back to life, send out little pulses of awareness—heat, pain, thirst, hunger, the death odors as if her body had already begun to decay. And the fear and the hate would come again, but only briefly and with less and less intensity. Even the desperate will to live had become muted, begun to give way to a desire for the peace that lay beyond the floating limbo.

Adrift again.

Aware again.

Sounds. The dog barking, always barking. Damn the dog.

Something else then, a roaring noise. Car engine. Outside, close.

Door slamming. Balfour, coming back.

She didn't care anymore. Let him come.

She tried to will the hovering spirit to take her back into the nowhere place. But awareness remained. Spasms of pain, thirst, hunger, fear, hate. Fragments of thought. And more sounds. Key scraping in the door lock. The truck engine, louder, throbbing. Heavy steps moving toward her.

His voice: "Didn't get loose this time, did you?"

Words came to her, bright and clear, as if they were being held up on a sign: *Fuck you*. But she couldn't say them. Her throat was closed tight, her vocal chords shriveled and frozen.

Bending over her, putting a hand on her.

Don't touch me!

Snick. Knife, he had a knife in the other hand.

No, don't. Go ahead, get it over with. No, please don't!

He didn't. Ripping sounds . . . he was using the knife to saw at the tape that held her against the bench support.

Another *snick* and the knife disappeared. His hands on her again then, pulling her away from the bench, turning her onto her back. A gurgling whimper came out of the hollowness inside as he bent over her, worked his hands under her and lifted her up tight against his body.

"Jesus, lady. You stink."

His breath was no better. The sour spew of it in her face jerked her head aside.

Grunting, he carried her out through the open door. The glare of sunlight was like needles poked into her eyes; she squeezed them shut. The dog was close by, its barks and growls loud.

"Shut up, Bruno. Shut up!"

The animal noises stopped and Kerry could hear the engine rumble again. She opened her eyes to slits. Blurred images settled into focus.

Pickup with a camper top, the camper's rear door open. He brought her up to it, lifted her inside, shoved her roughly across a hard floor. The back of her head thudded into something, her arm scraped against something else—cuts of pain that she barely felt. Things were piled up all around her . . . tools, camping equipment. And guns, big guns, rifles, automatic weapons, shoved into a space beneath a side-wall bench.

Balfour crawled in, up over her body, until he was kneeling astride her. He put his ugly face close to hers again, a white-and-black smear of beard-stubbled skin.

"Now you listen to me, lady. We're going for a ride. Gonna be a long one, maybe, depends on you. We stop anywhere and you thrash around back here, make noise, I'll kill you dead on the spot. You understand?"

She tried to tell him yes with her eyes. He didn't get the message. Slapped her, hard—more pain that she barely felt.

"Understand?"

The gurgling whimper.

"Okay. You do what I say, maybe I'll let you go later. Drop you off in the woods some place."

Liar. You're going to kill me.

He took something from his pocket, a roll of duct tape. Tore off a piece with his teeth and stretched it tight across her mouth.

Why don't you just get it over with? Why torture me like this?

Another piece of tape torn from the roll, larger than the first. This one, he stuck down over her eyes.

Blind, now. Mute and blind.

Another slap, not as hard, and he slid back off her.

Sounds: Him dropping out of the camper. The hinged door slamming shut. The pit bull barking again. The cab door opening, banging shut. The engine revving up, gears meshing.

And they were moving, jolting over uneven ground. Then stopping again. Then moving. Then stopping. Then moving, winding left and right over a smoother surface. The constant shifting motion bounced her up and down, but the tight-packed space held her where she lay.

Gray-wrapped, living mummy trapped in a moving sarcophagus driven by a madman.

Hot, hotter than the shed. Exhaust fumes choking the air, making breathing difficult through congested nostrils. Dulled hurt in her head, all through her body every time the wheels passed over a bump.

Bill, she thought once. And imagined his face, his hand reaching out to her. Then he was gone, swallowed by darkness.

Body and spirit seemed to separate again. The spirit once more withering, losing awareness, until she drifted into the floating limbo state—deep into it, to a place where there was no pain, no fear, only mercy.

24

It took us a while to track down Ned Verriker. The first place we went was to the sheriff's substation, but Broxmeyer was out somewhere, and the deputy manning the desk didn't know or wouldn't tell us where to find Verriker.

The man Runyon had talked to in the Buckhorn Tavern last night, Ernie Stivic, seemed to be the next best bet. We hunted up a public phone booth at one of the gas stations and looked him up in the directory. Listed, but there was no answer when Runyon tried his number.

Third stop: the Green Valley Café again. The plump blond waitress we'd talked to earlier knew where Verriker was, but wouldn't give out the information no matter how much we pleaded with her. "I know you're real worried," she said to me, "and I feel for you, but how could Ned know anything about your wife? The man's grieving bad, just wants to be left alone." But we did get one thing out of her, the name and address of the place where Ernie Stivic was employed—a restaurant called Burgers and More, near the high school at the north end of town. He worked there as a fry cook.

Burgers and More turned out to be a cafeteria-style restaurant, small, with a lattice-covered patio area along one side. There were no customers when we walked in, just a young tattooed guy getting the patio tables ready for the lunch trade. A second man was visible through an open kitchen window behind the service counter. Stivic. Runyon called out to him, and he came out wiping his hands on a clean apron.

Sure, he remembered Jake from the Buckhorn. Even before I opened my mouth, he knew who I was, gave me a nod of what appeared to be genuine sympathy. He was willing enough to talk until we asked him for Ned Verriker's whereabouts, then he closed up. "I don't know," he said. "Ned's in pretty bad shape. He don't want to be bothered right now."

"It's important we talk to him," I said.

"Why? He was at work all day Monday, he can't help you find your wife."

"We think maybe he can. Answers to a few questions is all we want from him."

"What kind of questions?"

"The private kind. Please, Mr. Stivic. There's a lot more at stake here than you realize."

"Like what?"

He'd already tried what was left of my patience. Before I started snapping at him, Runyon stepped in. "Like a criminal act, maybe more than one," he said. "That's all we can say at this point, except that Ned Verriker hasn't done anything wrong and we mean him no harm. All we want from him is information."

Stivic chewed his underlip, thinking it over. "Criminal acts, huh?" he said at length.

"That's right. You wouldn't want to impede our investigation?"

"No, hell no. Okay. Joe Ramsey's letting Ned stay at his cabin up at Eagle Rock Lake."

Eagle Rock Lake was the one in the mountains south of Six Pines that Kerry and I had driven around on Sunday, a lifetime ago. A mile or so in circumference, ringed by pine forest and roughly kidney-shaped like a giant's swimming pool. Cabins and cottages, half hidden among the trees, dotted its shoreline at widely spaced intervals.

The Ramsey cabin, Stivic had told us, was on the southeastern shore. We found it all right from his directions and description—small, plain, built of pine logs and redwood siding more than a generation past judging from the weathered look of the place, with a distinctive front door painted a rust red. A newish, dirt-streaked Ford van was parked in a cleared area in front, visible from the road, the same van that had barreled up to the scene of the conflagration on Monday afternoon and disgorged Ned Verriker. Runyon parked next to it, and we got out into blistering heat. Temperature must already be pushing ninety.

Nobody answered my raps on the door. There was a discernable path along one side; we followed that to the rear. A short dock jutted out into the glistening water, and near the end of it, a man in T-shirt and Levi's sat in a canvas sling chair staring out at the lake. Back straight, knees and feet together, hands resting palms up on his thighs—the rigid posture of a condemned prisoner about to be executed. Runyon and I made a little noise walking out onto the spongy wooden dock, but the man didn't seem to notice until we looped around to stand in front of him and block his view. Then he blinked and focused on us. Otherwise, he didn't move.

He was about forty, well built, lantern-jawed, with sparse ginger-colored hair cut close to his scalp. The face that had stared out at me from the bathroom mirror this morning had been haggard enough, but Verriker's was worse: gray and ravaged, lifeless red-rimmed eyes half buried in sacks of puckered flesh. The difference between fear of terrible loss and certain knowledge of it.

"Mr. Verriker?"

"Yeah. Who're you? What you want?" By-rote questions, without spirit or curiosity. I answered both, but I could have told him we were space invaders from another galaxy and gotten the same lack of reaction. His obvious grief was too great to permit concern for someone else's troubles.

"I don't want to talk to anybody," he said. "I lost my wife, my house, everything a couple days ago."

"We know, and we're sorry for your loss. But I may lose my wife, too, if we don't find her soon. You know, if anybody does, how desperate I am."

"I can't do nothing for you."

"You can answer a few questions about Pete Balfour."

Nothing for a few seconds. Then, "What about Balfour?" in the same dull, cracked voice.

"Does he own any other property besides his place on Crooked Creek Road? Hunting camp, cabin, anything like that?"

"No."

"You're sure?"

"Yeah, I'm sure."

"Know of any place he goes regularly to hunt, fish, camp?"

"No."

"He have any relatives in the area?"

"Only relatives he's got live under rocks."

Runyon said, "We understand you've had some trouble with him."

"I'm not the only one. He's an asshole."

"So we've heard. The Mayor of Asshole Valley."

"Yeah." Verriker's mouth twitched. "I nailed him good with that."

"And he didn't like it."

"Not anymore than I liked what he done to me one time."

"What was that?"

"Tried to cheat me on some repair work."

"Where? At your home?"

"My home. Yeah."

"And you confronted him," I said. "Then what happened?"

"Come skulking around one night, slashed all the tires on my van."

"How do you know it was Balfour?"

"Just his kind of mean trick, but I couldn't prove it. Lied through his teeth when I called him on it."

"Come to blows with him then, or any other time?"

"No. He won't fight a man, always backs down."

"But he'll beat up on a woman."

"His ex-wife, yeah. Goddamn coward."

"He ever hurt another woman that you know about?"

"Never had another woman. Too ugly, too mean."

"Violent. A violent coward."

"Cut your throat if he thought he could get away with it." Verriker stirred, showed a little animation for the first time. "Why you asking about Balfour? What's he got to do with your wife being missing?"

"We don't know that he has anything to do with it."

"But you think he might, or you wouldn't be here. Why?"

"He lied to us about his whereabouts the afternoon it happened. Told us he was working at the fairgrounds, but he wasn't."

"Where you think he was?"

"There's an old logging road in the east hills a few miles up-valley. My wife was walking there Monday afternoon— the house we're renting isn't far away."

"That's where she disappeared?"

"Yes."

"I know that road," Verriker said. "Nobody uses it much anymore. Balfour wouldn't have any reason to be up there."

"We don't know for sure that he was."

Silence for a stretch of seconds. Then Verriker blinked, blinked again, and said, "Wait a minute. Monday afternoon. That's when my house blew up, late Monday afternoon."

I didn't say anything. Neither did Runyon.

Verriker's gray face was mobile now, the dead eyes alive again. He gripped the wooden arms of his chair, lifted himself to his feet. "Accident, that's what everybody said, but I couldn't figure how it happened. We never had any gas leaks. I checked the lines and fittings regular."

Nothing for a few seconds, while he went on connecting the dots. Then, "That logging road runs near the south edge of my property. Be easy to slip down through the trees from the road. Easy to get inside the house, too. Nobody home during the day, nobody around." Blood-rush had darkened Verriker's face. He made a fist of one hand, slammed it into the palm of the other. "Balfour. He did it, didn't he. That son of a bitch made a death trap out of my house."

"It's possible," Runyon said, "but there's no proof—"

"The hell with proof. He killed my Alice, he tried to kill me—that's how you figure it, and how I figure it now, too. I'll fix him, I'll tear his fucking head off!"

Verriker pivoted away from us. Runyon and I hustled after him, got in his way as he came off the dock. I said, "No, let us handle this."

"He murdered my wife!"

"And my wife is still missing. Balfour may be responsible for that, too, but if he is, we don't have any idea where he might be holding her."

"She could be dead like Alice—"

"She's not dead. She's alive and we're going to find her, but it has to be done our way. I feel for you, I share your rage, but if you try to go after Balfour on your own, we'll have to stop you."

The words got through to him. He looked at me, at Runyon, saw that we were dead serious. Battle of wills for a few seconds, then the aggressive anger melted and he said, "All right. But I ain't gonna sit around here doing nothing."

"You won't have to. You can help us."

"How?"

"We're going back to the fairgrounds for another talk with Balfour. You come along. We'll put him in a three-way vise and squeeze him, hard. If he's guilty and as much of a coward as you say he is, we'll break him."

Verriker thought that over, nodded. "What if he doesn't break?"

"Then Jake will keep an eye on him and you and I'll take our suspicions to the county law."

"Broxmeyer? He wouldn't listen."

"We're wasting time. Are you coming or not?"

". . . Okay. I'll follow you in my van—"

"No. I'll ride with you and we'll follow Jake." I didn't want him changing his mind on the way in, veering off half-cocked on his own.

He went into the cabin for his keys and we got moving. Verriker and I didn't exchange a word on the drive into town. There was nothing more to say. From the grim set of his face, I knew the kind of thoughts that were tumbling around inside his head—they wouldn't be much different from the ones I was having.

It was a long fifteen minutes until we trailed Runyon through the open fairground gates. When we neared the construction site, my fingers dug tight into the palms of my hands. The same two cars parked in the same spots as earlier, that was all. No sign of Balfour's pickup.

The gray-haired Latino, Eladio Perez, and the red-haired kid were eating an early lunch in the shade under one of the trees. Runyon drove up near them, got out in a hurry. Verriker and I followed suit. I heard Jake asking where Balfour was, and Perez's answer as I ran up.

"He leave right after you talk to him, don't say where he goes."

"And he hasn't been back?"

"No. He don't come back."

Verriker said, "Shit!" a half-second before the same word jumped out of my mouth.

25

Balfour's front gate was still closed and padlocked. But he'd been there. I could tell that as soon as Runyon pulled into the driveway, confirmed it when I crossed the bridge to the gate and squinted through the chain links. The doors to the workshop had been shut when we'd stopped by earlier; now they stood wide open. And there was no sign of any vehicle on the property other than the stake-bed truck. Come and gone.

Jake hurried up. He'd taken his .357 Magnum out of the locked glove box, was stuffing it inside his belt; sunlight shone on its polymer frame. Just the two of us again—we'd sent Verriker to the sheriff's substation, to see if Broxmeyer was back from his north valley call and if he was, to try to convince him we were right about Balfour. We didn't tell Verriker where we were going; if the time had come to start breaking the law—and it had—it was our business.

Runyon said, "What do you think?"

"Balfour knows we're on to him. He wouldn't have come here if he didn't."

"After money, maybe, if he's panicked enough to run."

"And Kerry."

"If this is where he's been holding her."

"Where the hell else?"

"He didn't have to've taken her with him. She could still be here."

"Pray to God he's that scared and that stupid."

The gate and fence were eight-feet high, but not topped by anything like barbed wire that would've made for a difficult climb-over. Runyon gave me a boost up; I clawed my way astride the top bar, managed to slide down the other side without doing myself any damage. I was already running toward the workshop by the time he scrambled over.

Now that we were inside, I could see that a long length of staked-down cable had been strung in the grass between the workshop and the house. Dog-run line. Runyon spotted it, too, pulled the Magnum and held it down along his leg as we ran—defense against the guard dog if it attacked us. The animal was making a hell of a racket from behind the house, but it didn't come charging into sight. We were near the open workshop doors before I saw it: a big black-and-brown pit bull dancing around and half strangling itself in savage lunges at the end of long lead looped over the ground cable. Some sort of stake-hold in the line kept it from coming any closer than the house's rear corner.

The workshop's interior was cavernous, choked with the smells of heat and sawdust. The middle was open all the way to the rear, a space large enough for a couple of small trucks to park end to end. We split up to search among the rows of power tools, piles of lumber, construction business odds and ends. No sign that anyone other than Balfour had ever been in there. Both door halves standing open said that he'd driven inside today, but there was nothing I saw that told me why.

We made tracks for the house. The pit bull's leash let it come about halfway around one side, not far enough to keep us from going up onto the porch. The animal was in a frenzy now, yowling and snarling. The collar around its neck was one of those thick spiked jobs, the lead appeared to be more of the same type of cable, and the stake-hold must have been driven deep into the ground. If the dog had any chance of tearing loose, it would've happened by now.

The front door was unlocked; Runyon went in first. Half a dozen rooms plus one bathroom, all of them empty, all of them cluttered and unclean. My gorge rose when I stepped into what had to have been Balfour's bedroom, but not because of the smelly pile of unwashed clothing in one corner. The bed was a mess, blanket and sheets all twisted together. I made myself untangle them so I could examine the sheets. Gray, dirty, but without the kind of stains I dreaded finding.

Runyon was at the rear window in the other bedroom when I went in there, pulling the curtains back so he could see out. I took a look at the bed even though I knew he'd already checked it. Unmade, the bare mattress free of both stains and body marks. When I pushed down on it, a little cloud of dust puffed up. If anybody had ever lain on that mattress, it had been months, even years, ago.

Jake said my name, motioned me over to the dirt-streaked window.

I peered out. Another outbuilding sat across the rear yard to the right, small, squat, with a sheet-metal roof that threw off daggers of sunlight. Some kind of shed. A door in the facing wall stood open, but the distance and the angle of the sun kept me from seeing inside. The pit bull was back there now, racing frantically back and forth along a section of the ground cable that stretched to within a few yards of the shed; its lead was long enough to let it roam up close along the front wall.

I swallowed a reflux of stomach acid before I said, "That's where he had Kerry."

"How it looks."

"Staked the dog back there so it could guard the door in case she managed to get out. Sick son of a bitch! Be like an oven in there with that sheet-metal roof."

"Yeah."

Bad enough thinking of Kerry imprisoned in a sweatbox, but the likelihood that she'd been in there this morning was like a knife in my gut. I slammed my fist against the wall beside the window. "Goddamn it, if we'd come here right after we talked to Balfour, we might've found her."

"My fault," Runyon said. "I talked you out of it."

"No. I talked myself out of it. Too damn many years of playing it straight, staying within the law."

"You want to go over there now?"

"You'd have to shoot the dog first, and we'd just be wasting time. If she was still there, the door'd be shut."

He didn't look at me, didn't say anything. I knew what he was thinking: the door wouldn't need to be shut

if Kerry was lying in there dead. No way, Jake. No way.
I'd've sensed it by now, I'd be a basket case.

"He took her with him," I said. "Alive."

"Hostage."

"Yeah. Hostage. And that's why he'll keep her alive."

The pit bull's ceaseless racket echoed and re-echoed
inside my head, making it pound, and scraping like sand-
paper on my raw nerves. I turned away from the window,
hurried back into the front part of the house.

In the living room, on a scarred table next to a food-
and drink-stained easy chair, I spotted a pad with heavy
block printing on the top sheet. Pad of business invoices
headed BALFOUR CONSTRUCTION. The same inked words
scrawled over and over in a vertical line like column en-
tries, with such angry force that the point of the pen had
torn the paper in four or five places.

Verriker dead

Verriker dead

Verriker dead

Verriker dead

Verriker dead

VERRIKER DEAD!

I showed it to Runyon. "We've been chasing around
looking for evidence . . . all right, here's some even Broxmeyer can't ignore."

"Can't tell him we found it on an illegal entry."

"I'll claim we picked the pad up at the fairgrounds, it
must've fallen out of Balfour's truck. He can't prove any
different."

We finished up a quick search of the rest of the premises,
wading through clutter—stacks of dirty dishes, spilled

food, empty beer and whiskey bottles, other crap strewn around on tabletops and countertops and furniture, scattered over the floors. There was nothing else to connect Balfour with the death of Verriker's wife, nothing at all to connect him with Kerry.

But the search told us one thing: Balfour had no intention of coming back here. On the first pass-through, the place had seemed like the home of a typical bachelor slob, but there was too much disorder for it all to be the result of sloppy housekeeping. Drawers pulled half out of the bureau in his bedroom, several empty coat hangers in the closet and on the floor; cupboard doors hanging open and dropped utensils and food items in the kitchen; an empty glass-fronted gun cabinet in a room full of dead animal trophies—all indications of a hasty packing job. He'd stuffed that pickup of his with a full load while he was here: food, clothing, camping gear, weapons.

"Heading for the woods someplace," Runyon said as we beat it out of there, "maybe his favorite hunting ground. And getting ready for a siege. That was a big gun cabinet, and he's the type that keeps an arsenal— rifles, handguns, God knows what else."

Heading for the woods someplace. Which woods, where? Hundreds of square miles of timberland in this county alone, thousands more all across the state.

Where?

Broxmeyer was listening now. Verriker had got his attention when he came back from his north valley call; the two of them were talking in his office when Runyon and I walked in. The deputy frowned when he saw us, then motioned us to join them.

I showed him the Balfour Construction pad. Verriker went around to look at it over his shoulder, said through clamped teeth, "Crazy fuck!" I had to tell Broxmeyer that we'd been out to Balfour's place, that it looked like he'd gone there right after leaving the fairgrounds to take on supplies for a run-out. No, we hadn't gone onto the property; the gate was locked. He didn't buy that, or my story about where we'd found the invoice pad, but he didn't make an issue of it, either. Nor did he say anything to indicate he had any doubts that Balfour had made those "Verriker dead" scrawls.

I said, "Convinced, deputy?"

"That Balfour had it in for Mr. Verriker? Yes. But there's still no proof that he was responsible for the explosion, or that he kidnapped your wife."

"So you still think she's lost in the woods?"

"I didn't say that, did I?" Broxmeyer looked harassed, agitated, maybe a little embarrassed at his earlier treatment of Runyon and me. "Christ, man, I'm not your enemy. But I can't go off half cocked . . ."

"That mean you're not going to do anything about Balfour?"

"No. I'll put out a statewide BOLO on him and his vehicle."

"That won't do any good if he's planning to lose himself in the wilderness somewhere."

"You don't know that's what he intends to do."

Verriker said grimly, "Bet you it is. Always bragging on what a great hunter, great woodsman he is."

I said, "But you don't have any idea where he might go?"

"No. Heard him say once he had a favorite spot, but he wouldn't tell where it was."

I asked Broxmeyer, "Can't you make it an APB instead of a BOLO?"

"You know I can't. Nor request a search warrant, either, without more evidence that Balfour has committed even one felony. I don't have the authority."

"The sheriff does. Notify him yet?"

"He has my reports to date—"

"Not what I asked you."

"No, not yet. I will, but I guarantee he'll tell you the same thing."

"Do it right now, okay?"

Broxmeyer chased Runyon and Verriker out to the waiting area, but let me stay while he made his call to the county seat. He said when the sheriff came on the line, "I've got a situation here, Joe," and talked for three minutes, mostly listened for another three. I could tell from his expression and his monosyllabic responses that he was being told pretty much the same as he'd told me. I stood it as long as I could, hanging on to my temper, then made gestures until he reluctantly let me have the receiver.

The sheriff was an officious bastard, strictly by the book. He claimed to understand what I was going through, but he wouldn't listen to my arguments; nor did my not-insubstantial career in law enforcement or my acquaintance with Jack Logan, SFPD's assistant chief, cut any ice with him. Deputy Broxmeyer was following the correct protocol, he said: there was insufficient evidence to warrant any-

thing more than a wanted-for-questioning BOLO on Pete
Balfour.

When he ended the conversation, I had to make a conscious effort not to slam down the receiver. Broxmeyer
said, "I'm sorry, but I told you, our hands are tied." I
didn't trust myself to answer him.

I couldn't stay in the cubicle or the substation any longer; I'd come close to saying something that would have
alienated the sheriff, and I was afraid of losing it with
Broxmeyer. Outside, I said to Runyon, "BOLO, that's as
far as they'll go."

"We could try going over their heads to the FBI."

"And run smack into the same stone wall. Nobody's
going to do anything without having hard proof shoved
in their faces." I turned to Verriker. "That favorite wilderness spot of Balfour's. He always go hunting there by
himself?"

"Far as I know. Man don't have any friends."

"Anybody you can think of that he might've told
about it?"

"Well . . . Charlotte, maybe. His ex-wife. She'd be the
only one."

"She still live in the valley?"

"Right here in Six Pines. Works in the city manager's
office at city hall."

He took us over there, a refurbished brick building opposite the town park. Charlotte Samuels was a fat woman
with dyed-blond hair and dim little eyes; she and Balfour
must've been some pair. She didn't want to talk about
her ex-husband, but Verriker coaxed her into it—for all
the good it did. Balfour had never taken her hunting

with him—she liked venison, but hated seeing animals killed—and she had no idea where he went hunting, he'd never told her.

Outside again in the sticky heat, I asked Verriker, "You do much hunting?"

"Now and then."

"So you know the good spots, the more remote ones—say, within a fifty-mile radius."

"Some place Balfour might pick? A couple, maybe. But hell, we'd never find him if he's holed up."

"We can try. Unless you have another suggestion?"

"No. Wish I did."

Runyon hadn't said much since we'd driven back into Six Pines, but that was because he hadn't had anything to contribute. He'd been thinking though, more clearly than I had. Problem-solving.

He said now, "There's one other thing we can do if we can't find him, and the law can't. Long shot, but so is anything else we try."

"Let's hear it."

He laid it out. Long shot, yeah, but long shots come in sometimes, and if Runyon was reading the situation right, this one just might. The odds were no worse than those on the other long shots we had to depend on—blind luck, a spread-thin sheriff's department and a scattering of highway patrol officers, and the whims of an unbalanced mind.

26

PETE BALFOUR

Rosnikov had his order ready right on schedule. The Russian could get you just about anything you wanted in the way of ordinance, legal or illegal, and other stuff, too, such as a couple of clean license plates with current stickers for an '06 Dodge pickup. Didn't take him long, neither. Must've had a regular armory somewhere in the Stockton area, in addition to this old storage warehouse on the waterfront where he did business. Mob ties, too, probably, but who the hell cared about that?

Only problem was what the bugger charged. Arm and a leg for everything, and no haggling or the deal was off. Balfour had to fork over almost half his cash to get everything he'd asked for.

Place made him nervous while the deal was going down. Rosnikov, big and scowly, his two bodyguards or enforcers or whatever they were, standing there looking nasty with handguns bulging in their clothes. They'd told him to drive inside and then they'd shut the doors behind him; his pickup with the loaded camper shell was sitting right there in plain sight. What if Rosnikov got it into his head that he was carrying more cash than he'd showed, decided to double-cross him, knock him off? Wouldn't be anything he could do about it, one against three packing heat. They'd get the other $3,500, the truck, and his firepower. But that wouldn't be all they'd get. Big surprise when they saw what else he had in there.

Nothing like that happened. Hell, Rosnikov was a professional, wasn't he? Balfour hadn't had any trouble with the Russian when he bought the Bushmaster and the Sterling, he didn't have any trouble this time. Paid his money, Rosnikov counted it and handed over the package, nobody said a word until he was ready to leave. He asked if he could switch the plates on the pickup before he drove out, Rosnikov said okay, and even took the old ones off his hands.

Balfour was still a little shaky when the two body-guards opened the doors and let him drive on out. What he needed were a couple shots of Jack to steady his nerves, but he didn't dare take even one. Had to be cold sober the rest of today. Tomorrow and the next couple of days, too. His plans, his life, depended on it.

When he was back on the road again, he was even more careful than he'd been on the drive down. Not one mile over the speed limit, safe lane changes and only when necessary. Those two detectives in Six Pines might be after him right now, but the law wouldn't be. Suspicious, yeah, the woman's husband would see to that, but they couldn't prove nothing against him. Not yet, they couldn't. He didn't have no cause to worry unless he got stopped for some stupid traffic violation and that wasn't gonna happen. Still, he'd sweated all the way down from Asshole Valley, and he'd sweat some on the way back, even with the new plates.

The woman hadn't made a sound since he'd put her in there. Dead by now, for all he knew. While he was still up in the county, he'd thought about taking a detour into wilderness country and dumping her. Too risky, he'd decided, riskier than keeping her with him. Woods were crawling with fishermen and campers and sightseeing tourists this time of year. Somebody saw him do it or find her later, he'd never get to Stockton, much less make the return drive to Asshole Valley. Never get his revenge. That was all that mattered in the short run, paying Verriker and the rest of them back for what they'd done to him. Worry about the rest of it later, the long drive out of California and on up to Idaho. First things first.

But he had to think about something while he drove, so he thought about Idaho. He'd never been there, but that didn't matter. Lot of wilderness area in the north part of the state, he knew that. Go in deep enough and there'd be a remote spot for an experienced woodsman like himself to fort up. That Unabomber guy, Kaczynski, he didn't know Montana, didn't have any survival skills, when he went there and built himself a cabin and lived for, what, twenty years with nobody the wiser. FBI never would've caught him if his brother hadn't turned him in.

Nobody was gonna catch Pete Balfour once he built his own cabin way the hell out in the middle of nowhere and settled in. And if by some fluke they did track him down, well, he wouldn't just give up like Kaczynski had, he'd use his ordinance to take down as many as he could before they finished him.

Be kind of lonesome, living up there in the Idaho back-country. No TV, no Internet, none of the things he'd done for R&R most of his life. He'd get used to it, though. Wouldn't even miss his old life after a while. Never had needed people anyway, never would after what those bastards in Asshole Valley had done to him. Get along just fine by himself, hunting, fishing, trapping.

No, they'd never catch him because wasn't nobody could turn him in. As far as anybody knew, he'd've dropped right off the face of the earth. All he had to do was finish his business in Asshole Valley, then make it up to Northern Idaho without nobody being the wiser, and he'd be home free.

It was full dark when he reached the valley. He'd made sure it would be by taking a roundabout route and stopping twice on the way, once for gas, once for a Big Mac and fries. Pulling into places with lights and people didn't make him edgy. He wasn't worried, wasn't sweating anymore. Sure, he'd had his share of bad luck up to now, crap happening to spoil his plans, but that was all behind him. Everything from now on was going to go down without a hitch—he was sure of it. Nobody even looked at him once, much less twice, in the service station or the golden arches drive-through. And neither of the highway patrol cops that passed him on the roads glanced in his direction.

He wouldn't be recognized in the Six Pines area, neither. Not with the camper shell and clean plates on the pickup, and a cap he hardly ever wore except when he was hunting, pulled down low on his forehead. Just another tourist.

But once he got there, he'd have to be careful—real careful. Use the back roads, make sure nobody spotted him going in. Wouldn't take long to do what needed to be done, but if somebody saw him . . .

No, the hell with that. Wasn't nobody gonna see him. Dark tonight, drifting clouds hiding the moon. And it'd be late enough that there wouldn't be many people out driving around. He'd be all right. Just had to do what they were always saying you should—think positive. Yeah, think positive.

Wasn't nothing gonna screw up his plans *this* time.

Nothing did.

Less than thirty minutes, in and out.

Hellbox, baby. Hellbox!

On his way to Eagle Rock Lake, he passed a sheriff's department cruiser. He tensed a little, but the deputy driving didn't pay any attention to him, didn't brake or slow down. Nothing to worry about. Keep cool, keep thinking positive.

He thought positive about Verriker and the palms of his hands itched. He drove chewing on his hate, his blood singing with it.

Damn, though, he could still smell, still feel the woman.

He hadn't noticed the smell too much on the round-trip to Stockton, but now it seemed strong, like a gas filtering through the camper walls into the cab. He rolled down the window to let the night breeze in, but that didn't seem to help much. Lucky nobody'd noticed it at the gas station or the McDonald's drive-through. He'd have to stop somewhere tomorrow and buy something to fumigate the shell. Couldn't drive all the way to Idaho with that stink in his nose and throat.

The steering wheel felt gummy. So did his hands. He wiped one down his pant leg, then the other, but it didn't help any. Residue. And underneath the stickiness, a kind of residue from the woman, too, that he couldn't wipe off. Crazy notion, but there it was.

Hadn't had that feeling any of the other times he'd picked her up, carried her, but when he'd hauled her out tonight, he'd felt that residue come off her like flakes of dried skin, and his gorge had lifted right up into his throat. Had to put her down fast to keep from puking. Why? Because she was dead? Hadn't been a sound out of her, and he couldn't hear breathing or feel any heartbeat. Yeah, she must've died sometime on the round-trip to Stockton.

But why should that bother him? She'd of been dead tomorrow, anyway. And he'd handled dozens of dead animals, field-dressed deer and small game, without turning a hair. Carrying a dead woman shouldn't be any different. But somehow, it was. Her smell, the weight of her limp body on his hands and against his chest, a flash image of the way she'd looked alive . . . it all gave him the creeps.

It was as if her residue had gotten inside his head, too, and was working on him like some kind of drug, trying to make him think he should be sorry for what he'd done to her. He'd killed Verriker's wife and tonight he'd kill Verriker. Tomorrow there'd be plenty more blood on his hands. None of that made him feel sorry. So why should a woman he didn't even know be twisting up his insides?

He couldn't figure it out. She wasn't nothing to him. And she'd tried to put his eyes out with those tacks. Another of his enemies. Got in his way, gave him nothing but trouble, would've killed him if she could . . . an enemy the same as Verriker and the rest. You had every right to take revenge on your enemies, no matter who they were. Sure you did. Soldiers didn't have no qualms about killing, he didn't have none, either.

Then why was he bugged about the woman?

He put his head out the window, took some deep breaths. Told himself to quit thinking about her, she was dead, it was over and done with. But the smell and the residue wouldn't let him. His palms still itched, but now it was as much because of her as the thought of killing Verriker.

He wished he could stop somewhere, wash his hands, change his clothes. But there wasn't time. Later, after he was done with Verriker and out of the county. He'd have to park at a rest stop or campground somewhere and get a few hours' sleep—he was already dog-tired from the hours of road time he'd put in today, no way he could make it all the way to Northern Idaho or even out of California without some rest. He'd clean up the camper and himself then. Wash the woman out of his head at the same time.

The turnoff for the lake was just up ahead. He put on his turn signal even though there were no other cars on the road. Keep playing it safe, obeying the law, no matter where he was. One more survival skill.

The pickup rattled and bounced through the ruts until he passed the long limestone shelf. Lights on in the Ramsey cabin. Verriker was there and still up, but did he have company again tonight? If the Ramseys were holed up with him, they'd get theirs first thing. But it'd be a whole lot easier if Verriker was alone.

Balfour passed the place where he'd parked the last time, drove on past the cabin, slow. Grinned, his lips flattening against his teeth, when he saw that the only set of wheels down there was Verriker's van. All by himself tonight. Perfect. Now he could take his time, make Verriker sweat and beg before he blew him away.

The road jogged up ahead. On the far side, he found a place to turn around, rolled back past the Ramsey cabin to the hidden parking spot among the trees. He slid the Charter .38 into his pocket, locked the truck, and made his way along the verge of the empty road. Slower going tonight—he couldn't see as clear with the clouds keeping the moon covered up. But he could see the cabin lights all right through the trees.

He went all the way to the driveway this time, down along its edge. No need to go skulking around in the trees tonight. No need to look for an unlocked door or window. Just walk up, walk right inside if the lock was off. And if it wasn't, knock on the door—Verriker wouldn't have no reason not to open up for him. Wouldn't be afraid of him until he was looking down the barrel of the .38.

The closer Balfour got to the door, the softer he walked. Excitement made his heart hammer, sharpened his senses—the same as when he had a buck in his sights, ready for the kill. Only better, much better, because shooting a deer wasn't personal, and this was as personal as it got.

He had the revolver tight in his hand when he reached the door. He listened, didn't hear anything inside, reached out real quiet to test the latch. Locked. He let go of it, sucked in a breath, and rapped on the door panel. Not too heavy, not too loud.

Nothing for several seconds. The .38 felt big in his hand. Enormous. His palm was itching again, his mouth dry, his thoughts full of blood.

Come on, Verriker, come on!

Footsteps then, slow. "Who is it?"

He almost said, "The mayor." It was right there on the tip of his tongue. He bit it back, said his name instead.

"What do you want, Balfour?"

"I got something to tell you. Real important, Ned. Can I come in?"

A little more silence. Thinking it over. Open the fucking door!

Verriker opened it. The bolt lock snapped, light spilled out through a three-inch slit between the door and the jamb. Balfour shoved inward with his free hand, moving forward at the same time, bringing the .38 up. Saw Verriker backing away fast to one side, snapped at him, "Stay where you are!" as he bulled ahead into the room.

Movement at the edge of his vision.

Warning flash . . . too late.

Something slammed down on his forearm with enough force to paralyze his fingers, break his grip on the gun.

From the other side, something hit him across the side of the neck, took his breath away, and dropped him to his knees.

He tried to get up, but his legs and arms wouldn't work. Another blow sent him sprawling onto his back. He lay there dazed, staring up through a haze of pain. Two faces swam into focus above him, faces he recognized—

No!

Panicked disbelief surged through him. He tried to scuttle backward away from the hands that reached down for him, but all he could do was flop and jerk like a deer with a busted spine.

Verriker dead, Idaho . . . never happen now. Screwed again. Why couldn't nothing ever turn out the way he planned it, why did the shit always have to happen to *him?*

27

Runyon scooped up Balfour's snub-nosed revolver and shoved it into his pocket, then helped me haul him up off the floor. We dragged him to the couch and threw him down on it and slap-frisked him to find out if he had another weapon. He didn't. Runyon had brought in the set of handcuffs he keeps in his car; he snapped one circlet around Balfour's wrist, the other around the shaft of an old, heavy pole lamp.

While he was doing that, I got up beside Balfour on my knees, bunched my fingers in the neck of his shirt, and put my face close to his. He wouldn't look at me, kept jerking his head from side to side. I shook him, hard.

"Where's my wife, you son of a bitch?"

He made gurgling sounds, mouth twitching and spraying spittle, his little black rodent's eyes bright with fear and confusion. Kept up that rolling motion with his head to avoid eye contact.

"What did you do with her? Where is she?"

"Uh . . . uh . . ."

I cuffed him with the back of one hand. Shook him

again with the other, hard enough to snap his head forward this time. *"Where is she?"*

"Bill!" Runyon's voice sharp behind me. His hands on me then, wrestling me backward. The cloth of Balfour's shirt ripped before my fingers came loose; he bounced back against the cushion. "He can't talk if you break his neck."

I struggled a little, not much. Jake held onto me until I quit, but when he let go, his body was still blocking me from Balfour. The initial burst of rage had banked some; I leaned against the couch arm, trying to get my breathing under control. Balfour was still twitching, but only the right side of his body moved; his left arm hung limp across his lap. The gurgles had become grunts, and one of the grunts shaped out into a pair of words.

"Crippled me . . ."

Temporarily, that was all. Runyon had learned judo when he was on the Seattle PD; the nerve paralysis from his chop across Balfour's neck would fade pretty soon, but we weren't about to tell him that.

Verriker had crossed to stand alongside the pole lamp, his heavy face mottled with a fury that matched mine. I watched him lean down and spit in Balfour's face. "You miserable sack of shit, you blew up my house, you killed Alice."

"No, I never—"

"Yeah, but it was me you were after. Why? I never done anything to you."

"Hell you didn't. You and your mayor crap."

"Crazy, you're crazy as hell!" Verriker hit him hard on the side of the head, half punch, half slap. "I ought to—"

Runyon said, "You won't do anything," and shouldered him aside. "Stand over there by the fireplace, stay out of it."

Verriker glared, muttered something under his breath, but the look on Runyon's face pulled his gaze down. He went without argument.

I was all right now, in control again. I nodded to Runyon to let him know it, tried to push in next to him so that both of us would be looming over Balfour. It was like trying to push a hunk of cement.

"Let me handle this, Bill."

Taking charge. Okay with me. My thinking had straightened out enough to understand that he was the only one of the three of us who had his emotions in check. So I didn't put up an argument, just nodded again and backed off. He'd been a rock through all of this. If it hadn't been for him and his long shot idea, we wouldn't have been lucky enough to catch Balfour. Jake's reasoning had been that Balfour could have found out where Verriker was staying, hadn't been able to get at him last night because Verriker told us the cabin's owners had stayed over, and might risk delaying escape to come gunning for him tonight. So we'd staked out here before dark and waited, waited, waited. My screaming nerves wouldn't have stood much more of it.

The ugly little bastard was still twitching, sweat leaking out of him in oily pustules. But his shock and pain had diminished; his face was set tight again with some of the same belligerence he'd shown at the fairgrounds this morning. Only, it didn't run deep, and I could see behind it. Coward, all right. When push came to shove, the yellow would show through like jaundice, and he'd crack wide open.

Runyon leaned down close. "Where is she, Balfour?"

"Who? I dunno what you're talkin' about."

"The woman you kidnapped. Kerry Wade."

"I never kidnapped nobody."

"Monday afternoon, on that logging road. After you boobytrapped the Verriker house."

"Never done that, neither. You can't pin that on me."

Verriker said, "Lying bastard!"

Runyon waved him to silence without looking at him. He said to Balfour, "That's why you took her, we know that. We also know you had her locked up in a shed with the pit bull on guard."

Balfour hadn't expected that. Flesh rippled on his cheek, became a tick that fluttered one eye into a series of uncontrollable tics.

"There'll be DNA evidence in the shed to prove it," Runyon said. "You're going down for kidnapping and attempted murder, that much for sure. Maybe the law can prove you rigged the explosion that killed Mrs. Verriker, maybe they can't. If they can't, all you're facing is some jail time. But if we don't find Mrs. Wade alive, then it's kidnapping and murder with special circumstances— a capital offense. The death penalty for sure, Balfour."

Spitting mouth, but nothing came out of it.

"She's no good to you now, you can't use her as a hostage. Tell us where she is before it's too late."

Silence.

I looked away. If I hadn't, I'd've gone after him again. My mind crawled with vague images of dark, empty woods,

Kerry all alone, sick, hurt, eyes shining in the blackness around her . . . animals, bears, other prowling flesh-eaters . . .

"One way or another, she'll be found," Runyon was saying. "Alive, and you stay alive. Dead, and you're dead."

"Bullshit."

"Maybe you think you've got her hidden some place where she'll never be found. Doesn't matter. There'll be enough evidence against you for a no-body murder conviction. You'll still end up on death row."

"Bullshit," Balfour said again. He was looking down at his left arm, watching it jerk and flex as feeling came back. He rubbed it with his shackled right hand. There were flecks of something dark gray on his fingers, I saw then, dried mud or clay. "Go ahead, call the cops. I got nothing more to say to you."

His cowardice should've started fissures showing by now, and it hadn't. You could see the fear in his eyes, in the oozing sweat on his face, but still he kept holding out, blustering. Why? Stupidity? Psychosis? Something else going on inside his head that was stronger than the fear, some kind of dirty little secret?

I said, "This isn't getting us anywhere, Jake. We'll have to beat it out of him."

The words were intended to push Balfour's buttons, but I meant them just the same. The violence in me was hot and toxic, bubbling close to the surface with an intensity that scared me a little. I could pound this inhuman piece of waste to a bloody pulp and not turn a hair while I was doing it—an act of savagery I wouldn't have believed I was capable of until these past few days.

His buttons didn't push. "Go ahead," he said. "Beat on me all you want. Won't do you no good."

Verriker said, "Why don't we find out?" and started across the room.

Runyon said, "Stay put," and then reached down and began digging through Balfour's pockets, shoving him roughly to one side and then the other to get at the back ones. There was no resistance. Balfour sat there with that same expression on his ugly face, part fear, part defiance, part something else that I couldn't read.

Keys on a grubby chain jangled as Runyon yanked them free. The only other item that came out of the search was a thin leather wallet. Runyon opened the wallet, fanned through it; glanced at me when he was done, and shook his head. He threw the wallet in Balfour's lap. The keys went into his pocket before he straightened up.

"She wouldn't be in that pickup of yours, would she, Balfour?"

The facial tic that jumped again said she might be; his sneer said she wasn't. "Won't find it in the dark."

"We'll find it." Runyon turned to Verriker. "You stay here and keep an eye on Balfour. But don't go near him."

"Yeah. Okay."

One other thing Runyon had brought in from his car was a flashlight; he went for it, and I hunted up another one Verriker said was in the kitchen. We hurried outside. The night had turned chilly, a sharp wind blowing down from the Sierras' higher elevations. It dried the sweat on me, turned it cold and gummy.

"Jake. What happened in there—"

"Nothing happened in there. Except that Balfour wouldn't talk."

"All right. But we can make him talk."

"I don't think so. He's scared, he's a coward, he knows he's finished—pressuring him should've been enough to break him. But he's hiding something that's holding him together."

"It's not that Kerry's already dead. I won't believe that."

"No. Whatever it is, hurting him won't make him give it up."

Maybe not. But if we didn't find anything out here, I'd work him over anyway. And this time, I wouldn't let Runyon stop me.

We were at the road now. I said, "Vehicle that went by a few minutes before Balfour showed up must've been his pickup. Heading south first, then back to the north."

"Right. Figures to be hidden off the road in that direction, and not too far away."

It took us twenty minutes to find it, each of us working a side of the deserted road, and when we first uncovered it, it didn't look like the right vehicle. Dirty white Dodge pickup, but with a bulky camper shell on it and different license plates. But it was Balfour's, all right. He must've put the camper and the new plates on this morning—the reason for the open workshop on his property.

The driver's door was locked. I held my light up against the window long enough to be sure that the cab was empty. We went around to the back. The second key Runyon tried unlocked the camper door. I dragged in a breath as he pulled it open and shined his flash beam inside. Nothing to see except jammed-in goods and weapons, and a narrow open space on the floor in the middle, but the human body odor that came rolling out had the force of a blow to the face.

My empty stomach convulsed; I spun away, gagging. It took a few seconds for the sickness to pass. I sucked in more of the cold night air, leaned a hand against the side of the pickup away from the open camper door.

Runyon was still working the camper's interior with his light. He said in heavy tones, "Empty."

"She was in there. Today, tonight."

"Yeah. Unloaded her somewhere before he came here. He wouldn't waste time doing it before he went after Verriker."

"Take a quick look around anyway."

We looked. All around the pickup, up and down along the road, over on the other side. The trees and ground vegetation grew thickly in the area; Balfour couldn't have gone far carrying a heavy weight, and our lights would've picked up signs and there weren't any.

Back at the truck, I said, "I'll check the cab, you look in the camper. I can't go in there, Jake."

"I know. I'm on it."

I got the driver's door unlocked. Some of the body smell was in the cab, too; I locked my sinuses against it, breathed through my mouth. There was nothing on the seat except a light denim jacket, nothing on the floorboards. Usual papers and crap in the glove box, none of it that told me anything. I felt around under the seats, found a small box on the passenger side, and hauled it out. Cigar box with a rubber band looped around it. Inside was a lot of cash in small bills—Balfour's run-out money. I closed it up again, stuffed it back under the seat.

When I laid my free hand on the steering wheel to push myself back out, the rubber felt sticky, grainy. I put the flash beam on the wheel. Gray flecks adhered to it, the same kind I'd noticed on Balfour's hand. I picked off one of them, rolled it between my thumb and forefinger. It wasn't mud. Felt faintly moist, like clay or putty, but it didn't look like either one.

Runyon's light came bobbing around to where I was. "Nothing back there," he said, "except a one-man arsenal."

I showed him the flecks on the steering wheel, watched him rub one the way I had. "What do you make of it?"

"Not sure. Seems fresh."

"Balfour has the same stuff on his fingers."

"And under his fingernails. Something else I noticed, too, on one knee of his pants. Sawdust."

"Where the hell could he have been to get clay or whatever this is and sawdust on himself?"

"Wherever he left Kerry, maybe."

"We'll get it out of him," I said grimly, "one way or another."

The distant sound of a car engine cut through the stillness. We stayed put with the torches switched off as headlights flickered through the trees and the vehicle rattled past heading south. Passenger car of some kind, not a sheriff's cruiser. We waited another few seconds after its taillights disappeared before we hurried out along the road.

In the frigging perverse way of things, that car and

those couple of waiting minutes cost us dearly. Because
we'd just reached the driveway when the muffled popping
noise came from inside the cabin.

Once you've heard a gun go off in a closed space, you
never mistake the sound for something else. It had the
surge effect on us of a track starter's pistol firing: we both
broke immediately into a run, Runyon dragging the
Magnum free from his belt. He was a couple of paces
ahead of me when we pounded up to the door. Closed,
the way we'd left it; he twisted the knob, shoved it wide,
and went in in a shooter's crouch with me crowding up
behind.

Sweet Christ!

Balfour was on the floor, one side of his neck a gush-
ing red ruin, the pole lamp toppled into a slant across his
body. A few feet away, Verriker stood staring down at
him with a long-barreled target pistol in one hand.

Runyon shouted, "Put it down, Verriker! Now!"

Verriker must have obeyed, but I didn't see him do it.
I was past Runyon by then and down on one knee next
to Balfour. Still alive, but the way the blood was pumping out of the wound, he wouldn't be for long; the bullet
must have clipped his carotid artery. There wasn't anything I could do, anybody could do.

He clawed at his neck, the whites of his eyes showing,
bubbling sounds coming out of him that made the blood
froth on his mouth. But not just sounds—a disconnected
jumble of words. I could make out some of them when I
leaned forward.

". . . bastards . . . payback . . . asshole valley . . ."

A strangled noise then, that might have been laughter.

Another word that sounded like "hellbox." Then his body convulsed, jacknifed upward, fell back. And the wound quit spurting.

Our luck had just run out.

I scrambled back away from the body, staggered upright, sidestepped the spreading blood pool, and went after Verriker. Not thinking, goaded into action by a raging stew of emotions. Runyon had stripped Verriker of the target pistol, had it in his left hand, the Magnum still clenched in his right . . . two-gun Jake. He saw me coming, tried to stand in my way, but I dodged around him. Verriker was backpedaling, but he didn't have any place to go; I got my hands on him, drove him up hard against the fieldstone fireplace.

"No, listen, he tried to jump me, I had to protect myself—"

I hit him. Looping right, not quite flush on the temple. His head whacked into the stones, bringing a grunt out of him and buckling his knees; his sagging weight broke my grip. I let him fall, stood over him with my fists clenched.

He wasn't badly hurt. He shook himself, then crawled away until he was sitting with his back against a low burl table. "Self-defense," he said heavily, "it was self-defense. He didn't give me any choice."

Runyon had come up beside me, the guns put away and his hands free. "Balfour?"

"Dead."

He said to Verriker, "Didn't I tell you to stay away from him?"

"He started calling me names, yelling crazy stuff."

Talking to the floor, his chin down on his chest. "I wanted to shut him up, that's all, but I got too close and he jumped up and swung the lamp at me. I had to defend myself, didn't I?"

"Where'd the gun come from?"

"It's mine, I keep it in my van. Figured I might need some protection tonight—"

"Protection, hell," I said. "You snuck it in here hoping you'd have a chance to use it."

"No, I told you, it was self-defense. . . ."

He'd probably get away with that claim, true or not, with no witness to dispute it. I didn't care about that, it just didn't matter. The only thing that mattered was Balfour lying over there dead.

Verriker lifted his head, looked up at me with dull eyes. "I'm not gonna say I'm sorry. He killed my wife."

"Yeah, and you may have just killed mine."

28

JAKE RUNYON

Morning.

After a long, bad night. Two and a half more hours at Eagle Rock Lake with Verriker, Deputy Broxmeyer, and a crew of other sheriff's department people. Another hour at the Six Pines substation with a departmental investigator from the county seat named Sadler. Questions and more questions, a lot of finger-pointing and milling and scrambling around that didn't lead anywhere because nobody knew what the hell to do about Kerry. The FBI? Sadler hemmed and hawed on finally calling them in. They still weren't completely convinced Balfour had abducted her. And even if they had been, there was the usual jurisdictional bullshit: county law, especially small county law, always balked at relinquishing control to the feds because they usually got trampled when the FBI took over. Sadler did say he'd notified the ATF of the illegal weapons stash in Balfour's camper, but the ATF wasn't in a position to do Kerry a damn bit of good.

To make matters worse, the local law was miffed at the way Bill and Runyon had handled things, berating them for not reporting immediately after they'd caught Balfour. But there was as much embarrassment and frustration at the department's own bungling mixed in, at least on Broxmeyer's part, and enough concern for Kerry and how the media would react to the whole sorry business, to keep the browbeating to a minimum.

Verriker had been arrested, mandatory in a fatal shooting without eyewitnesses. But as far as the law was aware, he and Balfour were the only ones who'd broken any laws. There was no real cause to hold Runyon and Bill, so they'd finally been released. With nowhere to go at three A.M. except back to the rented house.

By then, Bill seemed to have settled into a zombielike melancholy, staring glassily into space and not tracking well, his voice flat and lifeless when he spoke at all. Plain enough that he blamed himself for leaving Verriker alone with Balfour, just as he blamed himself for not searching Balfour's property sooner; Runyon bore the same guilty weight. But at the same time, he knew they'd handled the situation as best they could under the circumstances, with their focus on finding Kerry and their emotions in turmoil. There just hadn't been any warning signs that Verriker might've smuggled in a gun or that he'd wanted revenge on Balfour as much as Balfour wanted it on him.

Bill had almost literally collapsed into bed when they got back to the house. Exhausted. Sick, too, maybe. His color wasn't good, his breathing heavy and labored.

As tired as Runyon was, he couldn't sleep except in fitful dozes. Once he got up to make sure Bill was all right.

The rest of the time he lay staring into the darkness, listening to the throbbing night rhythms of crickets and tree frogs and sorting through the fragments of information they had on Balfour.

The dark gray, sticky stuff on Balfour's fingers and the pickup's steering wheel. Nobody had been able to identify it. It wasn't mud, and there were no clay deposits in the area. Broxmeyer: "It looks like modeling clay." Being sent out for analysis ASAP, but with the holiday weekend, that meant sometime next week at the soonest.

The sawdust on Balfour's pant leg. He'd worked construction and lived and traveled within hundreds of square miles of timberland. He could have picked it up kneeling anywhere.

His dying words. "Bastards. Payback. Asshole valley. Hellbox." Bill was sure of all the words but the last. And fairly sure that Balfour had laughed with his final breath. None of it seemed to make much sense. Bastards . . . Runyon and Bill and Verriker? What kind of payback? Did "asshole valley" refer to the mayor tag Verriker had hung on him, or to Green Valley? Assume Bill had heard correctly and "hellbox" was the last word Balfour had uttered. A hellbox was a receptacle where old-fashioned cast-metal type was tossed after printing, but an uneducated carpenter and handyman wasn't likely to have known that. What else was a hellbox? That sheet metal–roofed shed where he'd kept Kerry was a hellbox in the middle of a hot summer, but even if that was how Balfour had thought of it, why would he say the word? And why would he laugh with his last breath?

Runyon sifted through what else they knew about the

man. Dishonest loner at odds with most of those who knew him, wife abuser, coward. Paranoid psychotic driven by hatred and revenge. Devious schemer: the blowing up of the Verrikers' home, the attempt on Verriker's life, the camper full of survival gear and weaponry . . . and the probable secret he'd been harboring that had kept him from breaking under pressure at the cabin. Kidnapper, but not by design—he'd grabbed Kerry because she'd seen him coming back from rigging the gas leak, an act of panic.

Why had he held her captive for four days? The obvious answer was rape, torture, only that didn't fit the revenge-obsessed profile. The fact that Balfour had beaten his ex-wife didn't necessarily make him a sexual sadist. If anything, according to those who knew him, he seemed to have shunned relationships with women. Kept Kerry as some kind of sick trophy? That didn't fit his profile, either. Unsure of what to do with her or her body? Squeamish about murdering a stranger in cold blood?

Pretty obvious why he'd taken her out of the shed yesterday morning: hadn't wanted her found there, alive or dead. All right, but why the decision to run in the first place? There was no proof that he'd booby-trapped the Verriker house, and if Verriker had been alone at the lake cabin and Balfour had succeeded in killing him, no proof that Balfour was the guilty party. Another panic reaction, maybe. Except that his actions yesterday and last night had been too calculated. The decision had to be connected to, or motivated by, whatever he'd been up to during the ten to twelve hours he'd been missing yesterday.

He'd kept Kerry in the camper for most of that time—the odor wouldn't have permeated everything inside the cramped space if she'd only been in there a short time. As a hostage, as they'd surmised? Or for some other reason that was also connected to that secret plan of his? Wherever he'd left her, it couldn't have been very long before he showed up at the cabin or very far from Eagle Rock Lake. . . .

Runyon had had enough of the lumpy bed. His watch told him it was a little after seven—time to be up and moving. The plumbing in the adjacent bathroom made loud grumbling noises; when he was done in there, he went again for a quick check on Bill. Still asleep in the same facedown sprawl, his breathing heavy, congestive. He needed to see a doctor pretty soon, before he suffered a complete breakdown.

In the kitchen, Runyon slaked his thirst with a glass of cold water from the fridge. He knew he should eat, but he would have choked on anything solid he tried to swallow. He went back through the living room, out onto the front deck.

Still early-morning cool, but the clouds were gone, and already there was a whitish dazzle in the blue overhead. You could feel the heat gathering. Another sweltering day coming up, probably hotter than yesterday.

But he didn't want to think about that. He sat at the table, his hands flat on the cold glass top, and stared out over the valley without seeing any of it. Going over the Balfour fragments yet again, trying to shape them into a pattern that had some meaning.

Psychotic driven by hate and hunger for vengeance.

Rigged the explosion that killed Verriker's wife. Tried to kill Verriker before heading for the backwoods with an arsenal of weapons.

Drove around with Kerry in that camper of his for half of another day before leaving her somewhere. *Had* to be a purpose in that. Nothing else he'd done had been aimless, unplanned.

Sticky gray substance that wasn't clay or mud. And couldn't have been on his hands or the steering wheel very long.

Sawdust.

Payback. Asshole valley.

Hellbox.

The pieces were like parts in a disassembled template that wouldn't connect. He strained to get a mental grip on them, manipulate and force them together. They kept glancing off each other, as if the pieces were antimagnetized.

Payback. Asshole Valley.

Dark gray stuff that looked and felt like modeling clay.

Sawdust.

Hellbox.

Last breath, last laugh—

From somewhere down on the road below, a sudden series of popping noises disturbed the morning stillness. Runyon tensed until he identified the sounds: a string of firecrackers going off. Undisciplined kids getting an early start on the Fourth. He'd almost forgotten the holiday, the big celebration coming up in Six Pines. Parade, picnic, speeches, fireworks—

Fireworks.

Explosions.

Explosive devices.

He went rigid. And the pieces came flying together like digital images interlocking, until they formed the template of Balfour's last planned act of vengeance. Insane, monstrous, but the pieces fit too well, explained too many things, for it not to be right.

Runyon stood so suddenly that the chair went skidding backward, toppled over. He ran inside, back to the master bedroom. Caught Bill's shoulder and shook him, lightly at first, then harder.

"Wake up, Bill. Wake up."

Bill's eyes flicked open, blinking up half focused and groggy. But the grogginess lasted only a few seconds; he threw it off as if it were a heavy blanket, sat up scraping a hand over his face. "What is it? You've heard something?"

"No," Runyon said, "but I think I may have figured out what Balfour was up to last night."

"My God, Jake . . . you mean what he did with Kerry?"

"If I'm right, yes. He was crazier than any of us realized. It wasn't just Verriker he hated and wanted revenge against, it was everybody in Green Valley. Asshole Valley to him. Pay back Asshole Valley for all the ridicule heaped on him . . . that's what his dying words meant."

"But how—?"

"That stuff on his hands . . . malleable plastic explosive, probably some crude homemade version of C-4 or Semtex. Got it from whoever supplied him with the illegal weapons. Rigged another explosive death trap last night, only this one in a place where it'd take out a whole bunch of people."

Bill saw it, too, now. He was off the bed, scrambling into his pants. "The fairgrounds. Somewhere under the grandstand . . ."

"No. Too open, too much chance of it being spotted."

"Then . . . Christ! That storage unit on the construction site."

"Has to be. The repair work was finished last night, there wouldn't've been time to have the unit hauled away. That's where the sawdust came from, that's what Balfour meant by hellbox."

"And where he left Kerry. Holy Mother, inside a hellbox packed with explosives!"

29

I was wild to get out of there, get to Six Pines. I tried to push past Runyon, but he blocked the doorway with his big body.

"Stay calm," he said. "Call the law before we do anything else, get a bomb squad out to the fairgrounds—"

"No. Broxmeyer won't be at the substation and Sadler's back in the county seat by now—we'd have to track them down, try to convince them. Closest bomb squad is probably Sacramento. All of that could take hours."

"We can't just go bulling in there on our own."

"The hell we can't. We've got to get her out of that death trap *now*."

"Fairgrounds won't be open yet. It's barely seven-thirty."

"Climb the goddamn fence—"

"There'll be people around, getting ready for the parade. And we'd need a key to the unit. Broxmeyer has Balfour's keys, or Sadler does—"

"Somebody else has keys. His helper, Perez."

I shook off Runyon's hand, shouldered past him, and

ran into the kitchen. There was a phone book on the counter; I grabbed it up. Two years old. But if Perez was listed, the number might still be good.

There was a listing, with an address in Six Pines. I fumbled in my pockets, didn't find my cell—couldn't remember what the hell I'd done with it. But I didn't need it; Runyon, grim-faced, had his out and flipped open. I read off the number, and he punched it in. While he waited for an answer, I stuck my head under the sink faucet and flipped on the cold-water tap. The chill shock cleared the last of the fuzz out of my head.

I grabbed a dishtowel to dry off, took the phone from Jake just as the line clicked open. A woman's voice chattered at me in Spanish, grumbling shrewishly about being woken up at such an early hour.

My command of the language is pretty fair, if rusty from disuse. I dredged up phrases, said them in loud and imperative tones. "Eladio Perez, *por favor. Es muy importante. Una cuestión de vida o muerte.*"

That got through to her. She shut up for a couple of seconds. Then, *"¿Quién está llamando?"*

"Dígale el detective cuya esposa falta."

"Ah, sí, sí. Momentito."

Five, ten, fifteen seconds. Then Eladio Perez's voice said, "Yes, señor, I remember you. What is it you want?"

I told him. Yes, he had keys to the main gate and another to a gate on the west side. Yes, he also had one to the storage unit. *Que pasa?* He hadn't heard about Balfour yet and there was no time to enlighten him. Instead, I did some fast talking, stressing urgency without telling him too much, and finally convinced him to meet us with the keys.

"Ten minutes, Eladio. *Gracias*." I broke the connection, tossed Runyon's cell back to him, and headed for the door. If he hesitated in following, it was for no more than a couple of seconds.

In the car, rolling, he said, "I don't like this, Bill."

"You don't have to like it. My decision."

"I know that. But it's a hell of a big risk. What if Balfour booby-trapped the shed door so it'll detonate when it's opened?"

As strung out as I was, the possibility hadn't occurred to me before. I thought about it as we cut down toward the valley road. "I don't see it, Jake. He wouldn't have expected anybody to open the storage unit today, a holiday—the construction work's finished, Perez wouldn't have any reason to use his key. And Balfour wasn't an explosives expert. Anybody can rig a gas-leak explosion—anybody can slap up a bunch of plastic explosive and wire detonators to a timer. That has to be what he did, all he did."

"You can't be sure. A timer, yeah, but set to blow this afternoon when the picnic's in full swing and the grounds are jammed with people. There's still time to do this the right way, the safe way."

"Maybe, but that's something we can't be sure of, either. Suppose it's set to go off this morning? Suppose he miscalculated or the timer malfunctions?"

Runyon didn't say anything.

"And Kerry could be badly hurt. Sick, drugged . . . God

knows. There can't be much air in that box. And it'll be damn hot pretty soon."

Still keeping his own counsel. I couldn't read the stoic set of his face, but I knew what he was thinking. Not that I blamed him; if our places were reversed, I'd be having doubts now, too. But I still had none: Kerry was alive.

"Don't try to change my mind, Jake. Go along when we get there, or back off and let me do it alone—I won't hold it against you."

The three miles to Six Pines seemed like thirty. There was traffic on the valley road, people heading in early for the holiday festivities, taking their time, clogging the road. Runyon drove as fast as he could, passing whenever he could without endangering anybody. I sat on the edge of the passenger seat, leaning forward with my hands braced against the dash, an image of that metal storage unit fire-bright behind my eyes.

People and parade vehicles were already starting to assemble at the high school—band members, one of the VFD fire trucks, horses and horse-drawn buggies, some kind of float draped with American flags. Parade started here at eleven, finished at the fairgrounds at one. If it started and finished at all.

They hadn't yet blocked off the main drag through town, but DETOUR and NO PARKING signs had been set out. Not too many people on the sidewalks yet, or down around the fairgrounds; I didn't see any sheriff's department cruisers. Runyon swung right on the street that paralleled the north side of the fairgrounds, then left along the western perimeter. That street was lined with trees and a handful of widely spaced houses. After dark, it'd be mostly deserted. Balfour's route last night, I thought—less risk of being seen going in and coming back out through the west gate.

Eladio Perez was waiting for us, standing alongside the old pickup we'd seen parked at the construction site yesterday. Runyon looped into the short driveway and braked nose up to the gate. Through the mesh I could see that it opened into the long parking area adjacent to the picnic grounds; blacktops branched off at an intersection not far inside.

I jumped out, ran over to Perez. He backed up a step, and I saw his eyes widen—probably a reaction to how I looked. "The keys, Eladio."

Wordlessly, he handed them over: three small padlock keys on a three-inch bead chain.

I said, "Quickest way to where you were working, left road or right?"

"Left."

"Okay. We'll get the keys back to you."

"Señor Balfour—"

"Don't worry about him. Go on home, thanks for your help."

I ran to the gate. The key with "West Gate" written on a piece of adhesive opened the padlock, but tension had made me clumsy-fingered, and it took three tries to get it slotted and turned. I shoved the gate inward, let Runyon push it out of the way with the Ford's bumper. Jerked the passenger door open, slid back in beside him saying, "Left at the intersection."

Shade trees flanked the blacktop in that direction, separating the parking area from the picnic grounds. Be dark along here at night, but you could drive it without lights if you knew the grounds as well as Balfour had. Where the row of trees ended, the road hooked right and intersected with the main road that led in from the front gates. Runyon cut to the right along the periphery of the grandstand and track.

After fifty yards, I could see the storage box squatting back between the concession booths and the restrooms. Sunlight shone on the metal roof and sides, giving it a glowing look like something being slowly heated in a forge. The image tied more knots in my stomach. I could feel sweat running down my back and sides.

Runyon pulled up under the tree where we'd parked yesterday. I was out of the car before it rocked to a complete stop, staggering a little on my run to the shed. He came up just as I reached the padlocked door, and when he pushed in next to me, I saw that he was carrying his flashlight.

I reached for the padlock, lost my grip on it; it clanged harshly off the metal. Runyon said, "Better let me do it."

"You don't have to be here—"

"The hell with that. Give me the keys."

I let him take them in exchange for the flashlight. From far off in the still morning, incongruous given what we were facing, I could hear the high school band warming up with "America the Beautiful."

Runyon got the padlock open, slid the staple out and let it drop on the ground with the key still in the slot. My heart had begun to race. I sucked in a breath as he eased the door open a crack.

Nothing happened.

The breath hissed out between my teeth. Jake was still holding the door in the same position, with maybe half an inch between its edge and the jamb. Carefully, he took the flashlight back with his other hand, switched it on, then put one eye close to the crack and squinted inside while he ran the beam up and down along the opening.

"Nothing that looks like a tripwire," he said.

He widened the crack another half inch, played the light again. When I moved closer to the opening, my nostrils dilated at the mingled odors from inside. Sawdust, machine oil—and that same sickening sourness that had come out of Balfour's camper.

"She's in there, Jake. Kerry's in there."

He gave me a sideways look, then a jerky nod. "Door's clear."

"Go!"

Again he widened the gap. But after a couple of inches, it bound up at the bottom. Grimacing, he yanked upward on the handle. That popped the bottom edge loose and the door wobbled open all the way. He swept the flash beam through the murky interior.

It was like looking into a chamber of horrors.

Half a dozen or more blocks of plastic explosive stuck to the inside of the door and to all three walls. Detonators poked into them, trailing wires that connected to a black-boxed timing device on the floor . . . glowing-red numerals showed it set for one-thirty, half an hour after the end of the parade when the fairgrounds would be packed with people. Other things embedded in the plastic—nails, screws. More of the same strewn over the floor, along with sharp-toothed saw blades and other stuff intended as shrapnel.

But I registered all of that only peripherally. The small, still figure encased in duct tape, lying supine on the floor surrounded by all that death, was all I really saw or needed to see.

I started to lunge inside, an animal noise rumbling in my throat. Runyon stopped me with an iron-fingered grip. "Pull the detonators first, all of them." I struggled, thinking *Kerry, Kerry!* He hung onto me, saying again, "Detonators, the detonators," and finally the sense of the words got through. I bobbed my head, pulled free, reached up to jerk the nearest metal cap out of the explosive.

We tore all of them loose, stepping carefully around Kerry, and threw them down; they were useless by themselves. Then I went to one knee beside her. That crazy son of a bitch Balfour had mummy-wrapped her from ankles to shoulders, with her hands and arms flat against her sides so she couldn't move. Strips of duct tape covered her eyes and mouth; what I could see of her face was ghostly pale. I touched the side of her neck . . . cold, so cold . . . and probed for an artery, a pulse that I couldn't feel.

Oh, please God, no!

Runyon had the light on her. "Is she . . . ?"

"I don't know, I can't tell. Help me get her out of here."

His shoes crunched on the shrapnel as he bent to take hold of her legs. I shoved upright, got my hands under her shoulders; my mind seemed to have gone blank. We carried her outside and over into the shade next to one of the concession booths, laid her down gently in the grass.

I dropped down beside her, felt again for a pulse. Had

to be one, had to! But I still couldn't find it. So faint only a doctor could detect it . . .

Runyon had backed off a couple of steps with his cell phone out, and I heard him making a 911 call as I hooked a fingernail under an edge of the tape over Kerry's eyes, eased it off. Both eyes shut tight, not even a twitch on the lids. As gently as I could I stripped the tape from her mouth. Her lips were cracked and smeared with dried blood. When I laid my cheek down close to them, I couldn't feel even the faintest whisper of a breath. With my thumb I raised one of the closed eyelids.

Vacant, blood-flecked stare.

Sick with anguish, I fumbled my pocket knife out. Opened it with fingers that shook so much now I had to steady my right hand with my left. Had to keep wiping sweat out of my eyes as I sawed slowly through the tape, trying not to cut her. Her left arm was free when Runyon finished his call. He dropped down on the other side and began freeing her right arm with a Swiss Army blade. Together, we sliced and stripped as much of the tape off her arms and legs as we dared.

Still no movement, no sign of life.

God, what that bastard had done to her! Finger and fingernail marks on her throat where she'd been grabbed and choked. Bruise on one cheekbone that had blackened the eye above. A scabbed-over wound above her left ear that had bled into her hair . . . but not much, not enough for it to be anything but superficial. Welts and lesions on her bare arms and legs from the tape. Blouse and shorts in place, but torn, soiled.

Balfour had died too easy, too easy, too easy—

Runyon was pressing fingers against the artery in her neck. He made a sudden low grunting sound, and when I looked up at him, I saw the tight grimace he wore smooth off.

"Pulse," he said.

I said something, I don't remember what, and caught up Kerry's hand and held my thumb on the wrist. Pulse, yes! I could feel it now—thin, thready, but discernible without putting on too much pressure.

Heartbeats. Life beats.

And all at once, the emotional dam inside me burst wide open. I'd cried before in my life, but never in public and never with such unashamed intensity as I did holding onto Kerry the way a drowning man holds onto a lifeline. Dimly, I saw Runyon stand, felt his hand on my shoulder before he moved away.

In the distance, there was the sound of sirens.

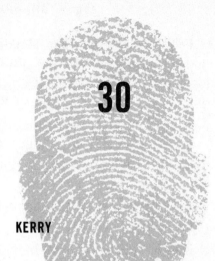

30

KERRY

Awake again, aware again.

Eyes opening to slits, bright light lancing in to painfully dilate the pupils. She squeezed the lids shut, but the light remained like a pressing weight against the outer skin. Slowly, she raised them again, squinting. The same dazzle, but it faded quickly this time . . . and she was looking at white walls, white composition ceiling, TV set on a wall stand, a window covered with partly open blinds.

Sounds intruded, a low steady mechanical beeping. She was aware, too, of a clean antiseptic odor. And of something clipped to the index finger of her left hand. She turned her head. Wires, tubes, lights flashing on some kind of monitor, an IV bag on a stand. Hospital room.

She rolled her head the other way. And saw Bill sitting in a chair alongside her bed, his eyes closed, his big hands lying palms up on his lap.

Didn't believe it at first. Hallucination, wishful think-ing. Her thoughts were fuzzy, disoriented . . . but it wasn't the same kind of body and mind disconnect as before. This was almost peacefully dreamlike. She raised her head slightly and blinked once, twice, three times.

The hospital room was still there. Bill was still there.

Acceptance came slowly, and with it, a kind of wonder. The last thing she remembered, and that only vaguely, was Balfour's hands on her, dragging her out of the camper, lifting and carrying her into a dark place. No, that wasn't quite the last thing. She seemed to recall a random thought, what might have been her last thought, the beginning of a childhood prayer: *If I should die before I wake . . .*

She tried to say Bill's name, but her mouth and throat were too clogged to form it coherently; it came out as a kind of mewling noise. Immediately, his eyes popped open; he hadn't been asleep, just resting. He came up out of the chair, emotions rippling like neon across his drawn, craggy face, smile on, smile off, smile on. He took her hand in both of his, leaned down to kiss her gently on the fore-head.

"About time you woke up." Trying to keep his voice light, but it cracked on the last two words. "How do you feel?"

She managed a word this time. "Weak."

"You've been out for a while. But you're going to be okay."

". . . Fuzzy."

"Drugs. Antibiotics, painkillers."

Pain? Yes, she was aware of that, too, now. Her body, her

arms and legs, seemed riddled with small, stinging hurts. One arm lay outside the bedclothes, gauze-bandaged. Her lips hurt; she licked at them with the tip of her tongue, winced at the deep splits and the taste of medicine.

"Thirsty," she said.

Bill lifted a cup from an aluminum table, held it so she could sip through a flex straw. The water was lukewarm, and she had some trouble swallowing, but it took away the dryness and let her speak more easily.

"What . . . hospital is this?"

"Marshall. Placerville."

"How long—?"

"Two days."

Two days unconscious. "I . . . must be in bad shape."

"Not so bad. Not anymore." But the muscle that jumped alongside his mouth, the moist shine in his eyes told her otherwise. She'd come close to dying. And maybe she wasn't out of the woods yet. Curiously, neither thought frightened her. Hospital. Bill. No, she wasn't afraid anymore.

"You found me?"

"With Jake Runyon's help. He deserves most of the credit."

"Where? How?"

"Long story. We'll talk about all that when you're up to it."

"Balfour?"

"He's dead."

"You didn't . . ."

"No. Wasn't me. Or Jake."

Good, she thought. Good that it wasn't you or Jake,

good that he's dead. I'd have killed him myself if I could, I really would have. But she didn't put the thought into words. Her secret.

Instead, she said, "He didn't rape me."

"I know. The doctors . . ."

"Just . . . tied me up, kept me prisoner. Don't know why."

"Later. Getting you well is what's important now."

Her eyelids had begun to feel heavy. So damn weak . . .

Bill said, "I'd better get the nurse. Said to call her when you woke up." He released her hand, started to turn away from the bed.

"Bill?"

He turned back.

"I knew you'd find me. I never lost hope."

Kerry wasn't sure if that was the truth or not, but it was what he needed to hear. And what she needed to believe.